SLEEPING ON JUPITER

A train stops at a railway station, and a young woman jumps off. She has wild hair, sloppy clothes, a distracted air. The sudden violence of what happens next leaves the other passengers gasping ... The train terminates at Jarmuli, a temple town by the sea. Here, among pilgrims, priests and ashrams, three old women disembark — only to encounter the girl once again. What is someone like her doing in this remote place? Over the next five days, the old women live out their long-planned dream of a holiday together; their temple guide finds ecstasy in forbidden love; and the girl is joined by a photographer battling his own demons. As the lives of these disparate people overlap and collide, Jarmuli is revealed as a place with a long, dark past that transforms all who encounter it ...

SLEEPING ON JUPITER

ANURADHA ROY

LARGE
PRINT

First published in Great Britain 2015
by
MacLehose Press
An imprint of Quercus Publishing Ltd.

First Isis Edition
published 2016
by arrangement with
Quercus Publishing Ltd.
An Hachette UK company

A catalogue record for this book is available
from the British Library.

ISBN 978–1–78541–186–1 (hb)
ISBN 978–1–78541–192–2 (pb)

Published by
F. A. Thorpe (Publishing)
Anstey, Leicestershire

Set by Words & Graphics Ltd.
Anstey, Leicestershire
Printed and bound in Great Britain by
T. J. International Ltd., Padstow, Cornwall
This book is printed on acid-free paper

for three beloved tyrants

Biscoot
Rukun
Christopher

"Would a circling surface vulture
know such depths of sky
as the moon would know?"

AKKA MAHADEVI, 12th century

BEFORE THE FIRST DAY

The year the war came closer I was six or seven and it did not matter to me. I lived with my brother, father and mother and our hut had two rooms with mats on the floor and a line of wooden pegs from which our clothes hung and in the evening we sat in the yard outside, watching our mother cook on the fire by the grapefruit tree. When the tree flowered I opened my mouth wide to swallow the scent. Little green beads of fruit appeared when the flowers fell off. One day, when some of the fruit had turned as round and yellow as full moons, my brother climbed the tree. He looked tall and strong clambering from branch to branch, my older brother. I stood holding the trunk, waiting for the fruit to come down. He snapped them off the stem, the branch shook hard, and I was showered with dust and dry leaves.

The grapefruits were pale yellow outside, with stippled skin. They were as big as melons and heavy with juice. My mother slid a knife into one and cut it in half and the flesh was pink and the smell of its juice was tart and fresh.

Our hut was all we knew, the four of us. I remember a fence around it, made of branches my father cut and brought home on his shoulders a few at a time, every day. The jungle was thick, the leaves of the tall trees were broad and green. I have tried to remember which trees they were, but I can only bring back the ones that gave me things to eat: mangoes, grapefruit, jackfruit and lime. We had hens that went mad cackling and crowing when they were laying eggs. Their eggs were brown. We had a cow, a few goats, and three pigs.

When the pigs were slaughtered for their meat they shrieked with a sound that made my teeth fall off and this was the sound I heard soon after my mother cut the grapefruit, and the men came in with axes. Their faces were wrapped in cloth. They shoved my brother outside, they pushed my mother and me to a corner of the room and then they flung my father at a wall. They slammed his face at the wall again and again. The whitewashed wall streamed red, they threw him to the floor and kicked him with their booted feet. Each time the boots hit him it was as if a limp bundle of clothes was being tossed this way and that. One of the men lifted an axe and brought it down on my father's forehead.

When they left they wrote something on the wall in his blood. They did not look at us.

In my sleep I hear the sound of pigs at slaughter, the sound my father made.

The next thing was a clump of bushes by a ditch. My mother was hiding me in the bushes. Smoke rose from the place our village was — not the smoke of cooking fires but a kind I had never seen before. It made the blue sky black and stilled the birds. There was not a sound. I started to shout for my brother, but my mother put her palm over my mouth. If only she hadn't stopped me. He always came when I called and he always knew what to do.

I was walking after that, as fast as I could, but still my mother kept pulling at my hand and dragging me, saying, "Faster, faster." Then she picked me up and I was on her back and my arms were wrapped around her. She ran through the jungle. My legs straddled her waist, my head reached her shoulders, but I could not look beyond. Her hair pricked my eyes, it was sticky with sweat and dirt. Her feet were bare. She stopped to pluck thorns from them and once she stopped to tear off a strip from her sari and wrap it around her foot when a stone gashed it. If I asked for my brother she said, "Quiet, not a word."

My mother's face was fierce. She had thick, straight eyebrows and she wore a nose pin that sparkled like a star. Her palm felt rough and hard when it slapped my cheek and when it rubbed oil into me before a bath. Although I scrape and scrape at my mind, there is not much else I can bring back.

We rested, we slept once or twice, then she hoisted me onto her back and walked again. It was for a day or maybe it was for two, and all of a sudden the leaves fell away, the ground grew soft, everything opened out and the ocean was before us. I had never seen the sea or sand. I ran towards the water. My mother came after me and held me back, but she let me paddle at the edge of the water. Then I saw a man. He came up to her and said something. My mother drew me away from the water and made me sit in the shadow of a boat. Her sari was wet to her knees. She bent down and wrung it out at the bottom. They moved away from me, they spoke softly to each other. She came back. "Wait here," she said, "don't move." She returned to the man. Her voice thinned and flew in the breeze. And then she was gone.

The sun hung over the sea, looking as if it would fall into it anytime. The water was high, there was too much of it. Waves came like white-toothed monsters and bit off the sand. They came closer and closer. I kept looking at the place where my mother had stood with the man. I was hungry. I called for her. My stomach ached with hunger. I stood up and opened my mouth as wide as I could and I shouted for my brother. Nobody.

When it was almost dark, two women appeared. They tried to take me away from the boat. I kept telling them my mother had told me to wait. One woman tugged at me. I shouted and struggled, my feet dragged in the sand, and she said, "Quiet!" She picked me up. The other woman forced water from a bottle into my mouth. They were taking me to my mother, she said. It would not be long.

I think it was the next morning that they put me into a van. There were other girls in the van, some smaller than me, some bigger. The van drove until it reached a town. There was a house in the town, painted pink and blue. It had a room with straw mats on the floor where we slept. We were given boiled rice to eat. The rice was red in colour instead of white. The grains were fat and chewy. I had never eaten rice like that. There was one girl who would not eat and she cried all the time. After a few days the women who fed us put that girl and her bedding out in the verandah for the night. Her wailing could still be heard inside, but not so loud, and we could all sleep. The next morning when the women went to get her from the verandah she was no longer there.

After that we were very quiet.

One of the women looked fat and kind and she held me tight every time I asked her when I could go back home. Her chest was as soft as a pillow. She rocked me back and forth saying, "My child, my child."

"I want my mother. I want my brother."

She said, "Your mother and your father and your brother have become stars. Whenever you want to be with them, look up at the sky and there they are." I thought of my mother's nose pin. The woman pointed upward and I followed her finger with my eyes. But although it was night, the sky was red from distant fires, and there was not a glimmer in it. "The stars are there," she said. "You can't see them, but they are there."

Then she held me close and wept. I had never seen a grown-up weep. My mother scolded us all the time, but when she was not scolding she joked and sang songs. This woman groaned and sighed. Each time she got up or sat down the woman held her knee and said, "Chuni, if only you would rub that oil in again." There was nobody called Chuni in that place.

One afternoon when I was sitting with the fat woman on the steps to the house, looking at the dust clouds in the street, she pulled out a pouch from inside her blouse. She had a needle that she held to a lit match until it went blue and black. She looked at my face as if she had not seen it before, and with a pen she made marks on both my ears. Before I knew what she was doing, she was pulling at one of my ears and I felt a sharp pain. Her face looked huge and ugly when it was so close. Her skin shone with sweat. Her nose had tiny pin-sized holes and black hair sprouted from some of them. I could smell her rotting breath. I tried to push her away, but she held me by the ear and kept pushing the burnt needle into the place that hurt.

She stopped. She turned my face towards the left and said, "Keep still, don't shout so much, or it will hurt more."

Again that terrible pinprick, then a burning pain. She looked at my ears and I heard her exclaim, "Jaah! They are up and down from each other. The things I do!" She picked something out of her pouch and prised it into my bleeding ear lobe. "Never mind, there it is. Up down or not."

My ears were still oozing blood when I looked at myself. Two loops of wire went through them now. One of them was higher than the other. The woman stood behind me, dark as a hill in the mirror that held us both. With the earrings on, I was different: I looked dressed up. I looked like a girl. The woman stroked my face and my hair and she kept saying, "Chuni, my Chuni, see how pretty they look, your rings." Another of the house's women came in at that moment and peered into the mirror. "That's gold! You gave her your gold rings?"

8

The fat woman said, "Better that a girl wears them."

Later, when we were alone and she was dabbing my earlobes with a stinging solution she said, "They are my daughter's. They are gold. I saved for many months to get them made. Chuni wore them all the time. You look after them. Keep them safe. Never take them off."

That night my ears swelled up and pus oozed from the holes. By morning the rings were stuck in the drying pus. The pain and later the itch made me want to tear the rings off my ears. It was worse the day after. Still, I looked at myself in the mirror and said in a whisper, "Chuni, Chuni, I'm wearing your rings. I will never take them off." The woman cleaned the wounds with her solution. "They really look as if they were made for your face, my child. They do. You are my girl reborn." She tapped the rings with her fingers to make them swing back and forth. The other women in the house gaped at her.

I stayed in that house a few weeks, maybe a few months, until more men came with cloth wrapped around their faces. One of them stood holding a gun. He shouted, "This is for your own good, this is for our motherland, this is for our mother tongue." A second man clapped his hands and told us to hold each other's shoulders and chug out of the house in a line as if we were a train. Outside, we had to keep chugging and whistling around the courtyard. It felt like a game. The man making us play seemed to be smiling under the cloth wrapped around his face. He was lanky and loose-limbed like my brother. He had that same kind of hair, scruffy and short. My brother. I broke the line to run towards him. The man stopped smiling and lifted his rifle butt towards me. I went back to the line of girls, but I no longer felt like a coach in a train.

The two other men took pots and pans, chairs, blankets and stoves from the house and loaded them into their jeep. The women stood by. Then the men sprinkled something all over the rooms and threw lit torches into the house. Flames leaped from the windows.

We spent that night in the open. We were twelve girls and the four women who looked after us. There was nowhere to go. In the morning we were put in another van and we left the buildings behind, we went through rough countryside, on and on, until the trees were behind us as well, the sky opened up, the sand stretched hot and bare, and there again was the sea. Again there was a boat. This time it was in the water. I ran towards it — my mother — I thought my mother would be there. All twelve of us were made to climb in. One of the women got in as well, but it was not the fat one. She stayed on the shore. The motor thudded to a start. Two men climbed into it and the boat rocked and swayed. Then it moved out into the ocean.

Until the sun whited out my eyes I kept them on the fat woman. The shore went further and further away from us and then there was nothing but water and sky. One of the girls vomited all over and the men threatened to throw the next one who did that into the sea. I touched my earrings.

THE FIRST DAY

At four in the afternoon, the sleeper train to Jarmuli shuddered to life and wheezed out of the station. Passengers locked into companionship for the next fourteen hours eyed each other sidelong, wondering how it would be. In Coach A2, three women were exchanging glances. "You ask her," Gouri's imploring look said to Latika and Vidya. Their eyes refused to meet hers.

The three of them, friends, were going on their first outing together. They were in a compartment, all grey and blue, with two large plate-glass windows and four berths. To climb to one of the upper berths you needed to be agile. Gouri, whose ticket number pointed her upwards, could just about manage stairs these days if she placed her weight on the right knee instead of the left. She turned to the fourth person in their compartment and said, "Excuse me, if you don't mind . . ."

The girl was bent over a travel guide, pen in hand. She turned a page and scribbled in the book's margin. Gouri waited. The girl did not look up. Gouri looked at Vidya for confirmation, murmured an excuse me again, then stepped closer and brushed the girl's shoulder with a finger.

At this the girl jerked to life and her hand flew to her mouth. "Oh! I didn't want to . . . I mean . . ." Gouri stepped back. You'd think she was a two-headed ogre and not a round-faced old woman.

The girl shook her head, as if to clear it. Her hair was a bird's nest, streaked brown and black, some of it braided with coloured threads. She reached under the braids and a pair of earphones emerged from ears spiral-bound with rings, silver or copper but for two tiny circles of gold at the lobes.

Gouri had not wanted to ask this intimidating young creature for a favour, but old bones left her little choice. She collected her breath and said, "My ticket is for the upper berth and you see, I no longer have the knees to be able to climb up — do you mind — you must sit at the window of course, as long as you like. Only at night, to sleep, if you could exchange . . ."

The girl wore a turquoise T-shirt over which the words "Been There Done That Binned It" undulated as though travelling over hills and valleys. Her pants were cut off at the calves and the fabric was held together with a dozen zips that traversed the legs. The women glimpsed tattoos and could not be sure if the glint at her eyebrows came from a stud. Vidya was longing to say, "Have you seen how young girls dress these days? And then they complain if men bother them!"

The girl shrugged. "No problem." Her face broke into a smile of unexpected sweetness. "I like the upper berth." She reached for her earphones again.

14

Huge black eyes in a pointed face, like a deer's, and she seems as jumpy as one too, Latika observed. She turned away and busied herself with her phone so that she would not stare.

Encouraged by the smile, Gouri beamed at the girl. "My friend Latika can still manage to climb to those upper berths, not me. Not many years left, you know, that we'll be able to travel! We said to each other, we've been friends all our lives and never been anywhere together. I said, Jarmuli! I've always wanted to go back to the Vishnu temple. And Latika, that's Latika, she just wants to sit by the sea and drink coconut water — so we left our children and grandchildren and here we are! My name's Gouri, by the way, and this is Vidya. And you?"

"Nomi," the girl said, her smile fading at Gouri's cascade of information. "Pleased to meet you." She fiddled with her earphones.

"Are you going on a holiday to Jarmuli?" This time the question came from Vidya, who looked at the girl over the rim of her glasses. "Where are you from?"

"From . . . I'm from lots of places. Mostly Oslo, I guess," the girl said. "Not a holiday. I'm here to . . . to research a documentary." Even as Vidya started saying, documentary about what, she added, "On religious tourism, temple towns, all of that. My boss wanted the Kumbh. Took some doing, but I persuaded her Jarmuli might work."

The girl took up her book, replugged her ears, and tried to find her page. In the corridor, a bullet-shaped child in red shorts narrowed his eyes, revved an imaginary motorbike, then hurtled up the aisle. From somewhere in the train came a woman's voice tight with anger: "No, *you* control him."

"Film! How interesting! My son, he does the same kind of work." Vidya smiled, delighted by the coincidence. She leaned forward to tell her story and the girl removed her earphones again, this time with obvious reluctance.

"Oh, the comings and goings when he was single and living at home — his madcap film friends, even famous actors! They'd be there all night! Such a racket, so much coffee, so much food cooked for hours and gone in seconds. Once . . ."

Surely anyone could see the young woman wanted to be left alone! Sometimes one's friends were so obtuse, yet however old the friendship there were things you could not say out loud for fear of offending. "Did you bring me that Dick Francis to read, Vidya?" Latika said. "Or did you forget?" Diversion tactics, her husband would have called it. Tact, that's what she called it.

The girl used the interruption conspicuously to return the earphones to her ears and go back to her book. Vidya stopped speaking mid-sentence, snubbed. She busied herself with a sheaf of blank cards that she took from her bag and placed on a book, the one Latika had asked for. She always brought herself back to an even keel with work. She began to write on the cards. She noticed Latika did not ask for the Dick Francis again. She hadn't wanted it in the first place, Vidya knew that, not right then.

Now, just outside the city, the train sped past slums that flowed down the banks of the railway lines. People had settled into their seats and taken out magazines, munchies, packs of cards. The boy who had been torpedoing through the aisles had been stationary for a while. Now he started his motorbike again and soon afterwards crashed into a woman coming the other way. "Whose child is this?" the woman shouted. "Why don't you keep an eye on him?" The boy lay prone on the floor at the woman's feet. Then after a whimper followed by a full-blown sob, he began to howl with rage. A man's voice said, "You go get him." A woman said, "Always me!"

"What a pest that child is, I'm sure it'll cry all night," Latika said. At once they chorused, as if at an old, shared joke: "*Badly brought up!*" Even Vidya had to laugh. She went back to writing in careful block letters, but now she had a smile on her face.

"What are you doing, Vidya?" Latika said, relieved the silence had been broken. "You're always so busy." Forty years in the bureaucracy and a preoccupied self-importance was now Vidya's natural way of being. She did not lift her head until she had finished inscribing her set of cards. Each one said:

GOURI GANGULY, STAYING AT SWIRLING SEA HOTEL, JARMULI, TILL 14 FEBRUARY 2006. PHONE 697565437. PERMANENT ADDRESS: TARINI APARTMENTS, 13A/5 HAZRA ROAD, CALCUTTA.

"I want you to put a card into every pocket of your handbag, Gouri," Vidya said. "If you drift off and can't remember where you are, it'll be easier for someone to bring you back to us."

Her voice exuded wisdom and forethought. Everyone who knew Vidya admired this about her: she thought of everything, and for everyone. She had a square, broad face in which eyes, eyebrows, nose and mouth, everything was in proportion and the right shape, yet the sum of it, inexplicably, did not go beyond symmetry. Her crisp cotton sari, her neat bun, the modesty of the plain gold studs in her ears all spoke of her habitual efficiency and practicality. She wore the waterproof sandals she had bought the day before specially for this trip to the seaside and in her bag was a bottle of hand sanitizer, a packet of rose-scented wet wipes, and phials containing basic homoeopathic medicines. After packing these she had sat for a full five minutes of quiet next to her luggage, to run through in her mind a list of the many things she and her friends might need that had not yet gone in.

Gouri, head against the train's window, was humming a bhajan under her breath. Her eyes slid over hutments, pylons, shops, drains, restive huddles of people at level crossings, and an advertisement repeated on every wall the train flashed past. It was painted in such tall black letters that she could not look away from it: HARD IN A MINUTE, PLEASURE FOR HOURS.

She turned her gaze to dogs rooting around a garbage heap. Soggy hovels of plastic, brick and mud in ditches of stagnant water. Forests of T.V. antennae on their roofs. A glimpse of a rice field and then it was gone. Only at times, for rushing seconds, she spotted silhouettes of mud huts and shining surfaces of ponds and thought of the village where she had climbed trees with her cousins and chased them through riverside grass gone cloud-white with flowers in the autumn, grass so high they lost each other, called out, held hands when they found each other again.

"Why must she carry so many cards?" Latika's voice broke into Gouri's reverie. "Isn't that a bit extreme?" She rummaged through her bag for a hairbrush, stealing a look at the girl. Did that hair ever need brushing? How did people manage with braids and beads and thread in their hair? Latika's own was cut into a crop that tended to fly around, but it was always clean, and it framed her fine-boned face nicely and set off the tortoiseshell glasses she wore. It was coloured to a glossy burgundy. She had agonized for weeks before settling on the shade, yearning for the simplicity of times when hair was either black or white, no shades in between, but was secretly pleased with herself for throwing caution to the winds and going for something bold.

Vidya's attention had not wavered. "Gouri needs many cards. She forgets where she's put what. Remember how we missed the first ten minutes of that film because she couldn't find the tickets in her bag?"

"That could have been any one of us," Latika said, "I can never find anything in my bag."

"Well, I just want to be prepared since we're going to be in an unknown place, that's all. Especially when she's even forgotten to bring her phone."

Did she sound too harsh? Vidya gave Gouri a nudge. It was meant to be affectionate, to show she meant no criticism, but her friend — she could not help thinking this — *wobbled* away from her. Every year that passed seemed to make Gouri more plump.

Vidya wondered how she and Latika would manage her. Her limbs were spindly, but her torso was a mound, a pumpkin perched on matchsticks. It was a small miracle she didn't topple. Her mind was on the edge as well. Over the last two years it was as if her brain had termites tunnelling through it. She repeated herself, she forgot where she put things, she forgot names. She would even forget that she had eaten and begin serving herself again. Gouri was usually meek, but now she needed handling. When she took offence she became combative: "No, you did not phone me yesterday," and "Of course not, I haven't yet had a fish roll." Vidya often woke at three in the morning and stared into the darkness. Those creatures turning Gouri's brain to dust might be biding their time for me. They must be there. Waiting.

"It's not so bad," Gouri said from the corner she had retreated into. "I just take a little longer with things, that's all." She wished they wouldn't discuss her this way, not in front of that young thing in the opposite seat — what was her name? Had she told them her name?

20

Gouri turned towards the window and saw that rainwater had rippled the glass. The countryside was now a barely legible shadow. A sagging face — her own, she realised — looked back at her. Behind her she could see Vidya, eyebrows arched, mouth opening to gather breath for more admonishing words. The deepening shadows outside had turned the train's windows into mirrors. Gouri noticed something and put her hands to her earlobes, wondering what she had done with the pearl studs she thought she had worn. She had taken them from the cupboard, put them on her dressing table last night, of that she was certain. Or had she? She leaned her forehead on the rain-flecked window, cupped her palms to shield her eyes from light, and peered into the early night. There was nothing to look at, but she kept her face there, staring into the void.

"Suppose you forget the name of the hotel. And you can't remember your home phone number. What then? What's the harm? These cards aren't heavy!"

Gouri picked up her handbag. The zips whined open and shut one after the other. She put a card into each of the compartments of the bag. When she finished she looked up without a word and Vidya turned away saying, "I'm sure I packed some of those sweets, you know, those chutney ones everyone used to eat on trams."

The train picked up speed and the awkwardness passed. They began to talk of neighbours and family, the drudgery of daily living. "She has to juggle a hundred things to come and see me," Latika said of her daughter who lived in Florence and came home every other year with her husband and their children. "But if she knew how many grey hairs each visit gives me! You know I'm not the greatest housekeeper in the world. Of course, I love seeing my grandchildren — and my son-in-law — but the amount of mineral water I have to stock up! Sausages, pasta! And cheese! The children eat nothing else."

In their own homes, surrounded by family or servants, they could never gossip this way, but here they didn't have to worry about being overheard. The girl was half dozing against her window now, book abandoned, her head and shoulders occasionally swaying to the music being pumped into her brain.

"Yes, the mineral water — cartons and cartons — each time my nephew from New York visits," Vidya said.

The ticket-checker arrived and his frown sobered them. They were all travelling on senior citizen concessions. The checker demanded proof that they were over sixty. Gouri and Latika obediently held out identity cards. Vidya rummaged through her handbag muttering, "I'm sure it was here, of course it was." Eventually she emptied everything onto the seat in a cascade of tissues, medicines, pens, safety pins, and rubber bands, but she could not find the driving licence she had thought would do the job for her.

The ticket-checker waited with a look on his face that said he was trying to be patient, but it was hard. His white uniform was stretched tight over his belly. The draughts from the air conditioning vents were icy yet his nose shone with sweat and he had to push his glasses back up every now and then with his forefinger. "There will be a fine if you can't give me proof," he said.

"You used to have an identity card from your office . . ."

"It's years since I retired, Latika!"

Gouri blinked at the man through her glasses. A sweet muffin with raisins for eyes, that's my Dida, her grandson always said. "Can't you see we are white-haired ladies, old enough to be your mother? Even her hair —" Gouri smiled at him and pointed at Latika. "Even her hair's not really that colour."

The ticket-checker's eyes wandered to Latika's head for a moment, then he turned to a careful study of the tip of his pen. Latika was appalled. She stuffed her hairbrush into her bag, seething. She had felt dubious about this outing from the start, she should have trusted her instincts and stayed at home. If they hadn't travelled together before, the three of them, there must be good reason: they would probably feel fed up in half a day together. Across the aisle she saw a couple sitting pressed against each other, staring at something only they could see. If only. In an earlier time, when her husband was alive, there was always someone to go on holidays with. So what if he had never sat like that with her, not even as a young man.

The train clacked over a bridge; a steward walked past thumping stacks of sheets and blankets onto empty berths. Vidya was hunting in yet another bag now, but something in the way Gouri had spoken had melted the man and he said, "Alright then." The clipboard arm relaxed, the tapping ceased. He wagged a finger at them as if they were errant schoolgirls. "This time I'll let you off. Don't try it on your way back. You'll have to pay double."

He turned to the girl next, and stood for a moment observing her. Nomi's shoulders and neck were twitching to her music. Her eyes were shut.

"Madam?" the ticket-checker said, making the word sound like an insult. He rapped the formica counter that jutted out from the wall between the facing berths. "Ticket!"

She sprang up at the noise and pulled out her earphones. Drowsy and confused, she unzipped first one trouser pocket, then the other, then a third. At length she prised out a sweat-damped, dog-eared piece of paper and sat back with a sigh of relief. The checker held it between his fingertips, as if it were too grubby to touch. "Nomita Frederiksen, Female, age twenty-five." He tallied the name on the ticket with the one in his chart, peering over his clipboard to look at her. Then, to show that he was merely doing his job, he turned back to her ticket and checked the details on it a second time.

The girl kept her eyes on the landscape outside the window which flared now and then with flashes of light from the villages and stations they sped through. When the checker at last gave her ticket back, she put it into her rucksack, pushed her earphones in again and once more shut her eyes. Bare, toe-ringed feet on the berth, chin resting on knees that she hugged close to herself, she occupied no more space than a curled-up dog might, and appeared to be just as self-contained.

An hour, perhaps two, had gone by when they stopped at a station. Lights glowed outside, white neon dimmed to a sickly yellow by the train's tinted windows. People surged towards their coach, suitcases and bags in hand. Just outside their window was a tea stall. A tattered woman hung around near it, hoping for food. She wore a grimy sari petticoat and a too-big man's shirt buttoned wrong. Her shapeless rags and matted hair somehow intensified the raw beauty of her face. Latika wanted immediately to get out of the train and rescue her before she came to harm.

The woman was sidling up to the people on the platform, tugging a shirt in passing or nudging an arm, as though she thought that their revulsion at her touch would make them cough up a rupee or two. Everyone sidestepped her as she edged closer. When she went up to a stocky, thuggish-looking man and put a hand out towards him, wheedling him with a smile, Latika shut her eyes. She didn't want to look. She would never know anything more about this ragged woman in the murky haze of this platform, what became of her on it. Their train was just a parcel of people rushing through a landscape they had no connection to. Already too many snatches of other people's lives were stored inside her, the built-up sediments from which bits and pieces floated up at times, into her dreams.

When she opened her eyes she had lost sight of the woman and the girl in their compartment was standing up. She hoisted her backpack onto her shoulder.

"Where are you going?" Vidya asked her.

"Just to look around? Everyone's getting off anyway." The girl gestured at the aisle, the people walking up and down, leaving the train, some coming back with bottles of fizzy drinks.

"But there's nothing to look at. How long will we stop here? Already so much of the stopping time is over." Vidya peered out. "I can't tell which station it is. Do you think it's Kathalbari? Then it's not a long halt."

The girl had disappeared into the aisle before Vidya was finished. They saw her reappear a minute or two later, on the platform. Separated by window glass and distance, she looked even more a foreigner. Gouri, who had just finished her evening prayers, put away her beads and opened her eyes. "What a thing to do," she said. "Getting off a train! Is she buying food? I'd rather starve than take these risks."

Latika laughed at the improbability of chubby, rosy-cheeked Gouri either starving or taking risks. "That would be the day! I'm sure you're thinking of dinner already."

The girl went towards the stall, jostled by crowds. Everyone was pushing at each other to get on the train or buy food at the stall before the train left. She was surrounded by men ogling her braided hair and ringed ears and the curves outlined in turquoise by her T-shirt. Inside the train, the women were shielded from all the noise and shouting on the platform, but they could see her lips move. She looked smaller and slighter among the men, and had to stand on tiptoe to be seen by the vendor. She waved a fifty rupee note over her head. The man reached out, took her money, gave her a long look, plucked a packet of bread rolls from his rack and handed it to her. Then a plastic cup of tea.

"Why doesn't she come back?" Vidya said. "She's got what she wanted, hasn't she? I should never have let her go. A foreign child!"

"She was hardly asking your permission," Latika said. "It feels long, but it's only been . . ." She checked her watch. "Two minutes."

They saw the girl walk past them on the platform with her tea and bread. When she veered left, to where the ragged woman had reappeared, they realised she must have bought the food for her. The girl went up to the woman and held out the packet. The woman did not notice her, so the girl tapped her elbow.

Latika noticed the famished gaze on them of two men idling on the platform. She drew a sharp breath, shook her head to dismiss her sudden sense of foreboding, told herself not to be melodramatic — then saw one of the men sidle closer to the girl. He was leering and saying something to her. She paid him no attention. As if by mistake, still grinning, he brushed an arm against her breasts. The girl stepped backward and in a single move that appeared to take no more than a second, she thrust the bread at the woman and flung the hot tea in the man's face. She kicked his shin and his crotch as his hands flew to his face. The man stumbled, fell to the platform.

All of a sudden, as if watching a silent film, the women in the train saw the food-stall outside starting to slide backwards. The lamp-post by the stall moved two feet back, then three. They saw the girl turning around to see her train moving out of the platform, the girl running towards the train, very fast despite her backpack, running as if her life depended on it, the second of the two men running after her. The crowds on the platform obliterated them for a moment, then they reappeared. They saw them falling further and further behind and Gouri let out an anguished cry. "What is she going to do, what is she going to *do?*"

"Pull the chain! We should pull the chain!" This was Latika, who had jumped out of her seat. They looked above their heads to where the emergency brake pull should have been and saw that it was hanging loose from the wall, its spring broken. "TO STOP TRAIN PULL CHAIN," a sign in red said below the broken chain. "*Penalty For Use Without Reasonable and Sufficient Cause. Fine Up to . . .*" The rest was obscured by graffiti.

They turned to look out again but the train had escaped the neon-lit confines of the platform and was already moving in inky countryside. Striped squares of light from the train's barred window glided alongside as it speeded ahead. It was too late to do anything. They sat back, hollowed out with anxiety. They stared at the empty window seat. It had all happened too quickly. Where was the girl? Had she managed to climb onto a different coach of their train, or had she been left behind at that nameless station? What if that man had caught up with her? What if she had fallen? Onto the tracks?

Latika said, "She can't have fallen trying to get on. The train would've been stopped."

Vidya peered under their seats. "Is that backpack all the luggage she had? There's nothing else here. Why did she carry it out?"

"Maybe she thought it would be stolen if she left it," Latika said. "That's what they're told when they come here."

The train, as if lighter from shedding the girl, swayed and began to move faster. It clattered over bridges, tore through village stations and roared past trains hurtling the other way into their own oblivion. Within the coach a low hum of conversation, boxes snapping open and shut. The boy on the imaginary motorbike had begun booming up and down the corridor again.

The three of them sat motionless, their holiday high spirits snuffed out by the absence of a girl they knew not at all. When the dinner trolleys came around they had to tell the attendant to take away the fourth meal. The man asked no questions. Expressionless, he shoved the unwanted steel tray of rice and dal and vegetables into his trolley and moved ahead. He came back to them a while later to collect the empty trays and saw they still hadn't opened the foil covering their food.

Later, Latika spread out her blankets and sheets and then hoisted herself to the upper berth. Vidya was already in her bunk, an inert shape on her side, eyes shut. Latika lay in the blue glow of the train's night light, listening to the rumble of a snoring man alternate with the train's rattling and clanking. The noise kept her awake all night — or so she thought until she opened her eyes and it was morning, the train had stopped, the sunlight was radiant, and her skin could feel the nearness of the sea. They got off at Jarmuli's station, saying nothing to one another, each of them searching the busy platform for a glimpse of coloured braids and turquoise.

There is a dream I often have. I am a baby in it, held aloft by a man. He is on his back on a bed, his legs are bent at the knee, he is holding me high above him, my face is above his face, his hands are under my arms, and he is rocking on his back until he almost somersaults. He takes me each time to the brink. Then is still for a second. After that he rocks backward again. I want to beg him to stop, but my voice has died and I can't say a word. I wake up soaked in sweat.

I knew that the place where I had grown up was near Jarmuli. Although I had left the place as a child, I thought it would all come back. I got off at the station in Jarmuli and on my way to the hotel I devoured the landscape and buildings as if they would fill me with memories. Nothing happened. I waited for a moment of recognition. It never came. When I reached my hotel room I did not pause to unpack, I reread my bunches of clippings to persuade myself I had it right. By afternoon I was tired out. I laid the clippings aside and closed my eyes. It was only after I woke from my old dream of the man rocking me as a baby, with the familiar terror suffocating me, that I felt certain I was in the place the boat had brought me to when I was six or seven.

After we had got off the boat, we travelled a long distance in another van. The road ran by the sea sometimes and sometimes we drove through villages and past ruins. My first milk tooth fell out in that van. I tried to find it under the seat, but when I knelt to look, it was lost in a forest of legs and fallen scraps of paper and bits of food.

In the end the van went through high gates made of metal sheets with a line of iron spikes above. The gates closed behind us. The van stopped and we got out. The woman with us led us further in. We walked down earthen pathways, red and pretty, through gardens in which there were small houses. We were taken to a square building. One by one we were put under a tap and bathed. I saw the other girls in their underclothes, wet like birds in rain. They were thin and knock-kneed. They looked like me. Newly washed, in cotton tunics, hand in hand, the twelve of us were shown into a cottage. The cottage was screened by creepers and trees. Inside, in the room where we waited, the sunlight in the windows had gone pale green and yellow.

The room had many pictures of a long-haired man. There was one that covered most of the wall on one side. It was much taller than any of us. I could not look away from it because his eyes in that picture seemed to follow me around. In front of it were incense sticks that smelled as sick-sweet as death. As we waited, the sticks turned into furry stems of ash. There were dark red mattresses and bolsters on the floor. I don't know if this

32

is exactly how the room was that day or if I am remembering it from all the later times when I went there and had to wait. It was always the same: the pictures, the incense, the red bolsters. Two women stood by the door, their palms full of rose petals. One was the woman who had come with us on the boat, the other had golden hair.

After a while, the man in the pictures walked through the door and both the women stood straighter. The golden-haired woman gestured towards his feet and said "Guruji". He hardly looked at us. He waved us away as we bowed down and strode past us into the second room, crushing the rose petals the women scattered in his path.

Now, when I think of the time my turn came, and I stood in front of that second door, my mind changes the image. The door stays shut. Before my turn, I slip out of the line and run into the garden outside. There, under a tree, is my brother. He is smiling at me in his gummy way. "Silly donkey! Where did you wander?" he says. He swings me onto his shoulder. "You've got no front teeth any more!" he says.

But that is not what happened. I couldn't have run to the garden because the women would not let us step out of the line. The one with the hair like spun gold and eyes as blue as two drops of sky was taller than anyone I had seen before. She placed a long finger on her lips, she rolled her eyes, shook her head. I could tell she was saying just as my mother used to: "Quiet, not a word."

The door opened. A square of light. I stepped into it. The door shut behind me. The man who had just walked past us was sitting on a wide chair at the other end of the room. Guruji. He wore yellow robes and he had glossy black hair to his shoulders. He was not like other sadhus I have seen since. His face was clean and smooth like a woman's, there were no matted locks nor a beard. He looked at me as if he saw nothing else. He sat there observing me for a long time, saying nothing. I thought he could see into me, through the tunic and my skin and bones, right inside. When he held up his hand to beckon me to come closer I saw that his arms had twice the girth of my father's arms. My father was a skinny man even though he could lift big branches and chop tree trunks with his axe.

Guruji patted his lap to make me climb on to it. Then he held me against him. His chest was warm and bare, and I could hear his heart beat.

"You think you have nobody," his voice said over my head, and I could feel its vibration enter my body. "That is not true. I am your father and your mother now. I am your country. I am your teacher. I am your God." He said it like a chant, as if they were words often repeated, and always the same.

His smile was kind. I must have smiled too because he put a finger into my mouth. He stroked the gap in my gums where my milk tooth had been.

"When did that fall out?" His voice was tender, as my father's used to be when I fell and hurt myself. He shut his eyes and murmured a mantra. "I have prayed for you. Whenever you are frightened, think of my face. I will keep you safe. You have come to my ashram now. This is your refuge. Nobody will harm you. There is food and there are clothes and you have friends to play with and you will go to school."

He put his hand into a steel box and brought out a laddu that he popped into my mouth. "Don't tell the other girls I gave you this, I haven't given it to them," he said. "Be very quiet, not a word about this to anyone. This is your Initiation. You are born again."

I remember the ashram very well although I cannot remember a single thing about what was around it. Were there mountains or tall buildings? Were there shops or houses nearby? Did a road go past it? Could we hear any traffic sounds when we were inside? In my head the ashram is in the middle of nowhere, it is the only building on earth. Sometimes I wonder how much of what I remember is true. I have read that your memories can be concrete and detailed even about things that never happened to you and places you have never been to. Like fungus that takes birth in warm and wet places, memories ooze from the crevices of your brain: spawned there, living and dying there, unrelated to anything in the world outside, the slime can coat everything until you can't tell the real from the imagined.

I remember clearly, though, how enormous the ashram was and dark with trees. At night we were scared to be out alone especially because we had heard that five dogs were let loose every night to patrol the place. There were cottages in the grounds that were set at a distance from ours, in which Guruji's disciples stayed. They came and went. There were many, from everywhere in the world. In our part we had Guruji's cottage and a few other cottages, our dormitory building, a dining room, a puja hall and our school.

Many years later, my new foster mother would ask, after another long silence at the dinner table: "Tell me about your school there, tell me about your friends, tell me about the building, tell me *something*." And I would wonder what to say, where to start. I could tell her my very first school, at the ashram, was in a yellow building — that was easy. It made her look hopeful. She waited for more. I said nothing. We both listened to the sound of a neighbour clipping his hedge. A boy cycling outside shouted to a friend. Still I found nothing to say. Then her sister phoned and my foster mother gave up waiting for me to speak.

Outside, I could see a blue and white bird and the hedge that went around her tiny lawn and, across the road, white houses with red roofs. Each house was exactly like the one next to it. The sun was like a moon in this country, and in its light I felt as if I was looking at everything through a pearl. It was cold and the trees had no leaves. I had never seen a leafless tree before. My foster mother dropped her voice, speaking fast and softly, even though I could not understand what she was saying to her sister.

What else could I tell her?

Of course she knew I had been in orphanages before I came to her, and when I spoke about the ashram I made it sound like yet another orphanage. I told her the school was not far from the dormitory where we slept. We went there after our morning's milk and banana. I told her the school had a courtyard with a jamun tree. I got stuck trying to explain what a jamun was: was it sour or sweet or bitter? How to explain its strange taste, and the way our tongues went purple and fat after eating them? And wondering how to explain jamuns, I would be distracted remembering how all day we did our lessons or our chores as if we boat girls were like other girls, but at night I would hear one girl grind her teeth fiercely enough to set mine on edge and another girl sob. Only when I felt my pillow wet with tears and spit would I know I had been listening to myself crying. How could I tell my foster mother this? I would begin to tear tiny shreds out from the paper napkin she never forgot to set beside my bowl of cereal. I dipped my spoon into the cereal and tried to count how many raisins there were in it, and how many bits of nut, and this way, by examining the cereal hard enough, I dissolved the lump that had somehow appeared in my throat. My foster mother watched me and waited for a while, then sighed and got up and began to wash dishes at the sink. I hunched over the shreds of tissue, unaware of her, the room, or the cereal I kept stirring around in its bowl uneaten, and in my head the rasping calls of crows grew deafening and I was back in that hot classroom, the bench hard and narrow under me.

Our ashram school had many students. There were girls and boys who came to it from outside for the day. They kept to themselves and in the classroom their seats were in rows away from ours. They were taller than us, their clothes fitted better, their shoes were less scuffed. They looked at us and then away, as if they had not seen us at all. We regarded them as people from another country, one that we would never go to, not even to visit. Some of the boys stayed at the ashram just as we did, but they came in through another door, they sat on the other side of the room, and when classes finished they left for their dormitories, which were so far away they were taken there in a van. We never saw them outside of school.

The first day at our school we were each given a set of books and a box of crayons. There were twelve crayons arranged in a row, like a rainbow inside a sheath of cardboard. There was also a metal box with a pencil and sharpener and rubber in it. I must have opened the box and shut it many times. I remember how those boxes shut with a click. I am sure I took out the rubber and smelled it, even pressed my teeth into it, as I like to do to this day.

The woman who handed us these things wore her hair in two plaits. Her eyes were painted black around the rims with kajal. "I am your teacher," she said. "You will call me Didi. Draw a balloon in your drawing book. Colour it with a crayon."

She turned her back to us and drew a balloon on the blackboard. It flew on the board attached to a long line. I opened my new drawing book and on the first page I copied her flying balloon. I picked out the navy blue from my row of new crayons. I started filling colour into my balloon. I pressed the crayon hard to the paper. The colour coated the page like grease. If I touched it, my fingertip turned blue.

The teacher's voice, very close to my ears said, "When you colour something, don't go in every direction, colour in one direction." She took the crayon from my hand and said, "Like this." Her strokes with crayon were sure and smooth. She said, "Stay inside the line, never go out. Understand?" This is what we were taught at the ashram: that we were never to go outside. Outside the line was danger. Outside we would be killed or locked up in jail.

The teacher's face had so much powder it was white like chalk. She had a black moustache. When she was bending over my drawing book, her plaits hung in front of my nose. They had ribbons at the ends. She had a smear of ash on her forehead and a red dot inside the smear. If I think of her the smell of the incense in Guruji's cottage and of coconut oil and soap comes back to me. She moved her face away, laid the crayon on my desk and walked to the rows ahead. I kept staring at her, the plaits with the ribbons that swung when she took a step.

Before I could stop it, my crayon had rolled off the desk to the floor.

I ducked under the bench to pick it up. Down below there were only legs — boys' legs, girls' legs, table and chair legs. It looked much bigger than the room above. It was a maze. I could not find my crayon because the maze made me as dizzy as when I was hunting for my fallen tooth in the van. I crouched there not daring to come back up without the crayon.

I don't know when it was that a girl came wriggling under the bench and crouched next to me. She had stalk-thin limbs. Her head looked too big for her. She crouched on the ground underneath our desks and she smiled at me. She had crooked buck teeth when she smiled. Where I had a shaggy mop, she had straight thin hair to her shoulders. Her eyes were watery, so big that they seemed to bulge. Later I found out that her name was Piku.

With Piku down below, everything became less strange. The furniture legs became furniture legs again. She crawled between the chairs — I was little myself, but she was even littler. It took her only moments and then she held the crayon up to me. That was how I became friends with Piku.

I don't remember many other things about my first year at the school, but I remember how one day we were told that our teacher had been taken ill. We made up stories about her. One of the girls said she had run away to get married and another said she had died and become a ghost who lived on top of the neem tree. But our teacher did come back: maybe it was days later, maybe weeks. A hush fell over the room as she entered. Her head and one of her eyes was wrapped in a bandage. Her ribboned plaits were missing. Her lips were like two swollen rubber chillies. We did not know we were staring, but after a while we remembered and stood up, chorusing Good Morning, Didi as we did every day.

She sat in her chair and her head dropped to the desk. The bandage on her head had a round patch of red on it right at the top. Under the bandage her head looked as smooth as a ball.

She pulled her head up after a while and said, "I had an accident." Then she took a sip of water from the glass on the table and replaced the cover on the glass. She held up the arithmetic textbook and said, "Page five."

There was shuffling and fluttering as all of us opened our books. From one of the other classrooms we heard a teacher shout, "Siddown!"

"Repeat after me," Didi said, "two wonza two, twotwoza four, twothreeza six, twofourza eight."

We repeated the tables. All of us were gaping at her.

Two wonza two, twotwoza four.

She had shut the unbandaged eye and clasped her arms and was swaying to the rhythm of our singsong version of her tables.

Twofivezaten, twosixza twell.

I kept losing track of the numbers. I repeated them without understanding what I was saying.

"Twoeightza sixteen," Didi said. "I had sixteen stitches in my head."

All of us repeated, "Twoeightza sixteen, I had sixteen stitches in my head."

At that she opened her eye. She stopped swaying. I saw that the eye had a cut at the edge. Blood was caked over the cut like a bit of burnt plastic. She said slowly, "My hair had to be shaved off for the stitches. My plaits had to be cut off."

We did not repeat that. Nobody said anything. The fan made a whirring and squeaking and clacking noise. Didi looked at us, expressionless. "That's what's waiting for you all," she said. "All." She had a glazed, dazed look. She put a hand to her head and touched the places where her plaits used to be. Without warning she got up. She did not pick up her books and the ruler with which she used to rap our knuckles. She left the room without saying another word.

For some time we waited for her to come back. Then we began murmuring to each other. After some time two of the girls got into a fight, started tugging each other's hair and scratching and biting. The rest of us watched the fun. The teacher from the next class stormed in and yelled, "What is this madhouse? Where is your Didi?"

"How long will you stare at your cereal and keep muttering to yourself, Nomi?" my foster mother's voice broke in. "Look what a mess you've made with all that torn up tissue." She cleared my bowl and brushed away the shredded paper, shaking her head to say she had given up all hope of sense from me. As if she had no idea what she was doing, she took a big jar of pasta shells and began to fling handfuls of pasta into a pan on the stove top in which she had put eggs to boil. "I asked at your school here, you know, and they said, What? Doesn't she talk at home?" Half the pasta missed the pan and fell to the floor, but she kept throwing in fistfuls, uncaring. Her voice sounded too high. She had been told by the teachers that I had friends in school, that I played football and went to kickboxing classes. She had looked in my room, she confessed, found that I had filled drawing books with dead birds, broken weathervanes and barbed wire. She wondered why I didn't draw some happy pictures. Flowers, the sun, green meadows. She wondered what she was doing wrong. Drops of boiling water splashed out, scalding her. She stopped throwing pasta shells into the pan. She stood there with her hand in the jar and her shoulders slumped.

THE SECOND DAY

Badal sat cross-legged in a padmasana, knees jutting out, meditating fingertips pressed together. His back was as straight as the wall behind him. His lips flickered, but his eyelids were sealed.

It was a two-storeyed house in Jarmuli, its rooms opening onto a small courtyard. Badal sat on the floor of the verandah that bordered the courtyard on three of its four sides. The way the house was built, sounds ricocheted off the mouldering walls. Somewhere upstairs he could hear his aunt threatening her son, "Are you going to get up or shall I empty a bucket of water on your head?" A knife scraping a steel plate, that was her voice. Chalk squealing across a blackboard. The screeching fan belt in a car.

From the room where his grandfather slept came coughs that sounded as if the old man was spilling his innards out. Each burst of coughing was followed by hoarse wails. "Call me to you, O Ram, O Vishnu, O Krishna, call me!"

Every morning at precisely four-thirty, a conch was blown in a house across the alley — once, twice, thrice. A long, high-pitched bleat that tottered towards the end as the blower's breath weakened and then gave way.

Every morning, Badal wanted to shut them up, blow it for them instead. He could produce flawless, melodious notes from any conch, however hoarse it might sound in other hands.

He took a breath and released it, "Ommmm." The choppy waves in his mind subsided.

At dawn it was his practice to sit and chant this way, longing for what used to come to him as naturally as breathing: a sense of the deep, everlasting hum of creation, an intimate, effortless closeness to God. He could not describe the sensation in words and he could not reach it by thinking about it. The more he tried to extricate himself from the quicksand of life, the more relentlessly it sucked him in. What was his work today? There were the errands for his uncle. Nothing else. It would be slow. And in the evening? He grimaced. "Three old biddies from Calcutta," the hotel had said, when booking him to take them around the Vishnu temple. An image of his father flitted through Badal's head. Large, grey-haired, and imperious. As a temple guide his father had exuded a dignity and authority that could crush whole squads of matrons, the kind who made Badal quail even though he had wandered Jarmuli's great temple with his father from childhood and few guides knew it as well as he did. He told himself the manager of the hotel had sounded anxious to book him for the women, and how many guides were trusted this way by good hotels? He counted them off in his head — no more than a dozen. The rest had to wait like scavengers for pilgrims at the temple gates.

The hotel took a cut from his earnings, it was the way the world functioned.

He took another breath and murmured, "Ommmmm."

His morning was free.

He could spend more than his usual few minutes at the tea stall.

He took a deeper breath.

Water thundered into a metal pail in the far corner of the courtyard. He opened his eyes a sliver and saw his uncle at the tap, bulbously naked. His chequered loincloth clung to his flesh like red and white skin. It was wedged between the cheeks of his uncle's shuddering buttocks.

A radio sang out from upstairs: "Tojo! Washing Powder Tojo!"

His uncle muttered, "Om Vishnu, Om Vishnu," twice for each jug of water he poured on himself. The stone paving around the tap was grey-green with moss. His uncle stepped warily. His head was bald, but his body was matted with coarse black hair. "Like a cautious water buffalo," Badal breathed out. "Ommmm."

A round pool of sunlight in the left side of the courtyard lasted from about nine until eleven in the morning. Within its circumference Badal had planted a shiuli sapling. In four or five years it would be taller than he was, reaching for the sky that the courtyard inscribed into a blue square, and it would sprinkle the earth beneath with creamy, sweet-scented flowers. Wider and wider the circle of flowers would grow over the years and one day it would bury the courtyard's squalor. Badal watered the shiuli every day, examined it for signs of new leaves.

When he opened his eyes to see how far his uncle was from finishing, he noticed someone had stepped on his sapling. Its stem jutted out at an angle, like a broken limb.

All at once he plucked his fingers apart, got up, and pulled open the iron latch on the door that separated the courtyard from the street outside. It was the main door to the house, but it was small and warped and faded and the latch was the old kind where a heavy iron chain climbed upward and fitted a loop on the doorframe. He had to bend not to knock his head as he stepped out — but that was the only change from when, as a child of two, he had found his way to the world outside for the first time. He swung the door open as he had for the past twenty-six years, with his foot, and slammed it shut. The door knew it was Badal. Kicked open and banged shut this way for years, it hung askew on its frame and responded to him with a series of creaks and groans.

Outside the house was a narrow alleyway where Badal's scooter was parked, but at this time of day he did not want his scooter. Instead he walked down the road to a shrine at the corner. The shrine was no more than two feet high, a few bricks at the foot of a tree, plastered together and whitewashed by the old woman who tended it. Badal took ten rupees out of his pocket and held it towards the woman who sat by the shrine threading flowers into a garland.

50

"What flower are you giving your God today? Hibiscus? Put in a few from me, will you?"

When the woman looked up at him, all that Badal saw were two squares of glass as thick as bottle-bottoms and crushed muslin for skin.

"He is your God too, and everyone else's."

She had a cackling, old-woman voice and smiled as she spoke. Her sari was threadbare, her body as bent as a sickle. She reached into her bowl of kumkum, dipped a finger into the paste and when Badal bent his forehead to her she planted a circle of red on it. She went back to making her garland as he kneeled and touched his head to the door of her shrine. He was still for a moment, then rose and walked away. He was out of earshot when the woman said, "Will you get me some gur and bananas on your way back?"

He was always in a hurry at this time of day, going to the sea. It was not far. Not so far that it was a tedious walk, yet enough to be a different world. Long before he reached it, he heard the waves roaring, receding, roaring, receding. He began walking faster as he neared the promenade and when a gap between buildings gave him the expanse of sand and water he knew so well, his steps slowed. He would turn the corner, he would see Raghu setting a bench before the tea stall, and old Johnny Toppo lighting the stove.

This early in the morning the beach was uncrowded, the breeze fresh, the day's heat gathering ferocity somewhere on the horizon. There were fishermen at work on their boats and nets. A monk as tall as a tree stood waist-deep in the seawater, wearing dark glasses

51

and yellow robes, saying his prayer beads. He was there every morning. Loose white hair cascaded to his shoulders.

Johnny Toppo took no notice of Badal. His tea stall was nothing more than a barrow and a bench, but he made a great to-do setting it up every day, lining up his charred pots and pans, the tea, spices, milk and sugar, the mortar and pestle for the ginger. Last, he put out his biscuit jars, the pair of them, their glass now clouded, blistered, finely cracked. They had grown old with him, he liked to say. He soaked stacks of clay cups in a deep iron pail of water. He hunched over his stove, fiddling with matches. His bare chest was rib-striped and a shark's tooth hung from his stringy neck on a length of black twine. His bald head gleamed in the sunlight as he lit the stove and breathed a song into it to get it going:

And the rain came again that night.
And again and again and again.

Badal scanned the beach in either direction, shading his eyes. It was a while before he spotted Raghu, not far away, to the left. There he was, on one of the concrete plinths by the beach, facing the sun, body stretched: sinking and rising, arching and drooping, as gracefully as if it were a dance, into stretches and push-ups. Sculpture that had stepped off the walls of a temple.

Badal stood motionless, his eyes fixed on the boy. He did not notice the fire-tipped waves or the fishermen pushing out a boat farther down the shore. His gaze did

52

not waver when Johnny Toppo's singing turned into curses: "This time I'm going to smash his pretty nose in two. Raghu! Come here and get to work. And where's that fifty I put into the biscuit box yesterday?"

Raghu straightened. A solid orange sun was floating out of the sea behind him, lighting up his mass of hair. He had taken off his T-shirt for the morning's exercises and Badal saw that it was true, what he had only imagined: the boy had no hair on his body but for a shadow that vanished into his grey shorts. He saw the beginnings of hard muscles, the faintest of bulges at the shoulders. Raghu reached for the red T-shirt on the plinth and his spine became a bow arching down the length of his back. He looked in Johnny Toppo's direction and noticed Badal's eyes on him. He shrugged himself into the T-shirt and when his face emerged through the neck it had a half-smile.

"One tea, no milk, no sugar, lemon only?" he said to Badal as he went past him to the stove.

The monk lurched in the waves as a breaker charged the beach. Buffeted, he seemed to be in danger of being washed away, but he went on fingering his rosary. You could not tell if the eyes behind the dark glasses were closed in prayer.

Jarmuli had white beaches and many miles of coastline, but the waters were treacherous. Riptides could suck in swimmers and innocuous waves could turn savage, picking people off the sand and sucking them into the ocean. Most people came to Jarmuli for the temples, not for swimming, and pilgrims too tended to stay away during the long monsoon when cyclones ravaged the bay, lashing it day after day with rain. The morning's lazy beauty had to end, work had to be done while the weather allowed. After the thrill of seeing Raghu at the beach was over, Badal stood at a food shop near the Vishnu temple, casting his eye around for possible clients, clinking the coins in his pocket. There wasn't enough money, there seldom was. His wallet too had barely a hundred in it. But he had eaten nothing at home and decided to spend his loose change on a samosa.

He had idled near the temple for only a little while when Hari, another temple guide, tapped his arm saying, "Bhai, Badal. I need to leave — something urgent — and I've two people waiting for me. You take them to the temple, give them a quick round."

Luck appeared to be on his side. It had to do with his early morning glimpse of shirtless Raghu, he was certain. Or perhaps it was those ten rupees and prayers at the old woman's shrine. He remained carefully unsmiling and continued chewing his samosa. Between bites he said, "I've no time, got another group soon. And in the afternoon I need to get home." He had no work till evening, but Hari did not need to know that. He looked towards the temple gates. He must not let Hari's clients escape. He had to slow it down to extract as much as he could from Hari, but not too much.

Although the street had been swept that morning it was a stewing mess already: fruit, flowers, spilled food, pulverised by the heat. A foul smell rose from the blackness in the drains and penetrated everything. It

54

was the only workplace he had ever known. He didn't mind the stench. He stuffed the last of his samosa into his mouth, then grabbed the plastic jug from the counter. He poured water into his palm, slurped it in, and with calculated slowness swilled his mouth and spat into the drain. They both knew what this was about, but it had to be gone through.

Hari said, "Once. This one time — only because — look, I'll tell you the reason later, it's at a delicate stage now, you get it? Be quick, just show them a couple of shrines. They won't know the difference. Or else I'll get it in the neck from you know who."

Badal drew a green plastic comb from his pocket, ran it through his oil-slicked hair, examined his nails. All clipped short apart from the long one on the little finger of his left hand. That nail was now about a quarter of the length of his finger, and he kept it coated with tomato-red nail polish. It was his good luck nail. He admired it for a moment, burped, then said, "I think I'll have something sweet too," and went back into the shop. He emerged with a leaf cup that held two creamy white squares. He offered one to Hari, who shook his head. "I'll give you my cut, don't refuse. I'll come and deliver the cash at your house. Tell me when and —"

"No," Badal interrupted. "Not to the house. I'll get it from you here tomorrow, same time." His uncle did not need to know about these extras. He had a bank account too that his uncle did not know about.

Negotiations completed, Badal stood before the main gate of the temple, talking into his phone. After several minutes of misunderstandings and misdirections he located Hari's clients waving at him from near the shack where visitors to the temple had to leave their shoes. A man and a girl. He walked up to them. The man had sleepy eyes and crazy hair; the girl looked puny, reduced by the massive temple gates and her tall companion, whose shoulders her head barely reached. The beggars and idlers on the street were gawping at her beads and tattoos and coloured braids. Badal turned away from her tentative smile. How was he to put this to her? He took the man aside.

"She can't go in like that."

The man seemed not to understand.

Badal switched from Hindi to English and enunciated the words: "Clothes. Not good." He gave the girl a rapid look, turned away as if embarrassed. How could she have come to a temple looking like that? Didn't every guide book make it clear how women must dress for this temple? Nothing shorter than ankle-length, no tight clothes, everyone knew that.

"The priest say no. Not allow." Badal pointed to the gates of the temple, which towered over the alley. Its stone arches were carved with gargoyles too high to see properly. Within the arches were heavy metal doors studded with brass clasps and rings. Half a dozen priest-like figures stood at the gates, bare-bodied but for their dhotis, chadars, and sacred threads. "She can rent something there," Badal said, Hindi again, the English eluding him. He was gesturing towards a counter by the gates. "A sari to wrap around herself."

56

Suraj, the sleepy-eyed man, followed Badal's gaze and assessed the girl called Nomi with new eyes. His just-met colleague. He had not taken much notice of her that morning, he was hung-over, headachy. He had drunk way too much and smoked too much the day before. His throat felt as if a thousand pins were pricking it all over. On the drive to the temple he had rested his head against the car window and dozed off. But even in better shape he wouldn't have noticed her clothes: olive green cargo pants cut off at the knees, pockets bulging with camera bits and pieces. An off-white shirt. Not loose, not tight. It was standard travel gear. But now that he was paying attention he saw that on her the shirt, its top three buttons undone, somehow looked quite unlike other shirts. Possibly not regulation temple gear.

Nomi's body stiffened into an uneasy self-consciousness. She turned her back on them, looked at the gargoyles.

Suraj ambled across to her. "Our man thinks you're not clad modestly enough for an audience with the Lord. He wants you to rent a sari from that counter over there."

"Really?" She looked down at herself, made a face. "I'm covered from neck to knees!" She began rummaging inside her bag, produced a long blue scarf. "Everything I read before coming here said the country had changed. What was it like before? The women were draped in curtains?"

Badal was a short distance away, frowning at her.

"This is dumb," she said as she wrapped the scarf around her shoulders. "Like I'm dressing in the street. I know what I'll do — I'll buy some Indian clothes today." She glanced over at Badal and said, "Will this work?"

Suraj wondered again at the way she spoke, as if she had no sure identity. She looked Indian, even spoke a faltering Hindi, but sounded at times American, at times like a German friend he had, Matthias. He remembered Matthias' fascination with the way Indian women in six-yard saris had no qualms showing off their midriffs. Now he noticed that Nomi's shirt ended at her waist, so that when she stretched to drape the scarf around her shoulders, they were allowed a glimpse of the whorls of her belly button. Tattooed, Suraj saw, with a red, five-petalled flower.

Badal said, "No, not allow."

"Still?" She sounded incredulous.

Badal shook his head and repeated, pointing again at her cargo pants and towards the priests at the gates: "Not allow."

His tone appeared to infuriate her. "Not allow, not allow!" She exclaimed, turning to Suraj. "I can't stand it, these temples, all these men laying down the law. Don't wear this, don't wear that, don't do this, don't do that. Half those men around the door aren't even wearing shirts. Fuck it. I'm not going in there."

"And you'll do what? Wait in the car? We can come back once you've changed. Or do this tomorrow." Suraj rubbed his aching eyes. A temper tantrum when they

58

hadn't even begun work. This was going to be a fun week.

She turned on her heel before he could say more. "I'll go for a spin, I'll look around. We need to put other stuff in the film, don't we? I'll go and see the temple later if you think anything will work in there — the permissions, space — all of that."

Suraj stopped on the brink of entering the temple gates. She had been paid good money by a television company to come all this distance to research their film. They had agreed to his over-the-top fee for being her point man. Here they were after more than a month of e-mail negotiations and preparation — and she was was giving up the very first day?

He snapped out of his shambling manner and loped off behind Nomi with surprising speed. After a moment's paralysis, Badal followed, shouting, "Where are you going? What is happening?" He had plans already for his morning's extra earning, it wasn't going to slip away, he would not let it.

The two men panted to a stop near the car just as it was revving to leave. Suraj pulled open the door and slid in. "Right. I'll do this later too. Go," he said to the driver. "My head's splitting," he explained to Nomi.

"But . . ."

"I'm not in good shape today . . . I'll miss too much . . . had thought you'd be the second pair of eyes. We'll do it together later. Whenever. Let's do something else today. The beach. Food shacks. Something not too exotic."

"It's daily life here! It's not exotic for them, they come to pray here every day. It's not exotic for him, see? It's how he earns a living!"

As if to prove her right, Badal was holding the window frame, banging on the car. "I left other people waiting, I turned them away, to take you to the temple." He thrust his face into the window, refusing to let the car move. Suraj saw the man's eyebrows came together in the middle of his forehead in such a way that his face was cut into two. The whites of his eyes were yellow and forked through with red lines. The hand that held the window had circles of rough skin on the knuckles and one long red nail stuck out like a painted talon. "You're not going to get in there without me, you know that?" Badal said. "Not today, not on any other day."

"We'll go tomorrow. We'll meet you here. We're not running away," Suraj said.

"Tomorrow's not O.K," Nomi said. "We haven't enough time, and we've got stuff to do tomorrow! Just finish this today. Could you please do that?" Was she begging him or was she ordering him? During their e-mailing, he had searched for her on the net but found not a single photograph. His repeated google-clicks had dredged up no information. Odd, when she was on the circuit. From the self-assurance of her e-mails he had built up an image of a tall, athletic, and he had to admit it — white — woman in his head. A sensuous blonde. Along the lines of Anita Ekberg or Britt Ekland, a Scandinavian Valkyrie ready for anything. They would zip around on a hired motorbike, their packed days of work followed by long swims in the sea and siestas in a big double bed. Then, yesterday, in the hotel's reception, there was this — this brown shrimp. He had looked past her, beyond her, around her, not wanting to believe that this was the woman he had been writing to. His boss for the next few days. Unbelievable. Just when he thought his luck had turned.

He got out of the car without another word and watched it crawl away from the parking lot through the crowds. When he turned back towards the temple again, he almost collided with Badal. The man was standing inches away, his close-set eyes drilling holes into Suraj.

"We will go into the temple now? Please remove your shoes."

Inside the temple, Suraj followed him around, nodding at everything Badal said. Shrine after shrine, square after square. He should have been looking out for possible camera angles, for the falling of light and shadow, for examples of striking sculpture, but within minutes of starting the tour he had discovered that the temple allowed no cameras. How would Nomi's company deal with this in their film? Would they use stock photos? Pictures of the exterior?

His head ached too blindingly to allow thought. He put one foot in front of another, dreaming of chilled beer. A tall glass beaded with a million drops of water, froth at the top. He stared at the square they were in as Badal said, "If you come here in the evening, you see a stunning sight — a priest climbing to the top of that tower."

Suraj looked up at the tower. The sun behind it turned it into a black mountain. He could not take it. Not with a piercing hangover. If he opened his eyes fully they might fuse like light bulbs. He said, "I'll sit for a while. I'll think of God. I want to pray."

Badal crossed the courtyard and stood in a corner pretending not to observe his client. He saw him take out a small piece of wood from his pocket, then a knife. The man scraped at the wood with his knife for only a minute or two before he stopped and sat there, gazing into space. He was taller than average, had a slight stoop. The short sleeves of his T-shirt exposed biceps starting to soften. The T-shirt was black but for a grey dragon that reared up its chest. The fellow had a shock of hair cut in such untidy tufts it was as if he had taken a paper knife to his head. A bristly salt and pepper stubble darkened his face. Badal had smelled soured alcohol on his breath.

He spotted a friend and nodded to him, pointing at Suraj across the square. "See that bastard? If I don't milk him like a prize cow my name's not Badal." His friend bowed low in a mock namaste, saying, "You're the king, we all know that."

Suraj leaned his aching head against a pillar. His eyes half closed, he was vaguely aware of the milling crowds around him. Such a swarm of people. Singing people, chanting people. People with beads, people ringing bells, people reading holy books, children, ancients. People everywhere, going from shrine to shrine, searching the stones for some traces of the salvation they had come to find. He was an impostor. Everyone

62

must know he wasn't there to pray. Not that they cared. They were too fired up by their proximity to the Lord, intoxicated with finding this hotline to paradise.

At the end of the courtyard was the entrance to a stone shrine. It might have been a stage door, the courtyard the stage, the pillars and arches around it the proscenium. He stared at the door. Surely someone would step out of its shadowed rectangle into the sun. A man. A muscular man with shaggy hair. An actor. He, Suraj. In those red robes he had worn at his college drama society's final-year performance, the spotlight on him, the rest of the stage dark, the audience below invisible, all eyes on him.

What were his lines? From an old poem: Ah, but a man's reach should exceed his grasp, Or what's a heaven for? There was tubby old dhoti-clad Mishraji flapping about like a wounded bird, certain he would screw up those precious lines. He had not. Despite that joker of a teacher he had made it to film school. And then what? Nothing. Zero. Reach exceeded grasp. It always did. Cut to now: he was not an actor, not a director, not even a real cameraman. Just some guy who lived off assignments, doing the homework for other film-makers. The real guys. Some day he would make his own film. He had a screenplay. He thought back two years, to the time a couple of producers were about to bite. Long telephone calls that left him sleepless with excitement. Then nothing. A good story, they had said. Award-winning stuff. Their chequebooks firmly in their deep pockets.

The pillar he was leaning his head against began to feel too hard. He straightened, remembered the wood in his hand. He rubbed it in his palm as if to warm it, started whittling again. It was a block of sandalwood, soft and responsive, which he had managed to get through a friend in the forest department. He loved the scented exhalations from the wood as he carved and scraped, growing steadily more focused, all but forgetting where he was, until he noticed a man coming towards him down the square. He was not walking. He was full-length on the stone floor of the courtyard. Painfully, slowly, he was rolling his bare body towards the next shrine, all the while chanting a mantra.

The knife froze in Suraj's hand. Inconceivable to feel as devout as this man, so certain of the existence of God and certain that this God looked after you personally. The ground was paved with rough granite and as the man came closer Suraj saw that grit had pierced his body all over, peeling skin away, making it bleed. Pink bits of his flesh clung to the courtyard's stone. His eyes betrayed no pain, they gazed skyward: entranced.

Suraj shut his eyes. His breakfast rose into his mouth — bitter coffee. He swallowed it back and shut his eyes, fending off thoughts of wounds and gore. His head filled with the yelping of a dog, his nose with blood, rum and night jasmine all mixed up into a familiar stink of rage and fear. He had to struggle not to throw up.

He opened his eyes and saw himself looking directly into Badal's face. The man had a mocking expression. He did not speak, only raised his joined-up eyebrows and curled his lips. He stood exactly where the blood-stained man had rolled past. He did not seem to notice that the dust below his feet was speckled pink.

Suraj stood up. He put his wood and his knife back into his pockets. He had seen enough, he would not go to another shrine. In fact if he could help it he would never go to a temple or church or mosque or monastery ever again. He would, instead, go and eat. He felt suddenly famished, as if he would pass out without food, his mouth flooding with salty drool at the thought of the crabs he had feasted on yesterday. He would have a whole plate of rice and that crab curry. It was rich and red and smelled insanely delicious. He felt his teeth crack the claws, he sucked out succulent white flesh, licked up every last drop of the gravy. Maybe they ought to shoot a test scene at that restaurant, right there, the air smoky with crab. Those shabby restaurants were made for travel films, with their turquoise walls and parrot-green chairs, the bottles filled with scarlet syrups and sauces, the gleaming brass pots and pans that stood in a row at the back.

Badal said, "So, shall we carry on? The next courtyard is the one where . . ."

Suraj said, "No more courtyards. Just show me the way out, and help me get my shoes back."

Badal smiled as if infinitely regretful. "My morning is gone. You'll need to pay me even if you don't complete the tour."

"I already paid your friend," Suraj said, "the other man . . . what was his name?"

"Ah, but that was just the advance. He must have told you."

"That definitely wasn't what he said," Suraj said, although he was too hungry to battle. "Not at all." He remembered his expense account and said, "Oh what the hell. How much?"

Badal stood looking at the money in his hand. Five hundred rupees. And he would get the rest from Hari later. More than he had ever made from one client in half an hour. Ripping off the ungodly was somehow more satisfying, it made the world a better place. He stood rubbing the crisp notes one against the other. Brand new. He hated folding new notes. He slid them into his wallet, taking care to keep them flat at the edges. He would use his free time and the windfall to buy something for Raghu — maybe a shirt, maybe a watch. One of those watches that told much more than the time.

Badal left the temple and scoured Jarmuli's main market for a present. He had never given Raghu anything and now that the thought had crossed his mind it had become a pressing need. He looked through stacks of resplendent polyester shirts at one clothing store after another, then watches. He changed his mind, thought he would buy the boy a radio and examined transistors of all prices and sizes, almost bought a sleek silver and black one shaped like a torpedo. After more than an hour of indecision, he settled on a made-in-China mobile phone. With a SIM card in it, it added up to quite a bit more than he could afford, but it would impress Raghu no end. He was sure of that.

He urged his scooter towards the beach until the old machine's rattle made it sound as if it were dying under him. He couldn't wait to give Raghu the mobile. He reached the promenade when it was well past the time Johnny Toppo shut the tea stall for his lunch and siesta. Business only took off much later in the afternoon when the beach swelled with stalls selling food, trinkets, souvenirs.

He skidded to a halt near the promenade and hurriedly parked the scooter, running to the beach. The sand felt hot enough to roast peanuts in. Not many people were about, only the diehards determined to make the most of their holiday, dashing in and out of the water. Badal made his way towards an isolated nook further down, where Raghu tended to laze most afternoons. The sun was a million crystalline pieces in the sea, glittering far into the distance. Badal never wore glasses against the sun, looking directly into it sometimes, daring it to do its worst.

He turned the curve and there Raghu was, half hidden by the prow of an upturned boat. The tea stall was shut. The boy could have gone off, but he had not. Had he been waiting for Badal? He must have been.

Badal came closer. He saw that the boy had gnawed at the skin on his chapping lips until the lower one — the fuller, fleshier, darker one — had bled. Burst open like a fig, Badal remembered from somewhere: your lips, bitten when kissed, burst open like a ripe fig.

Was it only two months ago that he had met Raghu? Three? He had been sitting on the tea-stall bench recovering from a quarrel with his uncle. Raghu had come to him and put down a tiny clay cup of tea unasked, saying, "Careful, it's hot," and Badal had looked up into the largest, darkest eyes he thought he had ever seen. The boy's voice had a husky edge that made the words taper off and retreat where you could not follow them. It left Badal wanting to hear him speak again, so he had said, "You're new?" Raghu had smiled in reply and Badal had caught sight of the dimple in his left cheek. All his annoyance had dissolved into euphoria.

It must have been the sight of the bleeding lip that made Badal sit closer now than he had dared before. Raghu said nothing, he held out his packet of gutka to Badal. They looked at the water. They never spoke much, but Badal had only to be within sight of Raghu to feel a deep contentment, as if he needed nothing more in the world than silence and the knowledge that Raghu was in it somewhere. He sensed that Raghu felt this too. Once or twice he had hidden himself behind the hull of a boat and watched Raghu look up each time a man approached the tea stall and droop with disappointment when it was just another customer. He was not a hundred per cent sure, but then what was a hundred per cent sure?

Badal's days now existed for the mornings and afternoons when he could escape clients, family, customers, priests, God himself — and run to the beach to sit holding a clay cup of Raghu's tea — just sit with his voice within hearing, his body within touching distance. Raghu brushed past him — on purpose, he was certain of it — as he went about serving customers, rinsing cups, doing whatever he did at Johnny Toppo's stall.

Ten days ago when he was at the tea stall and Johnny Toppo not there, Raghu had asked him out of the blue, "Have you ever been beaten? Thrashed?"

Raghu had not called him "Babu", as Johnny Toppo did. Badal paused over the thought. Raghu did not call him anything. He used neither his name, nor the deferential Babu, or Sahib, or Dada. It felt loaded with meaning, how he took care not to distance him that way.

"Many times," Badal had said. "After my father died, my uncle used to clobber me till my teeth ran around in my mouth like dice. With anything at hand — his shoes, his belt, even with the stick the bastard killed rats with." He smiled as he answered Raghu's question. He had suffered, he wanted Raghu to know, but he was nonchalant about it.

Raghu pulled up his shirt to show Badal a welt on his back. "Yesterday." He had said nothing more.

The rage and tenderness that had flooded Badal that afternoon came back again. He wanted to ask Raghu about the wound — had it healed? Was Johnny Toppo the bullying swine who had done it? The boy was gazing at the sea, a finger in one of his ears, then scratching something on his leg, his jaws working the tobacco in his mouth. The lusciousness of that itch, that hand moving from ear to leg — a boyish, scarred, beautiful

69

hand, the wrist bone jutting out in a knob. What beauty — how could such beauty possibly exist?

A red bead of betel-juiced spittle trickled from the corner of Raghu's mouth and he sucked it back in. The sun turned the sea into jagged blades of light. A faraway white-topped breaker gathered speed as it began its run for the beach. On the horizon was a grey, indefinable shape that might be a building or a small island. Was it an island Badal had failed to notice all his life? Arrow-like boats streaked past, criss-crossing. A group of brown dogs chased each other up and down the sand and into the water. Near Raghu's feet a coin-sized crab dug itself out of the sand and skittered away. Badal looked up from the crab, saw that his island had moved west. And then after a while, further west. Everything stood still and speeded up all at once. The faraway breaker came closer, it grew taller, it roared and bellowed, it flung itself at the sand, and without warning or preparation Badal found his lips on Raghu's, his hand roaming his smooth bare chest, following the line of the fine hair down into his shorts. The blood on Raghu's lips tasted of salt and sea and rust. He sucked the grainy tobacco off Raghu's tongue and felt it going straight to his head, making him dizzy, sending his hand deeper down. And then the boy pushed him off and ran away along the beach, leaving him empty and short of breath.

He clambered up. Everything was in disarray. He stumbled, hunting for his slippers. They had travelled over the sand in two different directions. His legs had turned into stilts, his feet would not fit into his slippers,

70

as if he had grown extra toes. By the time he managed to put them on, Raghu was nowhere to be seen.

He would not try to find him. Not right then. It was a kind of slow magic that had overtaken the day. The sky blazed. The sea shone. The waves came at a stately pace as if they had all eternity. There was time. He searched his pocket for his comb. The feel of its hard plastic teeth on his scalp made his eyelids droop with pleasure. There would always be time. He would give Raghu his gift the next time they met. They would talk, he would buy him a bottle of cola and Raghu would tell him everything. Who had beaten him, where his parents were, where he had come from, where he was headed. Badal knew the answer to that one. Raghu's wanderings were over, his lonely days were over. He would not go away. And if he did, Badal would be with him.

He covered his mouth and nose with his palm to breathe in the scent of Raghu. He touched his own lips to see how they had felt to kiss.

He wandered the beach that afternoon for longer than he knew, half expecting Raghu to return, running his tongue's tip over his lips at times. Where had he run off to? How had the boy vanished from a beach so empty? It was almost four by the time he snapped out of his stupor and remembered that he needed to get home, wash himself, change his clothes — all that to be done before he went to meet the Calcutta group at their hotel. Day after day, evening after evening, it was the same: gaggles of squawking hens in starched saris rustling through the temple in his wake without a notion of what it meant to be wasted, scorched, flayed, devoured with the passion of pure devotion. Was his whole life to pass in this way?

He hurried to his scooter. It was not far. He had not thought so — it now seemed further.

When he reached his parking place he saw that a tiny puddle of oil on the road was all that remained of his scooter.

He felt in his pocket for the key. There was his almost empty wallet, his green comb, a soiled handkerchief with which he mopped his sweating neck and face, but no key. He began to wonder if he *had* come on his scooter. Calm down, he said, starting an urgent conversation with himself: You didn't walk, did you? No, of course not. You came on the scooter. You locked it and put the key in your pocket. Maybe the other pocket — but no, the key wasn't there either.

He began to walk, trying not to run. He must have left the key hanging in the ignition, an invitation to any passing thief. He walked as if he had to reach somewhere, although he had no idea where he was going. Go home and tell his uncle the scooter had been stolen? What then? Scooter-less, how would he get to places in time for all his waiting clients? He was all of a sudden back where he had been after his father's death: a blubbering boy cringing from his uncle's blows. Grow up, Badal said to himself, what can he do to you? You're stronger than he is now. He needs you more than you need him.

He walked fast. He was alone on the road. He had not imagined a daytime street could be as eerie as this. It looked different. There was a powerful smell of

72

rotting fish he had never noticed before. The doors of the houses on either side of the street were closed against the afternoon sun. The heat had made a shimmering ribbon of the road, the sky pressed low upon it, and far down its length squares of water hardened into tarmac just when they came close enough to wet his feet. There were no shops. There were no people: not one person, not a dog or cat or cow — what street was he on? When he heard a scraping behind him and sensed rough feet dragging on the dirt, his heart thudded. Only an empty cardboard carton pummelled into imbecility by the late afternoon breeze. He walked on, faster. The sliding door of a van roared on its castors inches from him. The van's windows were covered with black sun-film and gave nothing away. But he could see in them the dark windblown reflection of his own high cheekbones and jutting chin. His hands went up to his chin, then his hair, and he smoothed it down before he remembered there must be someone inside the van looking at him — the person who had just slammed the door shut.

He turned and fled. He could not tell what unnerved him. Directionless he ran and it took him a few minutes to work out where he was and find the street going homeward. He dashed past the tiny shrine near his house. He did not notice the old woman in the thick glasses still sitting beside it. She beamed with anticipation as she saw him and called out: "The bananas and gur? Did you bring me the bananas and gur? I haven't eaten all day." He hurried on to his house, hearing nothing.

He stepped through the outer door into the half light of the courtyard, where saris, pyjamas, shirts, and underpants grey beyond the powers of detergent were strung on lines from end to end. Crows perched on the lines dribbling creamy droppings on the washed clothes. They rose in a cawing cloud as he went to the tap and poured a can of water on his head and shoulders. He flung himself into a rope-strung cot in a corner of his ground-floor room, too numb to throw off his wet shirt. He tried to stay awake, to push aside his anxiety about the scooter and relive instead the earlier part of the afternoon.

But in a minute he was asleep, and in a vivid dream: his shiuli sapling has grown to a tree with so many flowers that the courtyard is waist deep in the tiny blossoms. He is wading through them, in a white and fragrant sea, when his uncle waddles out in his wet towel and pours jug after jug of water over the yard to wash the flowers away. Their sweet scent fills the courtyard long after his uncle has destroyed every last flower.

Waking, he realised that his dream had been perfumed by the incense his aunt lit for her prayers at sunset. He looked at the screen of his mobile and sprang out of his cot. He was going to be late for the old hags from Calcutta. But for his aunt's determined blowing on the conch for her prayers, he would have kept them waiting half the evening, and then it would have been futile going to the temple at all.

When he stepped outside the house he saw it was twilight. The harsh magenta of the building across the

74

road had mellowed to a soft pink. A breeze was blowing in from the east, and children were screaming at a hopscotch game in the alleyway. The evening train hooted from the nearby tracks.

And there, against the wall, was his scooter, the key in the ignition.

Even as he was walking home, Badal's clients were resting in their hotel, readying themselves for the long evening ahead at the great temple. Gouri, however, could not lie still for thinking she had forgotten something. She turned her three bags inside out. She sat down on her bed, now strewn with her things, and wondered — what was she searching for? She looked around the room with a helpless gaze. The bed was covered with a red-and-blue striped sheet. The pillow was too bulky for her spondylosis so she had put it on the chair, a padded one covered with brown cloth of the kind some hotels favoured to save on cleaning costs. She heaved herself up from the bed to the chair and lifted the pillow to see if the thing she was searching for was underneath. No.

Sometimes it helped to go back to the room where the thing had originally been in order to remember. But where would she go? She opened the cupboard. Stared at the door leading to the verandah. She did not think she had gone out to the verandah yet. Curious, she opened the door, stepped out, lowered herself into a chair. The ocean was on her doorstep. She gazed outward at the slashes of sea and sky that lay beyond the verandah. A kite skimmed the sky, knife-sharp. It flew higher and higher. Her eyes followed it into the limitless emptiness of unblemished blue, not a wisp of cloud. The kite climbed further. It was a speck of sunlit red in the blue air.

Gouri's lips began to move unprompted through the lines of a sacred hymn she was in the habit of singing. She was a feather on the wings of the kite in that borderless sky. She was airborne. From high above she saw the waves in the sea frozen into white-topped serrations. The coast was a sand-white strip bristling with coconut trees. She could see herself as if from a great distance, as a mound of clothes in a plastic chair in a verandah facing an ocean. She soared higher. She was an immaterial speck, an atom dissolved in the elements. She was helpless to resist. She did not want to resist.

Loud, unfamiliar voices just below her verandah brought her down to earth. She could not move a limb. They felt heavy and alien, as if they didn't belong to her any longer. She became aware that her back hurt and her legs had pins and needles. Inch by inch, as she tried to move her painful muscles, she remembered why she was out in the verandah — she was meant to be looking for something. She should get up and look for whatever it was.

It was hopeless. She knew her friends were right about her ineptitude. She lost things, she forgot things. In spiritual matters she felt powerful and knowledge-able — but who valued that nowadays? It had long been evident to her that Vidya and Latika had the kind of minds that locked out spirituality. The deaf would not care if Tansen himself sat before them and sang. Nor had her friends the least sense of the ineffable, the God whom she experienced in a manner so real and moving and yet so unfathomable that she could not try communicating it. But she hoped they would admire the legendary Vishnu temple. It was her territory; she had arranged everything for this part of their trip. She wanted it to be perfect: it was after all the reason for coming to Jarmuli.

It began to trouble her again, that thing she had lost. Where else could she look to remind herself? She forced herself to get up from the chair.

Perhaps the solution was in the bathroom. It was a tiny cubicle in which she was finding it difficult to manoeuvre. She pushed open its door and ran her gaze over the white sink, the shower, the toilet bowl.

Then she spotted her face in the mirror and her hands went to her bare ear lobes. She broke into a triumphant smile. Of course. The pearl studs.

She went back to her things to search afresh. She wanted to wear the studs to the Vishnu temple, and the haldi-coloured sari that her husband had given her long years ago when they went on the Badrinath pilgrimage together. "Fire on the mountain," he had called her, as he photographed her in that sari against the white snow peaks. In the picture she looked daring and shy and delighted all at once.

Two doors away from Gouri, Latika lay on her back, staring at the pale, translucent lizard glued to the

78

ceiling by its belly, looking back at her upside down. It moved a fraction, its eyes now fixed on something she could not see. It had a streak of grey going down its back and although it was high above her, she shuddered to think of its skin: rubbery, cold, possibly damp to the touch. She remembered the time her daughter when still a toddler had stumbled towards a lizard before anyone could stop her and poked it with a pencil. It slithered away into hiding behind a cupboard but left a part of its tail on the floor, a fragment of beige flesh that wriggled and twitched before it fell still. Her daughter would not have slept a wink in this room. She would have summoned half the hotel's staff to drive out the lizard.

Latika turned on her side, wishing she had not complained in the train about her daughter's need for pasta and wet wipes. Why had she said all that to Gouri and Vidya, what need had she to talk so much? "You have no loyalties," her husband had said to Latika once in bitterness. "You'll say anything for a laugh. All you want is popularity." She could not remember what had brought on this particular caustic jab. He was often that way with her, especially in front of other people, reducing her to long, shamed silences.

She turned on her side again. An alarm clock by the bedside lamp counted the seconds. She had set it to 4.00, for a brief siesta to recover her energies. In the evening they were to go to the temple. It was their second day in Jarmuli. That morning, she had gone for a long walk on the beach, all by herself, and her ankles and calves still ached from the unaccustomed ploughing through sand. Vidya had predicted this would happen, and would tell her she had told her so. How was she going to survive the walking they would have to do this evening? She had heard the temple was enormous — a perfectly preserved medieval town — and that was the only reason she was going. She was not religious, not like Gouri in her sanctuary of gods and goddesses, meditating and chanting all the time. At times she wished she had her friend's faith — it must account for Gouri's tranquillity, she thought, her way of saying, "Oh well, whatever will be . . . What's the point of worrying?" Latika wasn't made like that. Her husband called her a high-tension wire, humming with faint vibrations, even when apparently still. Her flaming-red hair matched how she was inside, she thought, even if the red came from a bottle.

She stretched her legs, trying to rid them of the pain, then got up from her bed.

The three of them had rooms connected by a verandah that ran the length of the side that faced the sea. Latika opened the door to the verandah and a gust of wind plastered her hair to her face. Walking on the beach that morning, she had seen that their hotel was one among many set along the seafront. Next door was an opulently unobtrusive five-star, half hidden in foliage. On their other side was a shiny glass and stone building shaped like a boat with a vertical red sign going down its front saying, Pure Veg Meals, No Onion, No Garlic. Further along, the beach was fenced away by more hotels, and between the hotels now and then, like tiny rowboats stranded among cruise liners, were shuttered old houses whose owners must have refused to sell. She could hear the faint cries of children from the beach now. She smelled fish, and a spicy scent she could not place. Perhaps the blossoms on the tree that was on the other side of the verandah.

She walked past the windows to Vidya's room and then Gouri's. Vidya's curtains were drawn close. The curtains to the next room were open and she could see Gouri sitting in her bed surrounded by the contents of her handbag. Latika knocked on the glass and Gouri looked up with a start. She came to the window, wide-eyed with fright. Latika realised she had forgotten to put on her glasses and could not recognise her, so she called out, "It's me."

Gouri retrieved her glasses and opened the verandah door. "Is everything alright?" she said. "What's the matter?" And then, not waiting for an answer, "Do you know, I found my pearl studs. I hunted for them all over . . . and all the time, I had them in my handbag."

Gouri's bags, packed and locked, were by the door. She had strapped her sandals on securely. Her hair was tied in the two girlish plaits she always made at night, because it made sleeping easier. She was in her travel sari, an indestructible georgette.

Latika drew her back into the room and sat her down on the bed. She said in a gentle voice, "Didn't you say you would wear your orange sari for the temple? Did you change your mind? Why have you packed your things again?"

"But aren't we leaving in a bit? On the train? We are going to Jarmuli, aren't we? We're getting late. We need to reach the station in time."

That afternoon, Nomi stood by Johnny Toppo's stall drinking tea. There were no other customers yet, it was too early. They would come when the sun turned the waves into that molten copper he could not take his eyes off though he saw it every day.

Nomi asked him in halting Hindi, "What is that song you were just singing? It made me feel so sad."

Johnny Toppo looked the girl up and down — young, thin, with coloured threads in her hair, rings in her ears: to look at, like one of those starving hippies who reeked of old sweat, but this one smelled fresh and clean. One of her arms was covered in fine, shiny sand and she had a big camera hanging from her neck.

"You feel sad at a song if you are already sad, your eyes get wet if there are already tears. What's a girl like you got to be sad about?" He grinned at her, and his mouth looked like a piano's keyboard, black gaps alternating with white teeth. "Look at me, teeth gone, knees creaking, back bent. I'm the fellow who should be sad. But I feel like singing all day."

"I'm looking for my mother. She's here somewhere. I lost her by the sea. This sea, I think. This sea."

"What? Louder. I'm old, my ears are full of water."

"I said, I was looking for one more tea. One more like the last one, with ginger and cloves."

She sat on the sand and began to fiddle with the lens of her camera. She focused it on people paddling in the

82

foam. She scanned their faces through her telephoto lens. She did not know who or what she hoped to find. Since arriving the day before, everything seemed so familiar and so alien that she could not tell the remembered from the imagined. Like the time she got lost in a birch forest in Norway, trying to find her way back, starting up paths that looked right, realising they were wrong after she had walked a long way. Turning back again.

Johnny Toppo poured water into his aluminium pan, then crushed a piece of ginger and half a clove in a stone pestle. He could no longer afford to put in a whole clove. He scraped the contents of the pestle into the pan. When the tea was ready he came up to where she was sitting and handed it to her. "The sun is still strong. If you want an umbrella to sit under I can give you one, only five rupees," he said. She wondered where she had heard that voice before. Could it be — no it couldn't, of course.

The beach grew more crowded as the heat dwindled. Suraj appeared, faceless behind sunglasses, wandering in search of the right spot, choosing an upturned boat. He sat on it and took something out of his pocket — a piece of wood, she saw through her camera lens — and began to scrape at it with a knife. She observed him for a while. The piece was quite small and his movements with the knife precise and controlled. He gazed for long moments into the horizon, then went back to his work. His scowl, his dragon-black T-shirt, his stubble, made him daunting to vendors of seashells and beads. They left him alone, instead attaching themselves with the persistence of bluebottles to the girl with braids in her hair. Nomi ignored her clamorous followers and began strolling along the beach, lifting her camera occasionally for photographs, pausing at times with an assessing look that arced over the shoreline. She came back to the tea stall as if it were her new home, following the scent of cloves and ginger and kerosene, and the sound of the old man's gravelly voice. He was deep in his work now, noticing nothing but potential customers. She sat straight-backed in the shade of her newly-acquired umbrella, to listen.

> My little mud house as old as time,
> Is on a hill with pomegranate trees,
> Sweet lime grew there in the valley,
> And fields of tender green peas.

He pumped his stove, he smiled, at times he interrupted his song to call out "Cha! Chaaii!"

Nomi closed her eyes tight when he sang. It was unbearable. She wanted him to stop singing. At the same time she wanted him to sing this very same song forever. They would live in a hut and have hens and pigs and grow yam and bananas and play in the stream nearby, she had promised. Piku used to light up whenever she started talking about the hut, so Nomi had added more and more detail each day: new plants, new animals, new things they would do. That was the game, dreaming together. After the lights were put out Piku crept across the dormitory and snuggled up to her in her narrow bunk. Nomi would sleep comforted by

84

the sense of her breathing, her movements in the night. By dawn she was always gone.

"Sweet lime grew there in the valley, And fields of tender green peas," sang Johnny Toppo. And then shouted, "Chai, Babu, Chai! Jeera biscuit, elaichi biscuit!" When he turned to the girl to check if she wanted more tea he saw her eyes were shut and her lips were moving. Not a hippy, then, a meditating type. He shrugged her off and returned to his song.

"My little mud house as old as time,
Is on a hill with pomegranate trees."

Nomi's lips were barely moving as she whispered, "Do you remember, Piku, how we climbed the pomegranate tree? Was it a few months after that teacher had gone or was it much later? Were we seven or were we eight then?" They had been wandering outside, not sure what to do with themselves. It was a grey afternoon, the kind when it wants to rain but does not. They were kicking the dust somewhere near Guruji's cottage when they noticed the pomegranate trees. The ripe fruits hanging from the tree were red and bright. Nomi had never eaten a pomegranate and she had never seen what it looked like inside. There were so many that she did not think anyone would notice if they picked one. There was nobody about. It was the hour between school and evening prayers, when everyone was in the meditation hall. The tree had small leaves and it was bushy and green. Piku stood below it, skipping around, holding her skirt out like a basket while Nomi climbed the tree. She hoisted herself up to the first fork in the trunk. The next fork was easy. And then she was near a fruit. She plucked it and aimed for Piku's stretched skirt. She hoped Piku wouldn't shriek when the fruit came down: that was how she was, hopping up and down, shrieking when she pleased, and there was no stopping her. After the first fruit Nomi felt braver and climbed two more branches. She reached out her hand for another pomegranate inches away. That was when Piku made an odd sound. Nomi looked downward to tell her to shut up and saw that Piku's skirt had dropped and the first pomegranate lay at her feet. Her mouth was open, her eyes were bulging more than usual. Guruji was standing next to her.

He neither frowned nor smiled nor asked a question nor shouted a scolding. He did nothing. But Nomi remembered how he did not take his eyes off her, how she had that familiar sense he could see right into her. Did a breeze rustle the leaves of the tree or was it utterly, absolutely still? She thought maybe a low rumble of thunder had sounded from behind the clouds. She knew she had wanted to cry. She could not move a limb. She had the sickening feeling that if she moved she would wet herself. She clenched her muscles.

Guruji had said, "Come down. Just take one step at a time and you'll come down. Look at your feet, there's a fork in the branches near you." He sounded kind and was smiling. Nomi knew that punishments at the ashram were terrible, sometimes the girls could not walk for days after a beating. But if Guruji was smiling, she thought she might escape with just a cane on her palm. She started climbing down, knot after knot, fork after fork. It was only right at the end that she put her foot on a weak branch and it creaked and splintered and then broke. She crashed through the rest of the tree, down among the seeds of the broken fruit, at Guruji's feet.

He bent towards her. He put his hands under her arms and pulled her up. Nomi was shaking, she remembered that clearly: the way her whole body shook. She was hurting all over. Her foot had a cut, her toes were stubbed, the skin of her knees had been scraped away, her frock was torn where it had caught on the tree. Guruji held her hand and led her towards his cottage. He put her on his lap facing him, the way her mother used to when she oiled Nomi before a bath. She would make her lie flat on her outstretched legs, the child's feet towards her chest. I was so small then, Nomi thought, the whole length of me fitted along my mother's legs.

Guruji sat on the stairs to his cottage holding her foot. He looked at the bit that was bleeding. He wiped the blood away with his chadar. Through her pain and fear, Nomi had marvelled at how he didn't care that the blood and mud were spoiling his clothes. He had stroked the skin around the bleeding part of the foot and then lowered his head towards it. She thought he was going to put her toes into his mouth and suck the blood away the way she did when she cut herself. But he only blew on the cuts so that they felt cool. He said, "Don't do things that are forbidden. There is a reason why. When you want fruit, just ask me."

He set her down and stood up. And then, out of thin air, from the folds of his chadar, he had produced a ripe pomegranate. Just like that! Everyone said Guruji performed miracles, they said he could produce sweets and sacred ash from nothing. But the two girls had never seen it happen. At the sight of the miracle pomegranate, Piku squealed. Guruji merely smiled. He held the fruit out towards the children and said, "Share this."

How gentle was his voice that day, how his skin gleamed and his large eyes shone! His hair was a dark cloud that lay on his shoulders and his teeth were very white. She remembered he had looked and sounded as she used to think God must look and sound.

That night Nomi had stayed awake holding her half of the pomegranate. She had eaten a bead from it for the taste. It was sweeter than anything she knew. She had sucked on the seed until nothing was left of it but a tasteless grain. Then she chewed that and swallowed it. Next to her, Piku was mumbling in her sleep. She had clawed out the seeds from her half of the fruit, dripping red juice, the moment Guruji had gone into his cottage. Nomi had not eaten it then, and hours later, after sucking on that single bead, she did not eat any more. It was the only proof she had of what she had seen. Everyone said he was God. Now she knew they were right. She stayed awake for most of the night with the fruit next to her pillow. She did not know when she fell asleep. In the morning the fruit's pulp was like blood on her sheets. Dark red.

Nomi opened her eyes. As if she were rising from below water, she heard sounds again, saw that there were people everywhere, the tea man had many customers, and there were three children pointing at her and giggling from a few feet away. She must remain calm, she must remember why she was there. She had work to do. She lifted her camera, looking through the lens. Suraj swam into view again. She zoomed in until he was close enough for her to see the strands of grey in his hair and the dark brown handle of his knife. When they had met after weeks of talking on e-mail about the film locations they were to scout, he had looked at her in the way people did: with a certain wariness, the kind that comes from encountering up close an animal that might prove unpredictable. His eyes had rested on her when he thought she wouldn't notice, taking the measure of her. She was used to it and often played up to it, acting more erratic than she was. It was both method and disguise, one she had perfected as the eternal outsider, a way to disappear when physical escape was impossible.

As she turned her camera away from him out to the sea, she saw something else. Moving to find a better angle, she toppled her umbrella, tipped over her tea and crushed the cup. Her lens was now focused on a monk in the water. He was wearing dark glasses. His long white hair was loose to his shoulders. His chunky fingers were counting beads off a rosary.

She was about to take a photograph, but something made her stop: although far off, the monk appeared to be looking straight into her lens. His eyebrows, she could see, were as white as his hair.

She let go of the camera. She got up and started to run down the beach, past the hotels, around the upturned boats, away from the crowds and into a birch forest, threading her way through the bone-white trunks of trees, the glow of a burning house in the distance, away from blood streaming down its wall and in her head a girl's voice cried out again and again for her brother, so loudly that she did not hear Johnny Toppo agitating for his money until he was in front of her, blocking her way. She could see dark stars. She closed her eyes, opened them again, saw that the sun had gone and the sea had turned to foaming blood.

When I was eight I was given duties in the ashram, like the other boat girls. My new work was to help in the gardens. I knew nothing about plants and I was born clumsy. I would step on one plant when trying to reach another. I would uproot freshly-planted seedlings when weeding. Gradually I became better at it and in time it would become the only bond between me and my foster mother. I don't know why I became a sullen, monosyllabic lump around her. She persisted in being friendly, but her efforts only oppressed me. I felt trapped and restless, I would try to put up with her talk, try and try, then before I could stop myself I would leave her in mid-sentence and walk out through the door. One day, three long, fraught years after I had started living with her, I saw her looking out of the window at me. I was kneeling over the hard, cold earth planting bulbs for the spring. The fat promise of those bulbs: I had loved them even at the ashram, where we planted tuberoses and lilies. A bulb was a secret between the soil and me until the green tips of leaves poked out months later and gave it away. That day I was planting the crocuses, snowdrops, tulips, and daffodils my foster mother liked. When she saw me she came out and began to plant them too, some distance away. As we progressed along our patches, we moved closer and closer. Above us, the slate grey sky was low. There were powdery drops of rain on our anoraks. I said nothing, but I may have smiled at her. I saw her pale pink lips tremble, and when her glasses misted over she said it was the rain.

In the ashram's gardens I had to work with a man who had recently arrived. He once told me he had been a refugee like us, and from the same place, but he had spent a few years hiding in the forests between our old country and this one. Nobody knew what had happened to him in those years and nobody asked. We never spoke about that part of our lives.

The new man's name was Jugnu. He had a thin face and long arms and he walked like a monkey, with his shoulders drooping. His nose was twisted to one side. His neck had a scar that looked like wrinkled pink satin. He too had come by boat and his hair stood on end as if the sea breeze had never gone out of it. He lived in a corner of the garden shed that he had made his own, with a mat to sleep on and a stove on which he brewed sweet tea. He was known to be very devout. He sang hymns and was often found sitting in the ashram's puja hall as if in a trance. Usually, though, he was hunched over plants. His hands were scaly and big, the fingers looked like knots in a tree trunk, but when they went into soil they were so careful that he never broke the frailest, finest hair from the roots. After he came, the ashram started to look prettier and smelled sweet everywhere, especially in the evenings when the night flowers bloomed. He was devoted to Guruji and planted beautiful flowers all around his cottage.

During the morning the ashram was such a busy, bright place that I don't think anyone looking around would have known that there were twelve girls in it who had nobody. Everyone came to hear Guruji's discourses at the big audience hall. Holy men came from other ashrams to listen to him. I saw so many monks I could not tell one from the other. They all looked the same: long hair and yellow robes. Then there were our teachers, a cook, and Jugnu. In the afternoon the visitors left. The students who came from outside went off in their buses. The boys in our school went back in a van to their dormitory, which was in another building, far away. The teachers who did not belong to the ashram went home. The monks from the visitors' side of the ashram returned to their cottages across the fence. We were by ourselves then.

When school was over and everyone was gone, I had to work in the garden for two hours. I don't remember much about what I did for those two hours, but one such afternoon was so strange I can't forget it. Jugnu had told me to fork the earth below Guruji's window. I was doing that when I heard sounds from inside: grunting sounds, whimpering sounds, screaming, which stopped abruptly, the sound of something banging and thumping. Suddenly Champa shot out of the house. I dropped down behind the bush. I heard a man's voice: "You wait and see. See what happens." I could not tell whose voice it was, but it frightened me so I stayed behind the bush for a long while, being bitten by insects.

Champa was a favourite of Guruji's. She had her own room like all the older girls. Her bed had a striped bedspread and she had a vase for flowers and a picture of Guruji on the wall. The other older girls had none of these things. She used to worship the picture and light incense in front of it. I thought when I grew older I would have a room like that.

Champa was the only one among the boat girls who had a few things from long ago and these were never taken away from her. She kept her things in a brick-sized aluminium box with a clasp. A little lock went through the clasp. Nobody had ever seen the box unlocked. We did not know what was in it. In the evening of the day I overheard her screaming, Bhola made a fire in the quadrangle outside our dormitory. He was one of Guruji's trusted helpers and he had been at the ashram right from when the war started. Guruji had found him half dead and brought him back to life: it was one of the miracles he was famous for.

Bhola broke open the lock on Champa's box with a sharp rap of a stone. He picked something out and held it between two fingertips as if it were filthy. "A duster? A hanky?" he said. "Whose? Your father's?" Champa did not answer.

The heat from the fire in that warm evening made sweat pour down Bhola's pitted face. A bomb had left one side of him maimed. He hobbled to Champa with the rag. "What is this cloth? Give me an answer and nothing will happen to it," he hissed at her. Now I know he must have relished every second of being a villain who bared his fangs and growled to scare little girls, but at that time there was nobody more terrifying or cruel even in our nightmares.

I do not remember the exact sequence of the things that happened next — that evening is a series of dark images in my head. I think Champa mumbled something and Bhola tossed the cloth into the fire. He picked up a photograph from the box. "What an ugly fat woman," he said. After the photograph had sizzled to ashes he picked out a tiny doll. Its head lolled and its arms were limp and it wore a printed rag as a sari. When she saw that doll, something happened to Champa. She made a choking sound as if she would vomit and she turned away to run into the dormitory. Savita-di, our matron, held her back by her arm. "You can leave when Guruji tells you to, not before," she said.

It was only then that I noticed him in the shadows, watching everything. Guruji stood as expressionless as when he had caught me on the pomegranate tree. Champa was crying, "I won't run away again, I will never run away again." He said nothing. We did not know Champa had tried running away. We had been told never to leave the ashram. We knew if any of us was caught outside, every other boat girl would be in danger. We thought: if she ran away she deserves punishment. How just Guruji is, he punishes even his favourite.

After all the things in the box were burned, we were told to go back to our rooms and dormitories while

Champa was led away to Guruji's cottage for an audience with him.

Not many days after that it was my turn. I had been hiding between the bushes and trees in a complicated game with Piku, and before we knew it we had drifted to the outer boundary of the grounds. There was high barbed-wire fencing. Beyond the fences were rows of cottages and parks. It was the visitors' part of the ashram. I had only glimpsed it before from high up in the pomegranate tree. Now we could see men and women sitting at meditation. Many were just like us and some were foreigners with light hair.

If we had stayed quiet we would have got away with it. But Piku tried to make one of the foreigners notice her by standing up and shouting. She could be so stupid. The man turned. He was tall, with yellow robes, and he had a long beard and long hair and held prayer beads. I have never forgotten his face because he was young, but his hair was snow-white, his eyelashes were white, and his eyes seemed white too. He looked around, trying to find where the shouts had come from. I pulled Piku to the ground and behind the bushes. I knew there would be trouble if we were spotted. I led her away through the grass at a crawl. I thought we had made it. Then we heard a snuffling and growling and there, behind us, was Bhola and with him on a chain was one of the dogs that roamed the ashram's grounds at night.

Bhola's teeth were yellow and red because he chewed tobacco all day. Below his shirt he wore a lungi. Seeing us at the boundary he dropped the dog's chain to the

96

ground as if he had forgotten there was a fierce animal at the end of it. He only stepped on its chain at the last instant, when the dog was very close to us. He rolled his lungi to his knees and put his hands on his hips. One of his hands held a bamboo switch.

"So, shall I let him go?" he said. He said many more things, but for some reason this is what I recall. Maybe I thought I would be eaten alive by that dog.

Piku was smiling at Bhola, showing all her teeth. As if smiling would get us out of trouble. Bhola picked up the dog's chain and poked her with his freed foot. He said, "Hey, nothing to smile about, you dolt. Nothing at all."

I think of myself then, standing up very straight, hands on my waist, daring him to do his worst, saying, "We haven't done anything, you can't hurt us." Was I really so brave? My head must have been just about level with his waist. My hair was still in two plaits. I knew that only a fortnight had passed since Bhola burnt all Champa's things. I didn't care. I had no box full of things for him to burn.

Bhola tapped his switch against his hips. He prodded us with it towards Guruji's cottage. He kept stopping to chat with people he passed. Piku's hand was hot and sweaty in mine. I held it tight. The dog paused to lift a leg against the bushes. Bhola hit it with his switch and it yowled. The dog had pointed ears and red fur. It looked like a fox.

We waited by Guruji's cottage the whole morning. The other students, boys and girls, walked past giving us curious looks. We were left out of lessons and games.

We stood in the hot sun like beggars. Everyone went off for prayers and we kept standing in the sun. I can't remember how long we waited. When Guruji arrived, his hair was blowing in the breeze, a black halo. He kept his eyes on us as Bhola told him we had been found near the boundary, trying to cross the fence. I thought I glimpsed the shadow of a smile on his face and began to get my voice back. I opened my mouth. Guruji raised a hand to stop me saying anything. He told Piku to leave.

Guruji sometimes spoke Hindi with us, and sometimes English. People said he had never been to school, yet miraculously he could understand whichever language his devotees spoke in and he could speak them equally well. There were many stories about Guruji. They said he had divine powers even when he was a child. He could turn into a cat or horse or wolf, then come back to human form again. As a child he could tell what people were thinking and when he spoke out their thoughts a deep grown-up voice would come out of him even though he was only five or six at that time. Guruji's voice was soft. He never had to raise it, not even when he had a hundred people around him. When he spoke it was as if all other sounds stopped so that his every whisper could be heard from far away — that is what his devotees said. Now he only said, "Come inside".

I followed him into the inner room of his cottage. Padma Devi, who usually sat in the outer one, was not there that day. Guruji shut the door behind us. He locked it.

I remember every bit of that room. Its walls were covered with photographs of Guruji meeting people. They must have been grand people. I did not know who they were. In the photographs most of them were bowing to him and he had his palm raised to bless them. On one side of the room was a bed. It was low and wide, with carved animal paws for legs. It had white sheets and ochre bolsters and pillows. There was an equally low desk on another side with a square asan on the floor for sitting on. The desk had a book on it with a plain cardboard cover. A steel cupboard with glass doors stood against one wall and another wall had a row of pegs from which Guruji's robes were hanging.

I saw that one wall of this room was dark blue, and had framed pictures of birds on it. I could recognise red and blue birds I had seen at the ashram. There was a bulbul and also a house sparrow. The painted birds were brightly coloured and beautiful, nestling in green leaves among ripe mangoes or red hibiscus flowers.

Guruji drew the curtains. He sat down on the chair where he had first seated me on his lap all those years ago.

I had already forgotten I was there to be punished. "Who painted those birds?" I asked him. I had to stand on tiptoe to look at them from up close. I knew I could never do these with my school crayons.

"I painted them, of course," Guruji smiled. "Didn't you know that? Birds eat out of my hands. I can catch any bird I want to. I only have to sit and chirrup, Choo, choo, choo — like that, and they come. See that line of birds there? They are exactly like the real ones. Go on, touch the feathers."

He was pointing to a shelf in the room in which there were birds sitting in a row. I did not dare to touch them.

"They aren't alive, child, they won't peck you," he said. "They're stuffed. So that they are still enough to paint."

At one of the windows was a bird in a cage. This one was definitely alive: it hopped about and screeched. It had glossy green feathers on its back and a red band at its throat. Maybe when I was out on the flowerbed that time, it was the bird making those strange screaming noises.

"That one's next. It's a parakeet. It'll be a big painting," he said. "Go on, give it a chilli to eat."

When I did not go towards the bird he patted his lap and said, "Come here."

I climbed on to his lap as I had before and he settled me there and said, "Tell me why you went to that fence. You know you are not allowed, and there is a reason why. If people from outside see you, they might report you to the police. And then what? Do you want to be taken away and locked up? You must do as I say or God will be angry and you'll get into trouble."

I pulled away from him and said, "I was only looking. I didn't do anything."

He pressed me back against his chest. "Some things are forbidden, you know that, don't you? We need rules when we live together."

100

His face was very close to mine. I could see where his cheeks had tiny black bristles from shaving and I thought of the way my father used to sit at a mirror tacked on the wall outside our hut in the morning and shave. When I was very small, my father would rub his bristly cheek against mine and I used to squeal when he did that.

Guruji said, "You don't always understand the reasons why I tell you to do some things and not do other things, but there is a reason and one day you will understand it was for your own good. You have to hide for a while because there is a war. If you are found wandering outside now, they will lock you up in jail. Just wait a little, then you can do whatever you want to." He said, "Do you trust me? Don't you think I will always do everything for your good? Didn't I save you from the war and from starving on the streets without your parents?"

He said, "Didn't I tell you the day you came here that I am your father, mother and God? Can you disobey all of them?"

He stroked my hair and shoulders while he spoke. It was very cool in the room and the curtains had turned afternoon into evening. I could hardly hear his voice, it was no more than a murmur and the words sounded longer when they came from him because he stretched them out.

He stroked my arms and said, "You are like an insect. Don't you eat?" He held my leg and said, "Let me see that knee. Look, there is a scar from the time you fell off the pomegranate tree. That should teach you not to be naughty." He rubbed the scar and then another scrape with his fingertip and said, "What is this one from?"

"I was playing yesterday and I fell."

"Does it hurt?" he said. "I don't want any of my children to be in pain."

As his hand moved from scar to scar, it went under the skirt of my tunic and began to stroke the part between my legs. His hand went up my thighs and down. He shifted my weight and slipped down my knickers and put his hand right between my legs. He lifted his own robes and he pulled my hand towards himself and said, "Hold this, it is magic." It stuck out from between his legs like a stump.

Then he said, "Your hand is much too small, hold it with both." I had to turn to be able to do that. I did need both my hands because the stump was really big now, but I thought I did not have to hold it because it would keep standing on its own. When I took my hands away to see if I was right, Guruji pushed them back. I grew tired of just sitting there holding a stump. I did not know why he was making me do something so stupid. I wanted to get off his lap and go, but he shut his eyes and sat there stroking me for such a long time I wondered if he would ever let me leave and eat lunch. All of a sudden he groaned and said, "Enough." My hands had become wet and slimy. They felt as if I had squashed something. Guruji gave a deep sigh and opened his eyes. He picked me off his lap and told me to wipe my hands on a towel that hung from one of the pegs. I had to stand on my toes to reach the towel.

When I removed it from its peg, I saw it had been covering a picture on the wall.

"That picture is of a sculpture from an ancient temple's wall. Do you know how old?"

I shook my head.

"Nine hundred years. Can you see what the woman in the sculpture is doing?"

A nine-hundred-year-old woman. I stared at the picture. She had big, curved eyes and plump, curved lips and she was sitting at the feet of the man in the sculpture. Her fingers were as long as pencils. They were holding the cucumber between the man's legs just as I had been a few minutes ago.

Guruji hung a fresh towel from the cupboard on that peg. The picture was hidden again. I felt his hand caressing my head. "Go for lunch," he said. "Say nothing. I do not reveal myself in this form to anyone else. You are the chosen one. Not a word about this. I will call you and you will sit on my lap again."

I left his room. I scrubbed my hands at the kitchen tap for a long time, but I could not help feeling they had that ooze on them still. The dining room was empty. Everyone else had eaten and gone. I did not know where Piku was or whether she had eaten. I had a terrible, gnawing hunger after all that time. There was one piece of fish left in the pan, an especially big piece, and the cold gravy shuddered on it like jellied glue.

Badal had lost his scooter as inexplicably as he had found it, and that thought troubled him as he directed it towards the Swirling Sea Hotel that evening. How had it gone and why had it come back? Was it Raghu playing a prank? Or was his memory playing tricks? Perhaps he had left it at home that morning, never taken it to the beach at all.

He arrived at the hotel plagued by such thoughts. The three women were already outside, scanning the road for him. He was not late in the end, but they made him feel as if he was. He parked his scooter, taking a long time to lock it even though he knew he would be setting off on it again in a few minutes. He told himself he had put the key, as always, in his right-hand kurta pocket. Left pocket: comb, wallet, handkerchief. Right pocket: scooter key. At last he looked up towards his group for the evening. His uncle insisted he talk to clients and make them feel welcome, convince them they were in good hands, authoritative yet gentle hands that would direct them through the great temple in a manner that gave them to believe they were the chosen few. "Your father managed it, can't you? If you lose clients, you lose the roof over your head," his uncle would snarl. It did not come naturally to Badal, he was a man who spoke little, whose words came out wrong when he did speak. But still, in his taciturn way, he folded his hands in greeting, set his jaw muscles into an authentic-smile position, and mumbled something about saving them every sort of trouble. He sensed that the evening would be difficult. Clients like the bearded slob of that morning were bad enough, devout old women were disaster. They were always patronising, interrupting him with corrections, as if they knew better.

104

He summoned a rickshaw and Vidya and Latika clambered into it. Then they realised it had space only for two, and exclaimed, "What about Gouri? She's all alone. How will she go?"

"We can get her another rickshaw," Badal said. "Or she can come with me on my scooter." He felt deliriously oblivious of the mundane — of the rickshaw-wallas waiting at the hotel gates, the sensation of his shoes pinching at the toe, the old crone urging people, buy keyrings only ten rupees I'm hungry Babu need rice Ma — as if here, outside the Swirling Sea Hotel, arranging transport for his clients, he was no more than the shell of a coconut whose flesh was far away, in Raghu's mouth. Soon, soon he would give him that mobile. Such a fortunate windfall! As if God knew exactly what was needed, when.

He heard the three women clucking on about who would go with him on the scooter.

"Oh no," Vidya said. "Of course she can't, she'll fall off."

"But she can't go alone in a rickshaw either, what if we lose her?" Latika said. "Have you ever sat on a scooter, Gouri?"

They looked at her standing on the pavement in her too-young orange sari, and her pearl studs, round and unsteady as she balanced her bulk. Smiling at the thought of her on a scooter, Vidya volunteered in the brisk manner that came naturally to her at moments of crisis. "I'll go in another rickshaw. Gouri, you come into this one with Latika."

But Gouri had hoisted her sari and begun the process of sitting side-saddle on the scooter. "These old knees aren't gone yet!" she announced with glee. She leaned on Badal's shoulder to haul herself up and he had to dig his heels into the ground to keep the scooter upright. It was too tiny for the woman, what had he been thinking? Even so, she squeezed her flesh onto the pillion and clutched the front seat for safety.

There was a tense moment when Badal kicked the scooter to life and it tilted to one side, almost unseating her, but to feel the wind on her face and hair on that scooter was like going back to her village, running through fields of rushes. Weaving past buffaloes and children at play and flower stalls through such narrow lanes as even North Calcutta didn't have: she was flying! The rickshaw with Vidya and Latika was too large for those alleyways. It took a different route and they could not keep Gouri on the scooter in view for long.

They were reunited at the gateway of the Vishnu temple and hovered on the pavement, too nervous to push through the mass of people jostling for the shack where everyone had to leave their footwear before going in. Near them a blind beggar paused his singing to rattle his tin and assess how many coins he had collected. He made a face, then tapped his way towards them. "Ram, Ram. Spare a few coins, a few coins for one cursed by God, haven't eaten all day . . ."

Gouri fumbled for coins in her handbag. She unzipped one pocket after another, and one of the cards with her name and phone number fell out to the litter-strewn pavement.

"Close your bag, there are pickpockets here," Latika said, putting a protective arm around her. "What a relief you're here safe. We wondered what we'd do if the guide whisked you away somewhere! Stranger things have been known to happen in temple towns."

The beggar rattled his tin again. "Spare a coin, God will bless you, haven't eaten all day, Ma . . ."

"Ssh," Gouri said to Latika in a whisper, gesturing towards Badal. "He'll hear you!" But she was smiling.

The women walked barefoot on bricked paths and dirt tracks, buffetted by other pilgrims who pushed past them to get ahead. Inside the shrines the stone floors were so slippery with grease and water that they had to edge along the walls, holding them for support. They bowed their heads at a dozen altars. In the *sanctum sanctorum*, lit only with flaming torches, priests brought oil lamps towards them, dispensing benediction, their shadowy faces menacing in the flickering light. Latika wanted to find her slippers, run away, scrub her feet, never return, but she trudged behind the others admiring whatever she was told to admire: the austere grandeur of the stone Narasimha; the richness of the brocade that clothed an image of Krishna. Her legs were aching by the time Badal took them into a secluded square where an old banyan tree sheltered a tiny circular shrine. A particular guide to the temple many centuries ago, Badal said, a man who did the same kind of work that he did, had fallen into a dry well there. At that time this banyan tree was no more than a few leaves. Immediately the earth at the rim of

107

the well had collapsed inward and buried the man alive, as if God wanted to keep him close to Himself, within the temple forever. The shrine marked where the well had been. The tree had let out dozens of branch-thick aerial roots, enclosing it within a forest. Every year, when the caparisoned temple elephants were taken out in a holy procession, the dead man's effigy was mounted on one of the elephants as a reminder of his sacrifice. The temple's most respected guide was chosen to sit on that elephant, holding the effigy.

Badal's deep-set eyes glittered, and his ivory-coloured art silk kurta shone as he said, "The guide who holds that effigy on the elephant . . . he always dies within weeks of the ceremony."

He spoke to them, but he was far away, being churned in a heaving mass of pushing, milling, screaming, ecstatic pilgrims, watching the temple elephants lumber past, as huge up-close as hillocks, their gold headdresses gleaming in the light of flaming torches, their trunks swaying. It was at last year's procession. He still had not worked out how he had done it or where he had found the footholds, but insensible with passion he had flung himself towards one of the elephants and tried clambering up its flanks to reach the effigy of the guide and to sit holding it, up on the back of the elephant. He had not managed, of course. He had been pulled away by other pilgrims who had cried out in the din that he would be killed. Later, he was sure he had been possessed for those moments by some divine insanity, some primal urge for annihilation that would have fulfilled a destiny he could neither escape nor understand.

But he had not been crushed by the elephants. He was alive. God had wanted him to live.

Would He want him to live now — after what he had done with Raghu? A boy. So young.

He was saved from his agitated thoughts by Latika, who had heard his last few words and let out an involuntary giggle, which she tried to smother with her handkerchief. Badal looked at her with a questioning frown.

"If the temple guide knows he's going to die, how do you get any of them to do the ceremony?" she said. "How is the victim chosen?" Her voice had that mischievous lilt her friends dreaded as much as they enjoyed.

It was as if her words instantly rolled a set of iron shutters down Badal's face. Latika knew right away she should not have spoken. She should never have spoken. But it was too late, as always it was too late. She had resolved to cultivate the kind of solemnity expected of an elderly woman at this holiest of temples, but she felt too angular here, her hair felt too red, her malachite necklace too green. She could sense her friends were exasperated with her. Gouri began to babble: "She doesn't know much, she . . . she has always lived abroad." Vidya had moved away to the other side of the square and was feigning interest in a carved pillar. Latika felt her blouse stick damply against her shoulders. From beyond the courtyard she could hear the homeless widows chanting, and another guide's voice saying, "Now come this way, this way, this holiest of courtyards is where a temple guide hundreds of years ago fell into a dry well . . ."

Fury split Badal's words into syllables hard as stone chips. "Madam, for us temple guides, it is the greatest honour to be chosen, to be assured a death so holy. To die for God is what we live for."

It was true. He knew it to be so, had known it ever since his first lisping, toddling visit to the temple in his father's arms. He remembered his own fierce intensity, his infantile scholarship. He had mastered every twist and turn in the epics, the intricate ancestries in the *Mahabharata* unknotted themselves in his childish mind when he was only eight. If someone said "Arjuna", he would chirrup, "Born of Indra!" He knew even then that Vyasa was the father of Vidura and Gandhari the daughter of Subala. He could fast all day and never ask for a drop of water. Neighbours wondered if he was a child saint.

He longed to be with real seekers, those who would understand the depth and gravity of his words. He turned away from the women, knowing his contempt would show on his face. He cut short their round of the temple and shepherded them to another courtyard to watch the nightly pennant-changing ceremony. Hundreds of people waited there in orderly, patient anticipation. He showed them to a place where they could sit and then walked away, merging into the crowds.

One moment here, the next moment gone: had they not been warned never to lose sight of the man? Latika

110

wondered where he had disappeared to. Perhaps to a toilet? Were there toilets at the temple? She wanted one with a sudden desperation and made noises about following him. But Gouri was now even more ostentatiously the expedition leader and paid Latika no attention. She had been in a state of otherworldiness since they had entered the temple, and it was impossible to communicate with her about matters as lowly as toilets. Latika clenched her muscles and hoped she would survive.

The main shrine had three connected towers, the tallest of which seemed as high as a ten-storey building. They stared at the flags fluttering at their tips, trying not to blink and lose the first glimpse. A man began to climb the stone peaks of the temple's lowest tower. Latika saw Vidya clutch Gouri's hand, so she clutched Vidya's. Shouts and murmurs. How his yellow dhoti flared and fluttered against the black sky! As he climbed, unprotected by net or rope, his figure grew small, then smaller, until by the time he had reached the pinnacle of the tallest tower he was a tiny mannequin that might any moment be swept off by the gusts of wind gathering strength in the Bay of Bengal. Anxiety rippled through the crowd. There, on top, as frail as a scarecrow against the immense darkness, he began the process of taking down the old flag and unfurling and positioning the new. Would that flag billowing in the high wind twist around him and tug him into the sea beyond? Would it become his shroud?

With the new silk flag in its place at last, they realised that alongside the hundreds around them they had been holding their breath, which they let out all at once. The wind too seemed to sigh and die down. People began to exclaim and chatter, recognising an intermission. A child near them demanded a biscuit. Latika said, "Now I really must find a bathroom, or I'll burst." A few minutes later, at the end of an unusually hot day, it started to drizzle, the air grew dense with the scent of water meeting dry earth, and everyone fled for cover. Scurrying to the gates, saris over their heads to shield themselves from the rain, Gouri said to Vidya, "She has no sense of occasion. Couldn't she wait two minutes before she said something so tasteless?"

It was still drizzling but with a powdery lightness. The night air was fresh and cool. It had taken Badal quite a while to find his three old matrons after the pennant ceremony and take them back to the Swirling Sea Hotel, but now at last he was free. In his breast pocket he felt the reassuring shape of the new mobile phone. He had put in the prepaid SIM card, already topped up with fifty rupees. Raghu would be wonderstruck. And he himself would never again have to wander the beach looking for him; it would be the work of a fingertip now.

He rounded a corner and turned into Grand Road, usually crowded with stalls and vendors, now windswept and rain-dampened. Too late for shoppers or merchants. But it was not empty. Not far off in the deserted street, he could see two tall figures and two shorter ones lit by the one streetlamp that was working. They were strolling, pausing at times to drink from a

112

bottle. Coming closer, he saw that one of the men had dark, curly hair. The second man, in a kurta and pyjama, had white hair down to his shoulders and held a cigarette in one hand while his other hand kneaded a boy's buttocks.

He stopped his scooter.

The boy was Raghu. He had to be.

Raghu had an arm around the dark-haired man's waist and was begging for a swig of beer. Badal could hear his voice, unfamiliar in its archness: "Go on, just a few sips." And the man replying, "Hey, you're a kid, you know, it's illegal." His Hindi was strongly accented. He heard Raghu laugh as he ambled between the two, looking even slighter and smaller by contrast. He was not in his usual red T-shirt and grey shorts. He had on a black shirt tucked into tight black jeans. Badal had never seen those clothes on Raghu, did not know he possessed such clothes. His heart contracted at the thought, everything paused. And then he heard Raghu's coaxing voice again: "Just a sip."

The curly-haired man tipped the beer bottle into Raghu's mouth. Badal felt the hard glass edge of the bottle hit Raghu's teeth, involuntarily clenched his own. The man kept forcing in the beer until Raghu gagged and choked and his knees buckled. The white-haired one drawled through his cigarette, "Take it easy, Jacko. You'll break his teeth." He passed his cigarette to a lanky boy only a bit taller than Raghu. The second boy did not look in Raghu's direction. He took a drag and gave the cigarette back to the white-haired man.

Badal wanted to turn his scooter around so that he would not have to drive past them. But he carried on inexorably, until he was next to the group, until Raghu turned and saw him, until the white-haired man was staring at him, his gaze idle. Without his sunglasses and his yellow robes he looked different, but it was the monk who meditated waist-deep in the sea, Badal was sure of it.

Stationed in the sea every morning. Watching Raghu.

Badal speeded past the group and looped back through another set of alleys towards the empty beach. He drove into the sand until the scooter skidded and came to a stop. He threw it aside and ran to the beach. He flung himself at the sand. The hard oblong of the new mobile in his pocket slammed into his ribs, knocking his breath out.

The ocean was inside him, the impersonal immensity of it. It had frozen solid, it had exploded into a thousand icy pieces and each individual shard pierced him, made him cry out aloud.

The water was too far away to wet him, but the earth began to darken around his face. His nose was bleeding. He let it flow, he wanted it to bleed, he wanted the blood in his body to drain away.

The stubble that was a mark of slovenliness for Badal was achieved by Suraj with the help of a beard trimmer that could be set with millimetric precision. The stubble wasn't merely about cultivating an image, it was part of his strategy of attack and concealment, his daily war against the secret self he loathed but could not quell.

He could not bear people to know how, in truth, he needed everything just so, had to struggle not to set right a book upside down on a shelf or straighten a crooked carpet.

Having left the temple and shaken off Badal that afternoon, Suraj had eaten his crab curry and rice, then fallen asleep immediately afterwards in a heat and hangover-induced daze. By the time he woke it was dark. He had not met Nomi after she had driven off, leaving him stranded at the temple gates. He had not looked for her in her room, nor had she knocked on his door. Just as well. He did not like people in his hotel room. He did not want them to see the beard trimmer ready by the plug point on the bathroom counter beside all the other oddments that, over long years of travel, he had grown accustomed to having with him. Bug spray in case of mosquitoes. Antiseptic. Antacids. His own towel because hotel towels disgusted him. Plus his bottles of whisky, his carton of cigarettes. His photography equipment was in its own bag and inside his backpack was his stash of dope. On the table next to the bed were his wood-carving tools. There were four kinds of gouges. Three carving knives with short, sharp blades, each one differently shaped, and with broad handles that sat comfortably in his palm. The knife he used most had a lethal point that he took the greatest care never to blunt. The toolbox had slots for each instrument, including those for whetstones to sharpen the tools. When he felt in any way troubled, Suraj only had to open the box and look at the tools securely in their own niches for the universe to regain some semblance of order.

The last thing he did when checking into a hotel was to open the toolbox and put it on the bedside table. Until five months ago, he would have completed the ritual by placing a weathered little panda next to his toolbox: only then would the room have become his own. Ayesha had given him that bear before they were married, after a long-ago trip to China, and it had travelled everywhere with him since then. It was now a grimy black and white ball of nylon fur crushed into the depths of his rucksack. He could no longer bring himself to look at it, but neither could he throw it away.

Suraj tossed his rucksack to a corner and fell back into the mound of pillows on his bed. That last terrible evening of his marriage with Ayesha. It was five months to the day — an anniversary of sorts! The recollection sent a stab of pain to his chest. Was this how heart attacks began? His father had died of one when he was just about this age, mid-forties. Suraj lay inert, hardly daring to breathe, trying to take his mind off that evening five months ago. He had relived it almost every hour. The minute he allowed his mind to wander he was back in their rented house in Delhi, its enclosed courtyard lined with dessicated potted palms and straggly jasmine. For all the dust on them, he used to like the companionable way they rustled if there was a breeze. That evening there wasn't the whisper of a breeze, and the hot, dry air made noses bleed. He had not had much to drink, he had only been consumed by a black, bottomless despair, a sense of things ending, of hurtling into an abyss towards destruction. A dog had come into the yard after dark, looking for food. Suraj saw it ferreting around, sniffing the corners. A scrawny body and a tail that described a perfect circle. A cur. It tilted over the plastic garbage bin, clattering it to the concrete floor, spilling its foetid waste. Suraj had been sitting by himself, sweating quietly, holding his rum and coke. He did not know what got into him, but the glass fell through his fingers, he heard it shatter, and in a moment he was up, snatching his cricket bat. The dog cowered by the bin, everything else had blurred. Suraj knew only that he wanted to kill, smash the world into fragments. The dog looked for a way out, but it was too frightened to find the gap in the fencing through which it had come in. Suraj slammed the bat into its side, once, then again and again. He could not stop, his arms did not belong to him any more. The high-pitched yelps of the dog stoked his frenzy. He hit it harder and harder as if he needed to grind the animal into bonemeal. At some point, he became aware of his wife screaming. She threw herself against him and he pushed her away so savagely that she fell. That made him drop the bat. And then the only sounds were his panting, his wife sobbing, and low whimpers from the dog, a mess of broken bones held together by bloodied fur.

Ayesha had left the next day. They had been through partings before, when she had gone, her body a porcupine's, fending off touch, her silence the threat that she would never come back. This time too, after she left, he had told himself it would pass.

It would pass, he repeated to himself now, and meanwhile there was Johnnie Walker. Before he could think another black thought, Suraj swung himself up from the bed, washed one of the glasses in the minibar, dried it and poured himself a drink. He took a sip, placed the glass by his lamp, listened to the ice cubes clink. For a while he sat staring at the squat glass. He could hear the hum of the air conditioning, the fridge vibrating. It felt unbearable, the quiet. Alone he would plunge into deeper and deeper gloom; he needed company. It was about eight-thirty, purpled darkness, just the right time. He held his glass and bottle and stood up.

His room had French windows that opened onto a strip of garden shared by all the rooms on that section of the ground floor. The strip was divided by tall hedges and shrubs into sections, each with two chairs and a stone table so that you had the impression of owning a private garden. So private, that when Suraj stepped into the patch next to Nomi's room, he found her clothes drying on a bush. He smiled. She was saving money not giving her clothes to the hotel laundry. Or, like him, she knew laundries were hothouses for germs. It felt strangely intimate knowing this, to be with her drying clothes. His bottle-free hand went out towards them: a soft, damp, white scrap that must be the shirt she had been wearing in the morning. A pair of white knickers with lacy edges. A dark blue brassiere. He had just touched its strap when he sprang back. She was standing there in the half light, hunched, wrapped in a sheet as if it were cold — although stepping out of the air conditioning of his room, the briny air of the outdoors had felt to Suraj like a warm, moist slap.

He shuffled through his head for an explanation he could give her. Stepping closer to attempt an apology he saw that she was staring outward, mumuring to herself. She was glassy-eyed, and as he watched, a tremor shook her.

He spoke in a voice soft enough to be a whisper. "Hey? What's up?" Was she on coke? Did she have some on her? That would be interesting.

He heard her gasp of surprise and saw her eyes come back into focus. It took a few seconds before she said, "Nothing, just listening to the sea." And then, "Did you hear that strange sound? Such a hollow, scary, groaning sound."

Although their hotel faced the sea, it was at a distance from the water. A stretch of grassy wasteland that was now a mass of shadows stood between them and the pale sky over the sea. The sound came from that direction.

"Probably a buffalo." Suraj gestured at the expanse of the wasteland. "Someone must have left it tied there. I heard it too, there's nothing scary about it." He had already settled on a pretext for seeking her out. "Look, I'm sorry I was a bit . . . you know, rude this morning when you left the temple. Didn't want to . . . Anyway, I've a peace offering here. You want to get a glass from your room?"

Nomi went in and fetched a glass, then tucked herself into one of the two garden chairs. She drew her sheet closer, like a shawl, and nestled in it. Her head popped out about above the cloth, making her look like an anxious child at the barber's. Suraj said nothing. If she wanted to wear a bed sheet, who was he to ask her why. He set his bottle and glass on the table, and his mobile. Then a lighter and a packet of cigarettes. He poured whisky into the glass she had brought for herself and pushed it towards her. A tea light in the centre of the table cast a golden pool between them.

Nomi finished her first drink in two gulps. Suraj was surprised because he thought he had poured her a stiff one, but he filled her glass again without comment. Her eyes were on the candle's light as she spoke. "I should say sorry too — but I don't know what got into me . . . Can you believe it, I spent ages convincing them Jarmuli was the place to film — because of that temple? I plotted and planned . . . The fact is I've been wanting to come here for years, never had the money." She took a long sip. "I think I might have been born here. I'm adopted. And you know how it is, adopted kids have this well-known need to go back to their roots!" She shrugged, waggled her head as if she was not entirely serious.

She had a high voice and bright, very black eyes. She still wore her big beads around her neck — she was a jingling mass of beads, bangles, braids, and threads. He thought of the tattoo at her navel, felt a surprisingly violent need to examine all the others.

"Where did you grow up?" He looked only at his glass. "When did you leave here?"

"Oh, years ago. Years and years ago. And growing up — all over the place — mostly Oslo, I guess, but zillions of countries and trillions of airports. This is the first time I've come back. And guess what? On the train, I got down at one station and it left without me! Just slid off. Didn't whistle, nothing. One minute it was standing and the next minute it was moving off. I travel all the time and I've never done this kind of thing: I ran like hell after it and managed to climb back on. Thought my heart would explode."

Suraj looked up from his glass towards the shadowed trees. "Yeah, that happened to me once, and you know what, I didn't run or anything. I just let the train go. I saw it leaving and I thought, What the hell, let it go, I don't give a damn. I spent the night on a bench on the platform."

The hardness of that bench, the black gloom just beyond the dim-lit platform, the dark huddles nearby of postal bundles and sleeping tramps: he remembered it well. He was expected home that evening from a work trip. Ayesha was waiting up for him. Later she told him she had been sleepless all night trying to reach him and failing, phoning friends to ask if they had news of him, dreading the thought of the calls she might need to make next: police stations, hospitals. Morgues. "Such a simple thing to call! Why the *fuck* didn't you *call*?" She was so angry she had asked the question again and again, each time punching him in the ribs. "Why *didn't* you? *Why* didn't you?" But he hadn't. He couldn't. He had kept his phone switched off. He had dropped off the map for the night. The next day, back home, he sat out the raging storms of her anxiety and anger without a word. He would not tell her what had happened, nor explain why he had not called. He had no explanation for it himself.

To Nomi he said, "I hadn't a clue what station it was until I woke up. All my luggage was gone. Camera too. I didn't care."

"Didn't it feel good? Didn't it feel great?" Nomi was half out of chair with delight, sheet falling off, revealing the thinnest of noodle straps underneath, over a bare shoulder. It appeared and disappeared under her mass of hair. The shoulder was smooth and shiny, the brown of dark honey. If you dipped in a finger for a taste it would be sweet. The brown shrimp. She did not look such a shrimp in candlelight.

She gathered the sheet around her again and said, "Like stepping out of your life. Like leaving your own story. Like disappearing. Don't you feel like disappearing from your life sometimes?"

She took a sip of her whisky and said, "There were these women on the train, three ancients, coming on a holiday here. They were like schoolgirls, so thrilled. At first I thought, I've never felt this — this kind of straightforward happiness — they were full of it. They thought I wasn't listening to anything because I had my headphones on, but I'd kept the volume really low, because I love eavesdropping — don't you? Turned out they were sad old things, complaining about their children and their aches and pains. Like this was their last chance of fun."

Suraj shrugged. "They might go on twenty more trips and live longer than either of us."

122

"Sure." Nomi shook her head, impatient. "We'll both be hit by a bus tomorrow."

"Haven't seen too many buses in Jarmuli." He clicked his lighter on and his face turned into hills and dark hollows. He took his piece of wood from his pocket, began to work on it with his knife, and a woody perfume drifted across the table. A faint scraping from him, the whisky going down their throats, and then the lowing again, a deep sound of anguish that filled the night. Beyond the stone wall that enclosed their garden and beyond the darkness of the waste lot was a line of coconut palms that told them where the beach was. A new, cool breeze came from that direction, ruffling the air.

"I think it'll rain." Suraj looked up at the sky.

"What are you doing with that wood?" she said. "I saw you at it on the beach too. It's sandalwood, isn't it? I can smell it. Despite your smoke."

"Just helps to kill the time. Stops me smoking more." The lit cigarette dangled from his lips.

"Can I see the knife?" She put her hand out.

"Careful. It's sharp enough to kill." He handed it over. It looked much too big in her palm and that made him feel good somehow. It was a man-tool. Its dark wooden handle was silky with use. The handle was sheathed with brass at its tip and brass rivets and bands fixed the steel blade to it. His father had used it for years, it was a knife he had bought in Berlin. Suraj tapped his cigarette into the bowl on the table and told her that. He should have stopped — there was no need to say more — but he found himself telling her about his father, how he used to be good with his hands, especially making things with wood. He could make shelves and chairs and all of that, but what he really liked making were miniatures — model houses, minuscule windmills, boats. Everything he made actually worked: the doors and windows of the houses would open, the windmill would turn in the breeze, the boat would float. It was their yearly ritual to make one perfect boat, then go off together somewhere, to a river or a sea and float it away.

"But then you'd lose it," Nomi said. "Or did you have it on a string?"

"No strings. The whole idea was to let it go — we made it as perfect and seaworthy as we could. But after that it was on its own."

"Yes, but a thing I had spent months making? I wouldn't be able to abandon it like that."

"Not to abandon it, no. It was, well, supposed to be ready for life on its own. It felt like that. We'd stand on the shore and watch it going off. And keep looking till it became invisible. Never saw one sink, not in all these years. And I make one every year even now."

"With your father?"

"He died years ago. I was fifteen." Suraj stubbed out his cigarette. "I always give the boat a name. What do you say I call the new one Nomi? *S.S. Nomi.* And if I finish it in the next few days, we can put it into the sea right here."

She went so quiet he thought she had gone all glassy-eyed and weird again. What the hell was wrong with the kid? Wrapping herself in a bedsheet and

124

getting spaced out this way? He felt a twinge he had not felt for a long time towards anyone, of concern.

"Not a boat. I'm not a boat girl." She seemed to shake herself awake. "I'm a plane girl. I love airports — always bright, noisy, full of people, hot coffee and noodles round the clock. I feel like they should give me a room at an airport — you know — like that man in *Terminal*? I could live like that, easy. When you make a plane, you can name it after me."

"Planes don't have names," Suraj said "They have numbers." He saw a mosquito take position, spear Nomi's neck, rocking back and forth as it drew her blood. Its needle sucked her blood unnoticed for the moment. He stared at the mosquito, mesmerised by the silky brown of the skin it was feasting on. He felt the need to look away. Soon she would feel the sting and slap it off.

She did. Stared at her palm and screwed up her face. "I didn't go back to my coach on that train," she said. "I wonder what happened to those women. They must be here somewhere, no? Maybe next door? Maybe the fat one is drifting around in the maze inside that temple, lost forever. Maybe she'll forget to go back to her family. She'll turn into a holy woman. Years later her awful children will come here and fall at her feet."

She spoke faster and faster, riveted by the scenario she was conjuring up. "Don't you wish it could happen? Your mind wiped clean, like a hard drive? Start again without memories?"

Thinking of the day of the dog, he knew he would like his mind scoured spotless. He thought of his wife with her new man — his old friend. They played cricket together on Sundays, she had met him at one of their games when she brought them beer and chicken sandwiches. The three of them had had a picnic by the pitch. And then, all those times Suraj was away, travelling on work, more sandwiches. More than sandwiches. Plenty of memories he'd be better off without.

They had not heard the buffalo for a while. Perhaps the owner had taken it away. But for the far-off restiveness of the sea, there were no sounds. It seemed to Suraj that they were the only two people left alive on the earth.

Nomi began a vigorous scratching of her neck and in the light of the lamps concealed under the bushes near them Suraj saw a red patch form on her skin where the mosquito had bitten her. It was swollen, it would feel hotter to touch than the rest of her skin. Saliva. That's what made these weals subside.

He looked away from her neck. He thought out what he would say next with some care and spoke slowly after a pause, sounding tentative. "Do you usually talk so much with people you've just met? I don't. I haven't told anyone else that stuff about staying back at a random station." His voice was gruff, as if the words were being forced out of him. She was pleased, he could tell from the way she looked at him speechless with surprise. Every woman he'd ever known melted when you said this kind of rubbish. They felt they had some special quality that made men confide in them.

126

Nomi spoke only after she had drained her glass and risen from her chair. "I've no idea. It must be because we know we'll never see each other again after this assignment. Like people talk on planes and trains."

"Won't we? See each other again?" The thought made its slow way into his drowsy mind and never seeing her again appeared unlikely. They would see each other again and again. He sensed a tiny, almost imperceptible current between them. It would grow if he were careful. It had potential.

He felt drops of water on his face and looked up. "Here comes the rain," he said. He picked up his knife and the bottle and pushed back his chair.

Night seeped from the ground and spread from tree to tree and house to house, gathering them into a mass of darkness. In one alleyway a portly old man heaved himself into the rickshaw he had hired for the evening and grunted, "They're all like smelly old towels, and as much life in them. Get me a fresh young girl. With tomato-tight skin. With juice that spurts when you bite."

On a nearby rooftop, Johnny Toppo lay with his bundle of clothes as a pillow, gazing at the bloodshot sky. His money was in that bundle too. In his head he counted the notes. Ninety-six rupees. Not enough, but something. The wind had died down. It was so airless now he thought it would rain again. He had put a tarpaulin over his teacart. He had weighed the tarpaulin down with bricks. His pots and pans and jars were locked in his trunk. Nothing to worry about. He wiped the sweat from his gaunt face. He would sleep now. His knees did not ache that much tonight, his back did not hurt. He breathed out a deep sigh and closed his eyes.

Badal lay on his string cot in his stuffy room alternately opening and shutting the mobile he had bought for Raghu. Each time he flipped it open the blue glow of its screen lit up his face and his eyes glistened in the light. His nose was still smeared with blood. Grains of sand had got into the phone. He blew on it to tease them out.

Night smudged away the hovels, the hotels, the temples, the shuttered roadside stalls, the abandoned boats on the beach. The old woman Badal met every morning slept under the neem tree, the sweet jaggery in her dream making the drool trickle from her mouth.

On the dull grey sand of the beach a madman dug a hole and tenderly planted a twig. He dipped a clay cup into the sea, scampered back to water his twig, then lay down beside it, sighing at the coolness of its shade.

At the Swirling Sea Hotel, Latika slept, tense with anxiety, dreaming of herself tongue-tied on a spotlit stage. She had forgotten the song she was meant to sing or the reason for being on that stage. Down the corridor, Gouri lay awake holding a photograph of her dead husband, as she did every night, telling him all the things she could not share with anyone else.

Between their rooms and the luxury hotel next door was a shallow creek choked with rubbish, covered in reeds and gloom. Nomi lay in a large double bed in the hotel across the creek. She had fenced herself in on every side with pillows, her backpack, her travel guide, extra blankets rolled into barrels. The portion of the bed left for her was a small rectangle into which she just about fitted if she folded her knees into her chest. She clutched a pillow close. She was trying not to think of the monk on the beach. He was out there somewhere. Had he seen her? Had he recognised her? He must have, if she recognised him.

For years she had done nothing but gather information and courage. Bit by bit she had pieced together the details, waited for a chance to come back, to see for herself. Then this assignment. It had worked out. But now? She had spent much of last night sitting under the shower shivering in the cold but not able to turn off the water. She was a coward. That was what her foster mother used to say when she came back home bloodied from fist fights: she got into fights because she was in fact a coward.

A television voice started off in the next room. Not Suraj's room, the one on the other side. What was Suraj doing in his room? Carving his boat? An asinine thing to do, making all those boats just to float them away. What a fucking romantic. She could bet he put messages into bottles too, and threw them in the sea.

She put a pillow over her head to block out the sound from the television in the next room. Her thoughts went back to the morning, to the temple guide's strictures about her clothes. The bloody nerve. She had been on the brink of hitting someone, she had been so furious. It had taken all her self-control not to snap with those two men ogling her under the guise of judging the temple-worthiness of her cargo pants and shirt.

Her clothes always turned out to be wrong. The orphanage had sent her with a carefully-packed duffel bag to her foster mother, who lived at the time in Reading in England. The bag contained a pink comb, a matching toothbrush, a tube of translucent green toothpaste, shiny hairclips, undergarments, and four cotton frocks, each one a different colour. They were the first new clothes she had ever owned. She could not stop touching them, but her new mother had taken them out of the duffel bag and tossed them aside with barely a look, saying that they wouldn't do. She made a list of clothes Nomi had never heard of: tights, anorak, thermals. She was taken to a shop. It was huge, Nomi had never seen so many things in one place. She wandered from aisle to aisle, seeing nothing, hating the woman who had discarded her new frocks. She wanted to run away. She managed to slip off to a different section of the store, lurked among the merchandise. Now she was flanked by rows and rows of earrings, necklaces, hairclips, bracelets. Wonderstruck, she picked up a string of multicoloured beads. And before anyone saw, she put the necklace into her pocket. She could never explain why she stole the necklace, but it had given her a gloating sense of revenge. When she was leaving the shop, high-pitched beeps of piercing intensity began ringing around her. She knew nothing of burglar alarms and was taken aback when men in uniforms surrounded her. She hardly even reached their hips, she recalled, they were so tall. And she

130

remembered her vicious satisfaction when her new mother, checking her pockets, pulled out the beads, gasping, "It's just a mistake, I assure you! She's not a thief, it's just that she came two days ago from a different country!" One of the security guards had said, "Which country is it where they don't know stealing from buying?"

Despite the pillow over her head, the television voices rose, and over it she could hear men: loud talk, then guffawing laughter. It was always so quiet in her foster mother's house. Silent enough to hear leaves fall and rain drip from the roof, silent enough to make it hard for her to cry at night without being noticed. She tried to lie as motionless here as she had trained herself to do there. There was a wall between her and the television men. Thin, if it let through so much sound. But it was a wall.

A moment later, she sprang out of bed. She checked again if her cupboard was not in fact a door, looked under her bed. Ran her hands through the red curtains. Flung open the bathroom door for a look. No intruders. She fell back into bed.

She had to sleep. She shut her eyes. There was a way to sleep, it was always the same way. She made herself go back to the woods and the lake: cycling through the Norwegian countryside one midsummer — it is about one in the morning. She is with five other girls, they are straight out of school, sixteen, and she is on her first trip with girls her age. They are used to it, but to her it is new and strange. She is not saying much, just struggling to keep up, pedalling hard. She is smaller and thinner than they are, not able to cycle as fast, she gets out of breath. Around two, when they reach the woods, it is not dark and not light, it is a phosphorescent dusk, a mad light in which anything is possible. They put up two tents, she is inside one of them. The rest have not paused, they have run out to swim in the lake. She sits in the tent, not daring to come out of it. She can hear herself breathe: she breathes in the smell of the tent's nylon, her own sweat, the spilled shampoo in someone's backpack. Then she hears a bird. It doesn't call, it sings. A brief, ethereal song. Another bird sings back, then the first one sings again. On and on the birds sing to each other. She crawls out of the tent, sees a sheet of silver ahead, mirroring the unearthly midsummer night, the black trees, the glowing sky. Her friends' clothes are heaped on the bank. They are far off in the water, their voices ring out joyfully. She can glimpse flashes of gold — their hair. None of them are looking at her. She looks behind: there is nobody. She fiddles with a button. Her heart hammers her ribs. She has never done this before, not in changing rooms, or doctors' clinics, or dorms. Never before people. Tonight she unbuttons her shirt, shrugs it off. Unzips her jeans and peels them away, and then, very quickly before she has time to reconsider, she takes off every scrap of underclothing. She feels the warm midsummer air on her skin. There is nobody looking. Nobody to gape at her scraggy, stubby, knock-kneed body striped with welts and pockmarked with burns. She steps into the water. It is chilly and she gasps. As she slides in, it begins to feel warmer. It

132

covers her. There is nothing between herself and the water. The water flows into her and out, soft and cool. The birds are still singing to each other, she can hear them over her splashes and her friends' cries of delight. She is charged with a wild abandon, flips over, doesn't care who sees her breasts. Above her, the sky is opal.

By the time Nomi's eyelids dropped, all Jarmuli was asleep. At the great temple, the priests and guides and pilgrims had gone. Watchmen sat dozing outside the shrines. The temple idols gazed into oil lamps burning gold and red. Far out at sea, a fishing boat's solitary lantern bobbed on the dark water. The fish underneath swam in shoals towards its nets, eager to the end.

When I opened my eyes it was raining in the room, I could not see through the sheets of falling blood. I thought I was going blind, I thought I was losing my mind. As a child I had taught myself a game: whenever I was afraid, I pretended I was dead, the life in me had gone, nothing could happen to me again, there would be no pain, never again, and this is what I did now, I kept myself still, I willed myself hardly to breathe at all. I was a ragdoll, I was held together with thread, there was not a shred of flesh and blood in me, nothing that could hurt. When I opened my eyes again, everything was covered in a film of oil, rainbows shifted and melted and changed, my head felt undone, rearranged. A blazing skewer went through it, its pain made my stomach boil. But I could see again. I did not move a finger, only opened and shut my eyes until I was sure. The sheet below me was white and soft and pure, the ceiling above me was white and the doors were painted white as well. The red had gone, everything felt pale and damp, there were tuberoses in a vase by a lemon-coloured lamp.

My room was new, I had not seen it before, a hotel room — where was it, which city? It would not come back to me right then and I looked beyond the ceiling and the doors to the window to get a sense of where — and then I saw scarlet curtains against the sun, shifting and swelling as if they were alive, as if deciding what was to be done. Beyond the curtains through the window I could see the flesh-thick petals of crimson flowers on a leafless tree and then my heart thudded as if it would burst, the iron rod in my head was on fire, but that wasn't the worst of it, the rod twisted and turned, there was a burning wire around my skull, and I tore off all my clothes and ran to the door, I turned on the shower, I slid to the bathroom's polished floor. Over my head, my shoulders, my breasts, the water poured, I was sodden, I was sobbing, I scoured myself with my nails, my nails were thick and pitted and dirty and hard, they scratched my skin, but I could not stop. I don't know how many hours I passed inside, or maybe they were minutes, I was cold, my skin felt raw as just-flayed hide, I tried, but I could not go back into the room.

I thought I had torn the thing out, it would never come back. Nobody would cow me down, I would attack. I could slam my fist into a brick, not feel the pain, lick the blood away, hit the brick again. I would kick a ball hard and cry with joy. The boys sniggered, but it made me feel whole, it made me weep because that ball wasn't a ball, it was a man's head, it was that man I was kicking dead. This was the way I broke it, the thing was half-killed, I thought it had lost the will to fight but then I came to this hotel. It is by the sea, I had chosen that deliberately, to stare it down, to say you can't do anything more to me, but then at breakfast by the pool there was a man with a knife that he plunged into a melon not once but twice, thrice, and then again, and when he was done he prised the slices apart, and the juice inside poured out in red spurts. I told myself it was just fruit. A woman came around with glasses on a tray. Her eyelids were blue, her hair was gold, sapphires sparkled in her ears and I told myself it was just fruit, but my breath stuck in my throat, I thought I would choke, yet I picked up a glass, said thank you. It was all about willpower, I told myself, it was just a fruit and I would not look at it, but I did and there was the melon, cut in pieces on a flat white plate, red against white, just like the grapefruit we picked, my brother and I, that my mother sliced in half.

THE THIRD DAY

THE THIRD DAY

Vidya threw up in the early hours and lay in bed till late morning. Her head was spinning, her temples ached, her neck hurt. Quavering, she refused breakfast, even dry toast, and urged the other two to go out without her. "I'll be alright." She tried to sound brave. "It must be my B.P. Or the food I ate at that roadside stall yesterday." She had her zipper bag of medicine beside her and was dosing herself with Nux Vomica 30. "I'll be fit enough to play football by tomorrow, just wait and see."

Latika handed her some iced water. "Sip slowly. This has salt and sugar. You mustn't dehydrate. Really, Vidya, what a thing to do — it looked poisonous, all that prawn floating in oil and chillies. Whatever possessed you? The sea air?"

She clucked partly to mask her resentment. They had only two more days in Jarmuli. Could they afford a whole morning commiserating with Vidya? Latika longed to spend the day on the beach, feeling the waves lapping her ankles. It was many years since she had been to the sea: the last time, a decade ago, it was with her husband, in Goa. He stood on dry land shouting, "You are too rash, Latika! You'll float away and not

139

know until you're miles out and can't swim back."
Later they had eaten grilled salmon and drunk sweet
Goan port wine sitting in a rush-covered shack, looking
at the moonlit sea while in the distance someone sang
slow Portuguese fados. Her insides melted with certain
kinds of music. She felt herself twisted and wrung; tears
poked at her eyes. Forgotten things from years ago had
come back to her under that shack — doves in the
next-door house, the tamarind tree she climbed to pick
its stick-like fruit, stone images in a garden, the long
grey Buick — until she realised her husband was
speaking to her, waiting for a response, annoyed at her
farawayness. It was their first holiday alone in decades,
soon after their daughter had gone off to university in
Montreal.

In the early evening, only an hour left before sunset,
Latika stroked Vidya's sweat-dampened hair and told
her, "We are going for a walk on the beach. You must
phone me the minute you want us." Vidya shut her
eyes. "All I do is doze off, there's no need for the two of
you to waste a whole day as well."

Latika and Gouri left the hotel in a rickshaw that
took them towards the promenade. "Shouldn't we have
told someone at the hotel that she's alone?" Gouri said
anxiously as the rickshaw started to move. "What if she
feels dizzy and falls? I did that once and . . ."

"She's better now," Latika said, "all that a stomach
upset needs is rest and fluids." Their rickshaw rattled
along, the breeze carried salt and sea and as the
distance between them and the hotel increased, Vidya
and her troubles receded.

140

It was a Sunday. Walking away from their rickshaw, Latika and Gouri approached the crowded part of the beach. Here an open market tumbled over the sands, with makeshift stalls selling everything from conch shells to cowries and fried prawns. Children made gleeful sorties into the waves, then scampered back to land. Boys tugged at their saris, holding out seashell keyrings and bead necklaces, proclaiming unbelievable prices. The air smelled of drying fish, frying fish, old fish, fresh fish, but in the wind that gusted in from the sea none of it smelled bad.

Gouri held Latika's arm for balance and sloshed the water at the edge of the beach with her feet, dreamy in the heaving murmur of waves which snatched away the voices of people around them. The wind twisted their saris around their ankles. They laughed into it, pressed down blowaway hair. Abandoned their slippers to walk barefoot. Sidestepped tiny, translucent crabs which dug themselves out of the sand and skittered towards the water, disappearing again.

Looking at Gouri smiling, Latika thought their freedom from care was no more than a pause in time, a postponement of the inevitable even as the predator inside Gouri's mind rested, gathering strength, never letting her out of sight. Gouri appeared to have no recollection of the way Latika had found her in her room the afternoon before, packed and in her mind waiting to leave for Jarmuli — when they had scarcely arrived. How had she confused her hotel room with her home in Calcutta? And if she could not remember which city she was in, could she ever be left alone?

What future was in store for her now? A prisoner in her son's care? Or would he put her into a nursing home?

Her life was on the brink of catastrophe and yet she haggled over the price of a seashell, serenely ignorant. She bought a plaster model of the great temple. Then she noticed a man selling tea and the musky smell of rain-wet earth in tea served in clay cups came back to her. She could not remember when she had last had tea smelling of rain. She told herself she would get at least three cups right away, to make up. Where, back home in Calcutta, would she find terracotta tea? No, it could be many years; she was certain she wanted to drink three cups.

Or should it be two? She had a tiny sugar problem. Not yet diabetes, but she needed to be careful: her father had had diabetes.

As she dithered, Latika said, "Look, isn't that the guide who was showing us around the temple yesterday?"

"What? Oh yes, you're right, it is! Yes, Badal," Gouri said happily. "Let's go and —"

"He's a strange fellow — so silent and contemptuous — if he smiled a little he wouldn't look bad."

"He's not strange, Latika. He's not silent. On the scooter, when we were going to the temple, he told me all about himself. We had such a lovely chat. His father died when he was a child and his uncle stole everything he should have inherited and now he makes him do the work and takes away his money."

"How did you find all that out?" Latika began, but Gouri had started off towards the tea stall with a smile

142

ready on her face to greet Badal. Midway, she stopped. From a distance she could overhear an altercation between him and the vendor. Latika caught up with her and grabbed her arm. "Don't rush off like that into the crowd, I'll lose you."

"I'm not his mother or father," the stall man was saying. "He can go to hell."

"But where could he have gone? What if something's happened to him? He's just a boy." Badal's voice was anguished.

"A boy! And I'm a baby born yesterday, aren't I? What is it to you if he hasn't come? You don't pay him, do you?"

"Pay him?" Badal stammered. "Why would I —"

"What would you pay him for? The money going down the drain is mine. He's a waste of time, Babu. Look at me: now I have to wash the pans, make tea, collect money, attend to people — everything — did I hire the boy just so I would do his work for him?" He spotted Gouri faltering a few feet away. "Babu, I have customers, I've work to do."

Badal turned and saw the customers Johnny Toppo was getting agitated about. He looked away to avoid meeting their eye. The garrulous fat one who had sat on his scooter the day before — the woman's mouth opened and shut like a frog's all the time and words, words, words, endless words spewed out. Pointless observations, prying questions. And that thin red-haired one who had mocked him at the temple. There were questions he needed to ask Johnny Toppo about Raghu, who had not been seen since the night Badal had spotted him with the monk. But not now, not with these women around. He walked off swiftly as Johnny Toppo shouted past him, "Chai! Chaaai!" putting on a kind smile for the two women to forestall a migration to some other stall.

Gouri had already decided to have his tea, however, and now she hurried towards him in her wobbling, lopsided way. She leaned against his handcart and called out, "Look, Latika, clay cups!"

Latika followed saying, "I'd give anything for some coffee."

"Didi, biscuits? Will you have some biscuits also? Sweet and salt, jeera and elaichi?" Johnny Toppo pointed to the jars he had on his cart. His tea bubbled in a big dented saucepan that was leathery with old layers of burnt grease. A rag stained to dirty brown bandaged its handle. Johnny Toppo held the pan high up as he poured from it into the clay cups that he had lined up in a row. A finger of pale froth formed against the rims of the cups. It was a trick he had devised over years of practice, to half-fill the cups this way with froth.

Latika blew on her hot tea, dipped a chunky biscuit into it. It had an earthy crunch different from the packaged biscuits at home. Should she buy some to take with her? Of course it would not taste the same if it were eaten sitting alone at the coffee table in her seventh-floor flat, waiting for the phone to ring. It was different eating it here, out in the windy open, with Gouri next to her and the tea man crying "Chai, Chai!" every now and then. Soon the sun would begin its dip into the sea and the day would be over. She would not think of that. Gouri murmured, "The days go so fast."

Johnny Toppo had no other customers. Even so, he kept stirring the pan of milky brown tea on his stove, his way of telling the world he was still in business. He talked to himself in a mutter. "I'll sack the bastard, pity is the root of all trouble." Then, switching thoughts, he hummed lines of songs that Latika tried to follow, blocking out Gouri's chatter and every other sound. Was he singing of a village? Where was it?

Emerald green are the paddy fields, my love,
Black is the back of the crow,
But nothing is as dark or as deeply black
As those eyes that look at me now.
Your eyes are the light of my life, my love,
I am tied in the strands of your hair,
That red flower bush by the stream, my love,
It's for you. I planted it there.

Latika wanted to ask him — why should she not ask him?

"Is that a folk song?"

"Ah Ma, it is nothing, I make these things up in my head." Johnny Toppo laughed his gap-toothed laugh. "And they all have the same tune. There is only that one tune. It's a tune from my village."

He turned away, busying himself with soaking a stack of new clay cups in his bucket. Latika wondered why he wore a thick twist of cloth around his neck even when

145

the day was so hot. That was another thing she wanted to ask him, but she could not.

"Mostly, you know, Ma," he said over his shoulder, "I don't even know what I'm singing. I never sang before, not until I left everything and came here." He laughed again, his face creased, his eyes turned into lines between his crow's feet, and Latika wanted to sit on his bench and ask him, What about the woman in the song? Who is she? Where has she gone?

But Johnny Toppo now had other customers and was asking if they wanted the sweet biscuits or the salty ones in exactly the tones he had put those questions to Latika and Gouri. Latika turned away, disappointed that his voice was so indiscriminately distributed. Her discontent returned and she wished again that her tea were coffee.

It was when they were drinking their second cups of tea that Latika tugged at Gouri's hand and whispered, "Isn't he . . . ?"

For a while, Gouri couldn't tell what Latika had seen. "Who are you talking about?" And at that moment, she saw.

It was Vidya's son, Suraj, idling at one of the stands. With a girl. The stallkeeper urged trinkets upon them, picking up one thing, then another. Latika saw him thrust by turn a stone temple, a sea lion, and a keyring at the girl. Then a long shell necklace. The girl stared at it as if she had never seen a necklace before, turned away abruptly. The stallkeeper offered it to Suraj next, seeming to coax him into buying it. After some resistance, Suraj dug into his pocket, paid the man,

146

then followed the girl. He held the necklace out to her, got no reaction. He said something, touched her elbow. She seemed to pull herself back to the present. She smiled at him and took the necklace.

"That isn't Ayesha, is it?" Gouri adjusted her glasses. "I'm sure Ayesha has short hair. But maybe I'm mistaken. I have a bad memory for faces."

"Of course it isn't Ayesha, can't you see?" Ayesha, Vidya's daughter-in-law, was at least ten years older and ten kilos heavier than this chit of a girl who was now fingering the shells on the necklace.

"Can't you see, Gouri! It's the girl who was with us in the train!"

"In the train? What train?"

"God, Gouri! In our compartment! The train in which we came from Calcutta. That girl — you even spoke to her, you exchanged seats — the girl in our compartment who got off and never came back. Remember?"

Suraj and the girl began to stroll towards the tea stall and the women started away from it in a confused hurry. Johnny Toppo ran after them, scolding, "My money, my money!"

"We were going to have one more cup," Latika said to him. "We weren't leaving." She searched her bag with an urgent hand for the right amount of money, keeping an eye on Suraj, telling Gouri to carry on ahead, placating the vendor as he eyed a wavering pair of customers at his stall and complained, "Quickly. My boy hasn't come today, I'm managing alone."

On their way back to the hotel the two women didn't speak, too full of things to say. When they reached the hotel's gate they looked at each other and Latika said, "Not a word about this. We can't spoil the holiday for Vidya."

"But Latika, maybe the girl's just a friend of his. I thought she smiled politely, nothing more. You know how friendly children are with each other these days. Why the other day when —"

"Friendly! What's she doing walking on the beach with a married man, making him buy her necklaces? Didn't you see how come-hither she looked?"

"No, she didn't. Really, Latika, you're making too much of it." Gouri said in a soothing voice. "Just because your —"

She stopped herself, but it was too late. Latika's lips had tightened, her face had crumpled as if someone had let the air out of her. She straightened her back, said, "Never mind me." She took a breath to steady herself. "Vidya doesn't need to know about this right now. Forget that this ever happened."

But would she? There was something perverse about Gouri's amnesia, it had an unfailing way of making her blab about the wrong things. This time Latika wished she could put cards into Gouri's handbag to remind her to *forget*: not just Suraj and the girl, but also her own husband's escapade with his student. Such a wretchedly stupid thing to have confided in Gouri of all people! She had of course counselled refuge in God and told her that every misfortune hid a blessing. And ever since, brought up the topic when Latika least

148

expected it. It was thirty-one years ago. Yet the merest mention of those two months in her life turned the lights off inside her.

The good humour in Gouri's plump face had evaporated and she nodded at Latika solemnly. "You're right. What mothers have to put up with! There's no need for her to know about this now. First that boy married a girl Vidya didn't like. Remember how upset she was when he said Ayesha was years older than him? And now he's romancing another one half his age." If they let slip what they had seen, Vidya would be thrown into an immediate turmoil of shame and anxiety. She had never cared for her son's wife, she had often wished her away, true. But to chance upon her son with a lover on their own beach! For all they knew the fellow might be at the next hotel. What if he was in the *same* hotel, doing god-knows-what down the corridor?

Latika pushed her glasses up her nose and shook her head as if to reorder her mind. She would not allow herself to dwell upon long-ago things. She must live in the present. Suraj. Yes, she must focus on Suraj. She had known him from when he was a toddler, she had shared Vidya's jittery delight when he first climbed the steep stairs of her old house. Through his boyhood Latika had taught him how to recite lines from poems. When he first began to act in school plays, she had gone to all of them, clapped hard. They had thought he would be a famous actor. She had given him singing lessons. Suraj and her daughter, the same age, would stand next to each other, singing by her piano, both slightly off-key but persevering. He used to shut his eyes when he sang and frown until his little-boy forehead puckered like an old man's. As a boy he was irresistible, the most popular in school, the one the girls followed around. He had a beautiful face, and she remembered how, in the light of the sunset that came in through the window by the piano, his cheeks turned orange, his light-brown hair on fire as if he had become the sun he was named after. Once, she had her husband photograph him like that and gave the picture to Vidya, framed. She had wanted to caption it, "Suraj in the Sun," but it would have seemed too pat. The picture still stood on Vidya's bedside table, its black and white turning to sepia.

Nothing in that photograph predicted the Suraj she had seen today, dopey-eyed, degenerate, flirting with a virtual teenager. The girl from their train. She had looked such a child. How deceptive appearances could be. "It's true," she murmured, "what they say. They grow up quicker in the West."

"Best? Yes, that tea was the best. Why don't we go and have some more? Why did we leave in such a hurry?" Gouri was beaming up at Latika through her round glasses, her voice bubbling with enthusiasm.

When I landed after my first flight ever, my new mother was waiting inside the airport. I had a label on a string around my neck with my name and other details because I was travelling as an unaccompanied child. I was a parcel being sent from one country to another.

She came towards me with an eager smile. She had straw-yellow hair and grey eyes. She wore a frock. Nobody that old ever wore frocks where I came from. Her frock came to her knees, below which her legs were wax-white, with green veins running down the length of the calves. She had a necklace made of pink seashells in her hand. When she reached me she garlanded me with it and gave me a bright smile. She squeezed my hand, took my duffel bag from me, said, "How light this is! Is this all you've brought?" Later, in the taxi, she said she got me the necklace because she had found out that it was the custom in my country to welcome people with garlands — only she had not made it a flower garland because she wanted me to have something I could keep for always, something that would remind me of today, that would mark my passage across many seas.

I don't know why I took my rage out on that necklace the day I overheard her telling her sister on the phone that it was too much, maybe it had been a mistake. She meant me, I was the mistake, although I had been with her three years already. The necklace was hard to break because the string was nylon, but I was angry enough, I did tear it apart, and have loathed shell necklaces ever since. I hadn't asked to come to her either, to this lonely country where it was night all day and I had no friends. I flung the shells from my window into her garden where she would be sure to step on them. Later I saw her treading gingerly, picking shells from the grass.

Before the necklace I had had few presents. The gold earrings that had belonged to Chuni and oddments from Jugnu. He was the only person at the ashram who gave me things: flowers, fruits, oddly-coloured dry leaves, dead butterflies, flattened frogs, striped stones: these were his notion of presents for a girl. One day, he put together sheets of thin metal into a weathervane and said it would belong to both of us. He clambered to the top of his shed and fixed it there. He said when the wind pointed it northward, it would be time. Time for what, I asked him. Time to leave for a new country, he said. The weathervane screeched and squeaked on its spindle if it moved at all, but I was thrilled each time it shifted in the breeze and Jugnu said, "Look, it's going north. It'll be there soon. And then . . ." I would chorus, "And then we will leave." Sometimes at night I lay awake thinking of the weathervane, wondering which direction the wind was blowing it. What if it chose to turn northward when we were asleep? What if it had turned north already and we had missed seeing it? Each time I passed Jugnu's shed during the day I stared hard at the roof, willing that weathervane to turn. I made up all sorts of charms for it: if I saw seven green parakeets together, it was a sign that soon the weathervane would turn north. If a yellow butterfly sat on a blue flower, it would turn north.

Jugnu made a big to-do when he brought me something. You'll never believe what it is, he might say, nobody's ever had a thing so beautiful: as if he had brought me a pretty doll in a lace frock and not a twig wrapped in a dirty scrap of cloth. His mock ceremony made me giggle. I was wary of the other people at the ashram but never of Jugnu. He talked to me as if we were the same age. He made me feel grown-up and clever. He told me stories. He said that before he became a gardener he used to draw pictures for storybooks. His fingers looked too thick for pencils, though, so I would tell him he was making up a story about himself.

Jugnu would say, "What do you know about me? You don't know who I am or what I was before the war did this to me."

As the months passed, he changed. Some days, he would be in a bad temper and mutter to himself as he worked. Some days he would not talk to me at all except to scold me. He stopped going to the ashram's puja hall and he hardly ever went to serve Guruji. He would sing kirtans, but his singing was almost a whisper, as if he were talking to God and he did not want anyone else to overhear.

One of Jugnu's jobs was to pick the fruits and flowers to offer at the puja hall every day. He would pick them and I would follow him around with a basket. One day, after picking the fruit, he sat in a tree's shade and patted a spot beside him. "Come here, I'll tell you a story. From the *Ramayana*. It's about picking fruit for God."

I sat at the tree next to his feet. They were big, dirty feet with nails that looked as if they were made from the horns of cows, but I was used to them. I loved everything about him now. His face did not look ugly to me any longer, his scar did not look grotesque. I loved his hoarse voice, but I also loved the way we could work side by side together and he let me be.

Once there was a woman, he said, called Shabari. She was a hunter's daughter, yet she hated the thought of killing animals and she ran away from home on her wedding day when she realised animals would be sacrificed at her marriage ceremony. She lived in a deep forest after that, in a hermit's cave, serving the hermit. When the hermit grew very old and very ill and he was on his deathbed, he said in a sad voice to Shabari that he had spent all his life serving Lord Rama, and was leaving life without a glimpse of Him. That would not be her fate, he said, she would never be alone. She would always have Lord Rama by her side and one day He would appear before her, so she must be ready. After this, the hermit left his body.

Shabari understood his last words to mean that she would have to be prepared. She would have to feed Lord Rama and honour Him when He appeared before her. She would have to wait for Him in the very same place, otherwise how would He find her? Shabari was a simple-minded woman who thought of God as someone very like herself, as a friend of hers.

So she went on living in the forest, in her guru's cave, even though she was now all alone and sometimes she lost hope. Every day she cleared the forest path to her hut and every day she collected berries from all over the forest so that she would have something to offer the Lord if He came to her home. She tasted each of the berries after picking them, to see if they were sweet enough for Him.

In this way the years passed. She waited and waited. She became a crazed, half-starved, white-haired old woman in rags and the Lord did not come. Still, every day she hobbled out and swept the path and collected berries for him. And as always she tasted each berry for its sweetness, then arranged them on a clay plate and placed a pitcher of cool spring water beside them.

At last one day Lord Rama did arrive. He was with his brother Lakshmana and they were in the forest searching for Lord Rama's wife, Sita, who had been kidnapped. They came to Shabari's cottage. They told her who they were. The old woman wept. The Lord had come at last! She had her plate of berries ready, as every day. Lovingly she offered them to Lord Rama.

Just as the Lord was going to eat one of the berries, his brother said, "Stop! These are half-bitten, all of them." Lakshmana's eyes were fiery. He opened his mouth to scorch Shabari with a reprimand.

Rama, serene, put the once-bitten berry into his mouth. He picked up another and said, "These are the sweetest berries I have ever eaten. And they are sweet because they have been collected for me with such deep love. She has tasted each one because she could not bear to feed me a sour or poisonous berry. How can I do otherwise but bless her with heaven?"

"At last her wait ended," Jugnu said, "and why was that? Tell me? What is the moral of this story?"

He always asked me the moral of his stories. I usually came up with one, but that day I had to look away from Jugnu. I had no answer to give him.

Jugnu said, "The moral is that true, simple devotion is worth a hundred such . . ." He waved his hands around, pointing at our ashram. "A hundred such displays."

I went back to my own work feeling as sad as the first day, when I had cried out for my brother and he had not come. The story had done something to me. I thought I would cry, my throat felt stuffed with an emptiness I could not swallow. I thought of how Shabari had waited. In stories, waiting was never for nothing. But I knew by now that our weathervane would never point north. I would never be free. I would wait all my life and never again see my brother or my mother. Jugnu's story had made me older. It was then that I realised I was old enough to know fairy tales were not true.

The first time I saw a display of the kind that disgusted Jugnu was when we were taken to the grand audience hall beyond the barbed wire. It was in a winter month. I know this because we strung marigolds into garlands for three days before the event and the scent of those flowers still brings back that day. We had been at the ashram for four years or more but had never been allowed to cross to the other side until now.

Across the fence were cottages with red roofs among groves of fruit trees. Tall, shiny lamp posts with curly designs on them stood between the cottages. One of the squares between the cottages had a tiled pond filled with pink lotus. Each cottage was surrounded by a fence and inside the fence there were patches of garden. A fawn-coloured cat with fur that shone looked at us from the verandah of the first cottage. Its eyes were as cold as glass. Another cottage had birds in a cage.

We walked through the gardens, led by Padma Devi. We had not left the ashram since we were brought there. A few among us, I think Jui, Champa, and Minoti, who were older than me when they came, had clear memories of the world outside, but mine were muddled and faded. These cottages and the high-roofed auditorium that stood at the end of the path looked like a different world to me.

That morning, we had been told, the chief minister of the state was coming to the ashram. He was Guruji's disciple. Guruji had other rich and powerful disciples who respected his powers and this was why even illegal boat girls were safe inside the ashram. That morning, he was to preach a special sermon. Everyone who lived in the ashram would be there. Hundreds of his disciples visiting from all over the world would be there too. He had devotees everywhere, and ashrams everywhere. The outer room of his cottage on our side of the fence had photographs of beautiful ashram buildings in Vienna and Geneva and other places we knew about only from books. The ashrams abroad were in wooden buildings with sloping roofs and had pine trees and snow peaks behind them. Guruji even had his own aeroplane. There was a picture of him climbing into it to go to one of the foreign ashrams.

Everywhere Guruji went that morning, he was surrounded by followers who picked pinches of dust from the ground he had stepped on, and sprinkled it on their heads. We could see columns of people walking towards the hall. Although there were many people, there was no shouting or pushing, only the buzz of low voices and the shuffle of bare feet. We were taken in through a back entrance. We had been told we were to stay together, and to listen, not talk.

Guruji sat on a high stage on a velvet-covered throne with golden armrests. Behind him, all over the back wall of the stage, were oil paintings of the kind I had seen in his room, but much bigger, of birds in trees, among leaves and fruits. I saw a huge one with many parakeets, each of which looked like the bird I had seen in a cage during my first punishment.

A satin cushion kept Guruji's feet off the floor. Some favoured devotees sat at the edges of the stage. They came one by one, stretched themselves full length and touched their foreheads to the floor in front of his feet. Dazzling lights shone on Guruji, changing from gold to orange. His skin gleamed under the lights. The people in the hall craned their necks for a glimpse and chanted his name. Only I knew he had a stump between his legs oozing slime.

Guruji began his discourse and everyone went quiet. He spoke from the books of all religions and as he did in our own assembly every day, he said that all religions were paths to the same God. He spoke of how the Buddha left home in search of truth. He spoke of Sufi saints and Jain monks. He recited a sacred Hindu poem and then quoted from the Bible to show how the love for God sounded similar everywhere. He spoke of how true mystics, such as he was, had been thought of as madmen by ordinary people. Nobody understood where the mystic's strangeness came from. Would people not behave strangely if unseen by all, a star dropped into their hearts from the sky and lived on there, pulsing, burning? The things mystics did, or demanded of the people around them, these often seemed to make no sense, but this was only because ordinary people could not see the workings of God.

At times he referred to no books at all but spoke of daily things — problems between children and parents, husbands and wives, the price of vegetables — and at the end of each story he had a moral or a teaching that some of the people there wrote down in notebooks.

Every now and then Guruji paused in his sermon and went into a trance while his audience sang hymns. He would come out of the trance after a few hymns and look directly into the eyes of someone in the audience and say: "They say there are windows from one heart to another. How can there be windows where there are no walls?" Or, "How can we claim to know God when we cannot know our closest friends? Every other being is a mystery to us and God is the greatest enigma of all." He spoke to the person he had pinned with his eyes as if he were seeing right into them. Then he closed his eyes and was transported back into his trance.

At the end some people were in tears while others sat as if they had been turned to stone. I noticed a tall white-haired monk standing by the stage, looking at the twelve of us one by one. It was long ago, but I was sure he was the man who had spotted us when Piku and I had crept to the barbed wire fence that separated our part of the ashram from the other and Bhola had caught us.

When Guruji had left the stage after his discourse, the twelve of us were brought onto it. We had been told to smile and stand in a row holding the next girl's hand. We could not see the people in the audience because there were bright spotlights on us. Piku stumbled as we went up onto the stage. After that she clutched my hand throughout with her own clammy one. Her head only came to my shoulders. I had grown taller, but she was still a tadpole.

Padma Devi told the audience that we were a few of the destitute children that Guruji had adopted as his own. She said we were fed, clothed, and went to school at the ashram alongside paying students. Padma Devi's yellow hair and blue eyes looked brighter under the lights against her pink sari. Her lips twisted to one side when she spoke so her flat, shiny face went out of shape. She thanked the audience for their generous

160

support and gifts of old clothes and books. The audience clapped and cheered, but I saw that all of us were looking at our toes. I wanted to run out and throw away my clothes and books and pens and pencils. I plucked at my frock with my nails. I hated the pink flowers on it and the green polka dots between the flowers. I hated my round-toed shoes and the ribbons in my hair. When I grew up I would run away from here and have so many new clothes that ten cupboards would not be enough to hold them.

THE FOURTH DAY

By the next morning Vidya was well enough for toast and tea. But when she and Latika went to fetch Gouri for breakfast, she could not be found in her room: they knocked and waited, knocked and waited, then got the receptionist to open the room with a duplicate key. Gouri's handbag lay on the coffee table. When they went through it they saw her purse was missing, as were her prayer beads in their cloth bag. Nothing else that they could see was missing.

"Those address cards!" Latika said. "She's left them in her bag."

She must not appear over-anxious. She had not told Vidya about finding Gouri utterly muddled, packed and ready to go to the station the day after they had arrived in Jarmuli. Now she was too scared to confess it. What if Gouri had actually left the hotel this time, thinking she had to catch a train? She said, "She must be in the hotel somewhere. She didn't like her room, maybe she's still nagging them to change it."

Vidya replied, "I do all I can, what more could I have done? Look, two cards missing. What do you think that means?"

She sank down onto the bed. Perhaps she hadn't quite recovered after all and her head was swimming because of her stomach trouble yesterday.

"Oh, what will we say to her son!" Latika said. "He didn't want her travelling in the first place. He said so over and over, 'She can't be trusted alone any more, she forgets everything!'" What if Gouri became one of the missing whose grim, grainy faces one saw in black-outlined police advertisements in newspapers? And this wasn't even the worst of the possible calamities.

"We ought to phone her son . . ." Latika could see his bald, pompous face in her mind's eye. His thin moustache and his jowls. The way he said, "I'll try and make time, but I can't promise," whenever you asked if he could drop Gouri over on his way to work. The way he pursed his lips when called upon to smile.

"If that fellow had his way, Gouri would never leave the house at all. Remember what he said to me at the station?" Vidya put on a baritone. "So, Vidya Aunty, what mischief will you girls get up to on your wicked weekend, hmm?" She seemed to gather energy and resolve at the memory of his voice. "We'll find her, wait and see." She had dealt with many kinds of problems during her time in the bureaucracy, including an absconding typist.

They walked through their hotel describing Gouri to anyone they saw. They went into a satin-cushioned room they had never seen before which was called the Mumtaz Bar; they crossed the dining hall, the lobby, the corridors, the row of chairs around the

166

bathtub-sized swimming pool, the strip of land in front with its evenly-spaced columns of coconut trees — Gouri was nowhere. Vidya interrogated the chowkidar at the gate, who in turn asked the ragged bunch of rickshaw-wallas parked there if any of them had ferried an old, stout, white-haired woman that morning. They even tried going through a set of latched doors to the kitchen, but they were stopped by an agitated waiter.

At the back of the hotel was a garden. Along its edge ran an earthen pathway pillared by palms. It ended in a low iron gate. They had not noticed the gate before, but now they saw it opened directly onto the beach. Stepping through the gate, they were confronted by the white and blue of ocean and beach in limpid morning light. Bare-chested fishermen were pushing wooden boats into the surf, chanting prayers together for luck. Women in fluorescent knee-high saris walked past in pairs and threes, with fish-baskets on their heads.

Vidya and Latika took their slippers in their hands and walked barefoot, scanning the beach for a round form in a sari. They passed a scent of cloves and ginger. Latika remembered the tea stall and turned around to find it, but as she turned she glimpsed someone who looked very like Suraj from the back. She grabbed Vidya's hand to propel her the other way, babbling, "Look, they're selling lobsters there. And crabs too. By those boats." Upturned boats rose out of the sand like the carcasses of prehistoric animals. Latika pointed Vidya in their direction.

They hurried away, Vidya protesting. "If we walk this quickly, we'll never find her. Slow down!" The tea man's morning song came to them in snatches, "The rain came again that night. And again and again and again."

A familiar voice interrupted the song. "Awake at last. And I've been up and about since dawn! You should have seen the sunrise. Today I decided I would say my prayers out here by the sea."

She was parked on the hull of an abandoned boat. Despite her prayer beads and white hair and bulk, Gouri looked more sinister than grandmotherly. She wore round sunglasses that they had never seen on her before, and a necklace of rose-pink pearls acquired minutes earlier from a vendor who was offering them identical strings now. She bared her teeth in laughter at their furious faces and the stark white of her dentures gleamed in the sunlight. "Oh come, come," she said gaily. "I am not under house arrest here too, am I? And anyway, I have a stuffy old room, yours are much nicer."

They did not know what to say, feeling their pent-up emotions drift clear of their bodies.

"I can't bear to stay in my room, it suffocates me," Gouri stated as she rose from her throne.

"Why didn't you at least carry the cards I made for you?" Vidya's voice rained hailstones when she was this furious. The voice that was said to detonate bombs under the chairs of sleepy clerks when she was Director General, Social Welfare.

It did not intimidate Gouri. She whipped out one of Vidya's handwritten cards from somewhere inside the layers of her sari and waved it in her face. "I didn't carry my handbag, that's all. It's so heavy." She sounded even more smug now.

For a long time neither of them could speak to Gouri. It was only after breakfast, when they reached the bazaar, where they had to pool voices to discourage beggars, that they forgot their anger. They shopped, then found a restaurant to eat lunch in. Steaming mounds of white rice and dal and vegetables, too much for any of them to finish, were served by a waiter who seemed in a hurry to be somewhere else. Bells began ringing all over the town, bhajans battled each other on competing loudspeakers. From above, the first floor of the building, they heard voices chanting hymns, intoning the Sanskrit in exotic accents. A band of pilgrims passed them, singing kirtans, tinkling their cymbals. There were young women, men, even a child or two, all in saris and dhotis, their foreheads marked with the tilak of Vishnu. They smiled at the women through the glass front of the restaurant.

"Let's eat quickly," Vidya commanded. "We have other things to do."

As they began their meal the singing stopped and half a dozen men and women came down the stairs. They were foreigners in saffron and yellow robes. Sprigs of hair sprouted from the backs of their shaven heads like stalks from berries.

Gouri noticed that the foreigners were being served only bowls of grapes. Why was that, she asked their waiter in a whisper, "Don't they like the food?" He gave her a withering look. "They are fasting," he said. Then more emphatically, "For Shivaratri. Some of them won't touch water either all day. You've forgotten?"

The disdain in his voice, its air of authority, reminded her of home. It was how her son spoke when he said, "Your widow's pension was to be picked up, didn't you remember? The children were to reach their tennis lesson at two, didn't you remember?"

She remembered her terracotta tea and told herself she must have that third cup before returning home. And she would go back to the temple. By herself.

On the morning of Shivaratri the great temple was more crowded than usual. Badal was escorting a man in his eighties who hobbled along, trying to keep his footing in the cavernous inner sanctum. As always it was half dark, lit largely with flickering lamps.

"Please hold on to my arm, you might fall." Something about the man reminded Badal of his father. Perhaps the over-large ears. The sign of a good man, Badal's father used to say, pulling at his own elongated lobes. Look at the ears on statues of the Buddha.

The man said, "I may look feeble, son, but let me tell you, in my time I've climbed the Himalaya and swum half way across the English Channel. I just didn't reach the other side because . . ."

Inside the *sanctum sanctorum*, the image of Vishnu glowed red and gold and black. In his infancy, Badal had felt a sense of dread in the temple, even though his father held his hand. The oil lamps cast black shadows everywhere, the air thrummed with chanting, and there

170

were people in such raptures of devotion that they appeared insensible to the world. They frightened him then, with their swaying bodies, their dazed eyes, their delirious singing. He used to be frightened too by the temple's priests in their white dhotis, bare bodies melting into the gloom, the image of the Lord looming above them all with the impassive might of a mountain.

But what mountains had he seen? He had never left the shores of the sea he had been born by. A few nights ago, he had dreamt of them: snow peaks and ranges of blue hills. He was following people who were trudging up the rocks and ice. They had a dog with them. It was cold, the sounds were muffled. Everything was happening very slowly, every step took an aeon. All at once he was transported to a long, red-carpeted corridor and someone was shouting at him: "The doors are shut. They won't let you in." The shouting voice had woken him.

Awake, he had felt with superstitious certainty that he had dreamt of his own death, and the people he had been following were the Pandavas on their long trek to heaven. In the *Mahabharata*, the Pandavas too had been stopped at the gates of heaven. Indra had appeared and ordered them, "Abandon your dog, dog owners have no place in Heaven." And Yudhishtira, defiant, had declared to the king of the gods that he would abandon heaven before he gave up a friend.

Badal would never abandon Raghu, whatever happened. He would forget what he had seen: the monk, the beer bottle, the tight black jeans. He had not been able to find Raghu since. He had to have him back, he would not ask any questions. All he needed was to hold Raghu so close that he would not be able to tell their heartbeats apart.

A din of voices and exclamations broke into his thoughts. Commotion everywhere, people pushing each other, stumbling on the slippery floor. Badal realised he had been standing in a dream, his eyes shut tight. The old man he was meant to be looking after had wandered off. He tried to find his way through the crowds in the half light, damp with instant sweat. You must not panic, he told himself. Keep your head, you'll find him.

The old man's daughter, who had lost sight of him as well, heard a thin, shaking voice from some corner, turned to look for him, could not see anything in the dimness until she spotted a huddle around a figure on the floor. "Papa!! Papa!" she cried out.

Terror snaked through the crowd. People began to push each other aside to get out of the shrine, thinking something was wrong. A man fell and cried out. A voice shouted, "There must be a fire! Something's caught fire." The pushing and shoving grew more urgent.

Badal managed to reach the old man. "There's no fire. I have him safe," he called in a raised voice. "He's not hurt."

He sat the old man down on the steps at one of the smaller shrines outside. A shrunken widow singing kirtans for alms interrupted herself to bring them water in a small brass pot. "At such a great age," she said to the daughter, "it's hard. It's hard for us old people. The ground slips away." The old man's hands were shaking.

Badal held the pot to his lips and tipped it a fraction. Most of the water dribbled down the man's trembling chin to the front of his clothes. Over the man's head, he exchanged a look of shared relief with the daughter, whose eyes shone with unspilled tears. She dug into her handbag and brought out two hundred-rupee notes which she pressed into the hands of the widow, saying, "Please. For all of you. Sing a kirtan for us. God has been very good, He has seen to it that my father is not hurt." When they were leaving, she leaned out from the awning of their rickshaw towards Badal. "I don't know what we would have done without you. I should never have let him come. But he doesn't listen." She had a chubby face and a lopsided smile that gave her a rueful expression. The old man, who had recovered his spirits, quavered, "The next time I'll make sure you show me the whole temple. I want my money's worth, I'll be back!"

Badal waited, saw their rickshaw find its space in the crowds of cycles and rickshaws and scooters in the narrow lane. He stayed where he was till he lost sight of it. He met so many people in a year, his head had become a room filled with a faceless crowd. Even so, he knew he would never forget this woman and her father. He felt he had been responsible for the old man's fall. He should have been taking better care of him. The irony of their gratitude! If the man had come to any harm — he did not want to think about it. He felt reduced by their generosity.

Yet the afternoon filled him with contentment. Usually he had no interest in the pilgrims he had to conduct around the temple. They were work, and when they were gone it was over. But these people — he wanted to show them around Jarmuli now, take care of them, see that father and daughter came to no harm, feed them the special fish and rice at Manoj's lean-to behind the bazaar, then the warm, succulent sweets at Mahaprabhu. Take them to Johnny Toppo's tea stall.

That tea stall! The shadows from the night before lifted as if by magic, the mid-afternoon sun dazzled. Badal went off to the lane where he had parked his scooter. He would eat something. Then he would go and look for Raghu. Maybe he was back and waiting. At long last, he would give him the mobile. He sang aloud as he turned the corner. One of Johnny Toppo's songs, sung every day:

> Dark, gleaming gold are my love's bare legs,
> Deep in the emerald paddy.
> Red as rose are her bangles that shine,
> Bright in the emerald paddy.
> Wary as a thief is that watching egret
> White in the emerald paddy.
> And the rain came again and again that night,
> Soaked all the emerald paddy.

Business was slow at the tea stall. Not many people on the beach and so many women fasting because of Shivaratri, it halved the number of customers. Johnny Toppo was by himself, pottering about. White spikes of stubble stuck out from his chin and his bald head shone. Raghu had wanted time off and he had told him

174

to disappear. It was a relief to be rid of that boy. Johnny Toppo was sure the rascal was stealing; he was a sly fox, that one. Just thinking of Raghu today was putting him in a bad temper even though he had woken that morning feeling as light as the froth on his tea. More often than not, he found himself grinning about nothing even when alone, and at times he was gleeful without reason, like a simpleton or a child. The other day he had been gazing at the madman watering his dry twig and then making his day-long sorties into the water when he had abandoned his stall and sprinted off in daft pursuit. He wasn't thinking, he hadn't planned it, it was the end of a tiring stint, almost night, and there he was, racing the lunatic into the froth and back again, shouting nonsense, and then the two of them had laughed like hyenas and pissed into the sea side by side. Yet today he could not stand the sight of that filthy, ugly loon. And he wished his customers would disappear as well. But he needed to earn, didn't he? He had to grin at tourists and brew tea and grin again. Some days he wanted to turn his table into a raft and sail off into the Bay of Bengal. He'd be washed up on an island nobody knew, and live on fresh fish, beeris, and palm toddy. And not one drop of tea.

He was lost in these thoughts when Nomi appeared and said too close to his ears, "One. With ginger and cloves."

For some reason, whenever he was startled this way, pinpricks of an itch started all over him and took time to subside. He scratched his head, then scratched his shoulders, fought not to scratch his armpits and groin.

He tried to summon up a smile and his patter. "Done shopping today? Gone to the temple? Buy a few saris while you're here. And don't forget to eat fried prawn by the sea. That's what Jarmuli's famous for! That and my tea." It was what he rolled out for everyone and he forgot that she had heard it all from him twice or three times already. This girl made him uncomfortable, he could not tell why. Maybe the way she kept staring at him with those big, black eyes of hers.

On the beach, the madman scurried around, planting his twig, watering it from the sea, stepping back to admire it, then plucking it out from the ground and planting it in a better place.

Johnny Toppo had not covered the scar on his neck with the cotton square he used sometimes as scarf and sometimes dishcloth. He felt her eyes upon his patch of raw, buckled-up flesh. Quickly, he adjusted the cloth. He straightened, took shelter behind his stove. He stirred his pan with great vigour, he clattered dishes and cups around. His smile was gone, he was not singing.

Nomi strolled down to the water, kicked a dented plastic bottle out of her way. It flew seaward in a shower of sand and the madman rushed out chasing it into the waves. She turned around to look at Johnny Toppo at his stall pounding the ginger and cloves in his mortar as if they were fighting back. He picked up a jar filled with what looked like black dust and tossed some into the water boiling on his stove. When she came back, the mixture was bubbling, dark and frothy like the beers she had drunk in Germany. She took a deep breath of

176

the tea in the pan and said, "Sometimes I feel I've seen you before. Don't you feel sometimes . . . as if you've seen someone before, been somewhere before?"

"I don't think too much, or feel too much." Johnny Toppo poured out her tea. "If you think too hard you just get a headache and lose your hair. And I don't have any hair to lose, see?"

They stood in silence. She finished the tea in her cup and peered inside it. She said, "Do you know, people tell fortunes from tea leaves?"

"I don't know. People will say anything to make money."

"No, really, I had my fortune told once. And the woman — she was a very old woman in New York — that's in America — her room had bead curtains and a mini tree — this small — in a pot by the window. She told me that if there was one place I should visit on earth, it should be a place in the east by the ocean. So here I am."

"My tea has no leaves, it's all boiled up. I can't tell you where to go next."

Nomi smiled and ran her finger over her beads. "Can I have another?" She was not going to leave, Johnny Toppo could see. He poured milk into the pan and more water, tipped in a spoonful of sugar.

"You sing so often of trees and flowers and paddy fields. Are you a farmer or a gardener?"

"I am what you see. I sell tea and biscuits."

"But wasn't there a time when you looked after plants?" She sounded braver now, her voice was louder.

"Everyone's looked after plants some time or other. That crazy goat out there? He's watering one, see? You must have had a plant or two in your life as well."

She blew on the tea he handed her. "I mean, did you ever look after plants as your work? Somehow, because of your songs . . ."

"No," Johnny Toppo said. "And it will be ten rupees for the tea." He turned away from her and stood behind his stove. His bones stood out more than usual now, as if he had sucked in his hollow cheeks and sealed his mouth against further talk.

"I'll take one of your umbrellas," Nomi said, "and sit here."

"I have no umbrellas for hire today," Johnny Toppo said. He had three umbrellas propped up in the iron bucket behind him, but if she persisted, he would say they were spoken for.

She looked out to the sea. Johnny Toppo clattered his pots and pans. Then she said, "Do you know of an ashram here in Jarmuli?" Her gaze was fixed on the madman, who was now stamping on the twig he had been watering.

A band of pilgrims passed them just then: young women, men. They smiled as they went down the beach, swaying and singing.

"Ashram?" Johnny Toppo said, after the pilgrims had gone. "There are hundreds of ashrams here, this is a temple town. All you hear is the sea and bells. And fools like these every five minutes, braying like donkeys, buying an advance booking to heaven. Temples. Ashrams. Devotees. That's Jarmuli."

"A big ashram. Run by a guru. It had a school. Since you've lived here for many years, surely you'd know?"

Johnny Toppo stalked towards her and growled, "Who's to tell how long I've lived here? I've lived in a thousand places. Tomorrow I might be somewhere else. All ashrams are run by gurus, how do I know where yours is?"

Before she could ask another of her questions, two tourists soaked in seawater came up to the stall panting. "Hot tea! Hot tea is what we need!" one of them cried out.

"Arre Babu! Look what you have done to your clothes!" Johnny Toppo's transformation took no more than a second. He sounded like a mother delighted by the waywardness of her toddlers. "What kind of tea? With ginger? Or with lemon? With sugar or without?" He turned away from the girl and produced the genial chuckle all his customers were given. He stirred his pot and started humming to himself. The tourists said, "What are you singing? Sing it aloud."

"Oh, it's nothing!" Johnny Toppo's tone of practised cordiality had come back. "Just a folksong. That's all I brought with me when I came here to Jarmuli. A few songs and the clothes on my back." He began to sing again.

Nomi sat on the sand a short distance away, listening. It was a voice from long ago, a voice that contained grains of sand, winds from the sea. Why hadn't she heard it as clearly before?

The tourists sat on the tea bench. One of them said to the other, "Did I bring you to the right place or not?

Have you ever heard anything so beautiful?" The man turned to Johnny Toppo. "Bhai, I want to record you. I'll record you, I'll sell your songs, I'll make you a star. And I'll make me some money."

Johnny Toppo stirred his pot. "People like me, our dreams were beaten out of us long ago. I have no time for stars, I just want a patch of ground to sleep on, a bit of cloth to wear and my next meal."

The man paid up, saying, "We can do something — folk songs are in fashion now!" As they walked away he smiled and slapped his friend's shoulder. "You'll buy his songs or not?"

Johnny Toppo had heard many such conversations. He turned his back to them and scraped his saucepan clean, swilled it out with water from the iron bucket at hand. Nomi sat watching, and before she fully understood what she was saying, the words were out of her mouth and once they had started she could not stop them.

"Once there was a woman called Shabari and she ran away from home on her wedding day. She lived in deep forest after that, in a hermit's ashram, serving the hermit."

Johnny Toppo's head jerked violently and the saucepan fell to the sand. A shudder seemed to go through him. When he bent to pick the pan up he looked old and creaky. "Do you want more tea? I've work to do," he said. He pulled the cloth tight around his neck. He picked up a packet of beeris. He looked for his matches. His hands were trembling when he lit up.

180

"When the hermit was on his deathbed, he said in a sad voice to Shabari that he had spent all his life serving God, yet was leaving life without a glimpse of Him. But that would not be her fate, he said. One day God would appear before her, so she must be ready. After this, the hermit died."

Johnny Toppo said, "So what's the moral, eh? Do I look like a child who needs fairy tales?"

Nomi carried on, talking softly, as if to herself. "Shabari understood his last words to mean that she would have to be prepared. She would have to wait for God in the very same place, otherwise how would He find her? Shabari was a simple-minded woman. She waited and she waited, all her life."

Johnny Toppo stormed out from behind the tea stall towards Nomi. "I thought you only *looked* crazy, with all these beads and rings and that madwoman hair." He let out a jet of spittle that shone on the sand like a blob of jelly. "That screw-loose gardener there, see? *He's* the one you're looking for! Ask him if *he* remembers anything."

He went back to his stall and turned off his stove. He had a trunk below the barrow into which he locked everything each evening and began to stack his pots and pans and cups and jars, pell mell, cursing as a few of the terracotta cups broke inside the trunk. He muttered furiously to himself as he packed up. "All words and no money: some days start bad and get worse."

Nomi sat alone in a car, watching the suburbs of Jarmuli go by. She stared out as if she could not afford to miss the landscape for a minute, even though the suburbs of Jarmuli looked much like those of any other town. Boxy houses on either side of the road, their verandahs curtained by wet clothes on lines. The few trees covered in dust. Ragged oleander hedges with drooping pink flowers. Grocery stalls garlanded with foil packs of chips at street corners. Here she was far away from the sea, the temples, the tourists, the radiant, suspended disbelief of the beach.

Johnny Toppo had not wanted to help her. She had been overtaken by a staggering sense of recognition, of joy — he was not dead after all, he was alive and she had found him! But he had spat at her and turned away. She could handle that, she would feel nothing, she was used to having doors slammed in her face. And I might be wrong, she told herself, many men have scars on their necks and everyone asks for morals of stories. What makes me so sure it was him? A memory she thought she had lost came back to her, its every feature sharp: Jugnu unloading the manure truck at the ashram. First he would spade the manure into a big metal basin. Then he would lift it to his head. He would walk with it on his head to the manure pile near the shed. Tip it out, come back with the empty basin, start the whole process again. He was bent under the stinking manure. His thin, bare body was lean and hard as wood. He spoke to nobody. The remote look he had then was on Johnny Toppo's face today. Neither of them wanted to have anything to do with other people. Who was she to try and make a man remember what he wanted to forget?

A sudden exhaustion permeated every bone, muscle, and tissue in her body. It was futile. She should never have come. The roads through the town grew narrower and bumpier. Here, only a short distance away from the broad promenade along the sea, trucks bore down on them from the opposite side, and dented, rattling tempos scraped past the car. She could no longer smell the salt and fish. Exhaust fumes made her eyes sting. She asked the driver to switch on the air conditioning and soon her window was coated with a film of grey dust. She stared at the houses and street markets they were passing, hoping, as she had on the first drive from Jarmuli station, for a moment of recognition.

After a while, the distance between the houses grew until there were no houses at all. Beside her on the seat she had a map, but like most maps it seemed to bear no relation to what she saw. The driver made a sharp turn towards the highway. Here, the road outside cor-responded with the map in one detail at least — as they drove, she caught glimpses of the sea across the road, beyond a stretch of scrub and trees. She did not know for sure if they were going in the right direction, but she leaned over and said to the driver, "Take a left at the crossroads."

She picked up the map again. It was wrinkled now, frayed at the folds. She had scribbled on it, drawn arrows. There was nothing to connect the represented with the real or the present with the past, not if you went by the road names. But she knew from her research that the place she was looking for was somewhere on the Kanakot-Jarmuli highway.

The sun hung orange between branches and leaves by the time her driver stopped the car two hours later. She had left Jarmuli too late, she realised, not knowing the drive would take so long. Long shadows of trees already barcoded the road, nightfall came swiftly here. She felt a prickle of fear at her neck, wanted to lock the doors of the car, turn back without getting out. They were at a pair of metal gates. The driver looked over his shoulder, despite herself she nodded, and he turned the engine off.

The silence was sudden. Nothing seemed to move, the air humid and heavy. The driver felt as if he was having to push the heat outward to make room for the door when he opened it. He got out, stretched and looked into the car. The girl was still sitting there, making no move.

He went to her window. "What, madam? This place is shut. Nobody here. Is it the right place?" He wiped the nape of his neck, making a face. Only moments away from the air conditioning of the car and his shirt was damp.

She sat without moving. Like water's flooded her limbs, he thought. Or did she expect him to hold open the door for her? She was looking towards the gates, scabby with rust. One of them hung askew, as if it had broken a bone. A sign on it said: SITE FOR PEACOCK AYURVEDIC SPA. He said, "This place has been a ruin for years. If you had told me before where you wanted to go, I would have told you. Even the builders abandoned it. It's a godforsaken place. They say bad things happened here long ago."

184

His words seemed to bring the girl to a decision. She got out of the car, saying only, "Wait here." The earthen pathway leading from the gate to the grounds inside was covered with dry leaves. The driver watched her trudge forward as if she were ill. When she reached the gates she peeped through them as a child might, frightened of encountering ghosts.

He locked the car and followed her. It wasn't safe out here on the empty highway, wandering in a derelict estate. What would he do if she disappeared in there?

He walked a short distance in, his feet crunching the dry leaves. She had stopped at a shed-like house beside the path. A pelt of moss covered its walls. The windows she was looking into were broken, the door missing. Inside, it was a brutal concrete cube. There were platforms shaped like beds along the wall and tiny cell-like windows with bars on them. When they walked further in they found more ruined cottages of the same kind, surrounded by warped iron railings, fallen masonry and broken tiles. A few of the cottages had been demolished and turned into piles of bricks, hairy now with grass and weeds. A grey old tree trunk lay on the ground in a ruffled skirt of frilly toadstools.

They walked through groves of old trees, twisted, chopped, vandalised. Pomegranate trees hung with what looked like organs cut in half: shrivelled fruit opened by age. Some of the trees had red flowers. The girl hunched before the trees, her arms wrapped around herself, holding her own body in an embrace.

They came into what appeared to be a central courtyard which had the remnants of a large structure,

185

the pile of bricks and construction material was almost as high as a building. Beyond it was the outer boundary wall of the place. She walked back in the opposite direction, almost colliding with the driver. "Can you see a jamun tree anywhere?" she asked him. "Would you recognise one?"

Swatting early evening mosquitoes the driver said, "Half the trees are chopped down, Madam, can't you see?"

She went back to the outer edge of the compound and ran her finger tips over sections of the boundary wall that had fallen to the ground. It was tipped with shards of broken glass and upturned nails.

"It looked big from outside, but inside it's not so big," the driver ventured. "I think there's no more to see." The girl was unstable, he was sure, and the oddness of her interest in the ruin was unnerving him now.

She murmured, "It isn't. I always told Piku it was too far for her to walk to the gates. It wasn't."

They walked to where the frame for another gate stood, a smaller one, entirely off its hinges. At its edge, where the wall curved into an inlet, a giant banyan tree shaded the clearing. Tarnished brass bells hung from its aerial roots and were strewn around its trunk. Fragments of cloth, ribbons, pieces of tin, evidence of long-ago worship, now dead, were visible in the dust. The girl bent and prised out from the ground something barely visible to the driver — a rusted metal cross, he saw, once she had rubbed the earth away from it with her fingers, with an arrow on one of its arms. It

186

was rubbish, yet she held on to it, swivelled the arms this way and that.

"Madam, we must go now," the driver said, his voice insistent. He did not like driving in the dark. The tree formed a canopy under which a few grass-thatched huts nestled in even greater darkness than the road beyond it. All around the courtyard were shapeless forms like corpses wrapped in sheets.

The girl turned to follow him, then appeared to take fright. She scurried closer to him. "Did you see something? Isn't there a man — behind those bushes? There, look. In robes?"

The driver squinted. "I didn't see anyone."

"I'm sure I saw someone. A tall man in robes? We should leave."

"That's what have I been saying . . . all along," the driver panted, trying to keep up with her. She was moving too quickly for him. Then he noticed it wasn't dark any more. There was lamplight, dancing among the trees, giving their bodies long, irregular shadows. A man had materialised behind them, and was now blocking their way. A tall, hunched form shrouded in yards of cloth — a lungi below, a cloth over his head and shoulders. An arm as thin as a bamboo cane stuck out from the folds of his clothes, holding a hurricane lantern. He was shining it in the girl's face, lighting up the coloured threads in her hair and all the gold and silver in her ears. He swung it towards the driver, saying, "Come. This way."

As their eyes adjusted to the new brightness of the light, Nomi saw that there was a congregation of stone

187

figures in the courtyard, some quite small, some so large their faces were too high to make out. Gryphons, elephants, Buddha figures, apsaras. Most appeared fully finished, a few were still struggling out from the stone. The man shone the light close on one of the statues. A woman made of flowing lines and blind eyes, nearly ready for a temple niche.

The man shuffled forward, swung the lantern on another piece of sculpture, this one a winged horse. Then a dancing girl. A lion with moustaches and potbelly. He would not hold the lantern still long enough for them to look properly at the pieces.

"My family has been sculptors to the emperors of this land since the time of the Buddha," the man said. His voice was reedy and he sucked his gums between words. "They were sculptors when the great old temples came up — and let me tell you truthfully, my family has a chisel hidden away in a place so secret nobody else knows about it — a chisel that carved the walls of temples then, eight hundred years ago."

The man stopped and swung his lantern on to a gargoyle. "That one's no good." He coughed between his words. "The eyes aren't right. I will always tell you if something isn't right."

"Have you been here many years? Were you always here?" Nomi said.

"Always. For generations. If you came here a hundred years ago, you would still have heard the sound of a hammer on a chisel in these parts. Why, it was a flourishing village then, of people from our caste. Now we're only a few left, all dying of hunger. Who wants these statues? Everyone wants things made in a factory. Of plastic."

She hesitated, drew a breath. "This ruined place next door to you — what was it before?"

"What was it before?" The man brought his lamp down. "I don't know. I don't know anything but my own work. I kept to myself, never went in there."

He moved ahead. "Will you buy something? Look around, a gift for a friend, all the way from the Bay of Bengal? There are smaller ones too, easy to pack." He went from statue to statue, shining the light on them. "That one is made from sandstone . . . that is pure marble . . . that is black granite, the Buddha, you can see. Foreign people like Buddha statues. Elephants too, all sizes, look."

"All I want to know is . . . Do you know what happened to the people who lived next door? The children?"

"This one, see? It's a replica of the chariot in the Sun Temple. Been to the Sun Temple?"

The driver said, "Madam, we should leave now."

Something caught the girl's eye. "There, I want to see that one."

The man brought the lamp across and shone it to where she was pointing, at a statue that sat in a corner of a verandah, as if cast aside. There was a tulsi plant next to it in a terracotta pot and a plate of stone-carved food lay before it as an offering. This one was different from the gryphons and apsaras and Buddhas they had been looking at. Only about a foot high, carved in black marble, soft folds of clothing shaping the form beneath, the sculpture showed a young girl squatting on the ground with her elbows resting on her knees, her palms cradling her chin. Her ears stuck out saucer-like from a large head, her hair fell in two plaits on either side of her face. She had a squat nose and her stone eyes had been given a slight squint. The eyebrows were bunched together in a frown as if she had been too impatient to sit still while being sculpted, she wanted to run off and play instead.

The man swung the lamp away from that statue and it went back into the cover of darkness. "That one is not for sale," he said.

I remember the sculptor who once came to the ashram and sat there chiselling an idol. It was going to be huge. Slowly the rock yielded some parts of a face, then a neck, then the shape of an arm. He didn't finish making it. He went away one day and we never saw him again. We wondered for a day or two, but we never asked. So many things happened around us that we did not ask about — and whom would we have asked? The half-made idol lay under a tree saying nothing either, unfinished, half a head, a blind eye, an arm and the curve of a shoulder, the rest a block of mouldy grey stone.

I remember many other things that happened, things we could not talk about. How Piku lay in bed and whimpered all night. When she was beaten she didn't understand why, when she was left alone she had no idea why. The older girls bullied her too. Sometimes they would pin her frock to the bed so she would tear it trying to get up. They would steal her food and the oddments she collected and hid. They would hold those things out as if to give them back to her and when she ran towards them looking delighted, they would fling them far away, out of reach, and guffaw at her tears. I was always getting into fights because of her. I could never fight with words, I didn't know the right ones, so I would fling myself at girls much bigger and older. I might be bleeding and screaming, but I wouldn't let go, I tore out clumps of hair from the other girls' heads if they did anything to Piku. She stuck to me, she trusted only me. I was her protector.

I remember a cat. Its face was in the stomach of a pigeon. When the cat noticed me it lifted its head out of the bird. It was gluey with blood and feathers. Its eyes were shining amber.

I remember how Jugnu would stand in the quadrangle at dawn, screaming, "Evil sucks you in. It's sucked everyone in! Wake up, you fools! Look around you! Wake up!" He would groan, "Weep, little children, weep that you didn't die."

Jugnu would tell me the sea was nearby, pointing at the horizon, saying softly, "Listen and you'll hear it." I tried, but I couldn't hear it. His weathervane had rusted now and hardly moved at all. Still I thought I would wake one morning to find the arrow had turned northward and we were setting off, sailing away.

I remember the boat that had brought us to the ashram, an open motorboat with an oil-tarred hold in which we were hidden, stacked against each other because there was no space. The boat rocking, then steadying itself for long hours, then rocking again. The creamy yellow of the vomit flowing into the pools of black grease all over the floor of the hold. Its stench. Girls crying "Ma-go, Ma-go", as if moaning would bring our mothers back.

192

I remember once we got mutton stew to eat for lunch. Why? We did not ask. Its gravy was dark brown and thick. There was a bone in my helping which I saved till the last. I sucked the marrow out of the bone. It slipped into my mouth and down my throat before I had tasted it properly. We never got meat again so I forgot the taste.

I remember the time when Champa was brought back by the police. She had gone to them when she ran away the second time and they brought her back because she was a ward of the ashram. She was dragged in by her plaits and locked up in a cottage. I remember the thorny rose branch which Bhola cut and took with him into the cottage. How he grinned at us standing outside and then went in and locked the door. We stood there with our eyes fixed on the cottage. There were banging and thumping sounds. Shouts, and then the screams for help so loud it was as if there was no sound in the world but Champa's frenzy.

I remember the silences in between that only made her cries more terrible. When Bhola came out of the cottage his white lungi was flecked red. The rose branch was bloodied and bent.

I remember when Jugnu was locked up for a week with hardly any food. He could not stand up, he crawled on the ground when he was let out. He tried protecting his head with his hands. Bhola was kicking him. When he saw us he shouted, "Come on, you all, come and play football with this bastard." We stood there in our coffee and cream school skirts and blouses and neat braids, rooted to the ground as Jugnu moaned in pain. Bhola screeched again, "Come on, I'm ordering you!" He kicked him again to show what he meant. I remember how Minoti, a girl with a deformed leg, prodded Jugnu in his stomach with her crutch. How Jui hit him with her geometry box, how the instruments inside the metal box rattled as she raised it and brought it down. How the box made a sound like stone hitting wood when she banged it on his head. How one girl stamped on his palm with her foot again and again with her teeth bared. I remember the way Bhola kept saying, "That's the way! One more time! Break the fucker's bones."

I remember the first time I went to a church, somewhere in Italy. The coloured glass windows, the death-stench of incense and the enormous painted stone statues of Christ dripping blood, the priests in their robes. I ran down the aisle and out into the square and in the bright, hard day my head spun, my eyes went sun-blind and I threw up near the fountain. The tissue with which my foster mother wiped my face smelled of lavender.

I remember the day my first period came, at the ashram. I had just turned twelve. My legs were sticky with blood and there was a damp red patch on my sheets. I was put away in the hut where every girl who got her first period was locked up. My stomach, my back, my thighs, everything hurt. The pain made me throw up. It gave me a runny stomach. I sat all day looking out of the tiny window, waiting for someone to come, feeling desperately alone.

194

I will never forget what I saw when I was locked up that time. The smell of smoke. The huge whoosh of flames going up somewhere in the direction of the coconut grove. Drumming feet. Jugnu standing at my window, shouting, "Set the child free! Unlock that child, set this whole place on fire! Fire burns evil!" The girls told me later that when he saw me being locked up Jugnu had gone mad with rage. He had crept to my hut on two nights to open the door and let me out, but they had found him and beaten him half to death. The minute he could stand and walk again he went from tree to tree with a flaming torch. The dried up coconut fronds had needed only a touch to start burning.

I crouched by the window watching in the dark as Bhola and the others appeared, dragging Jugnu behind them. They tied him to a tree. And then they kicked and punched him. In the orange light of the flames I could tell that they were using rods, stones, feet, belts, and fists.

I remember I saw Guruji poking Jugnu with his feet in the end. I remember Guruji's face in the firelight. It had no expression, as if his feet were nudging a sack of mud.

They carried Jugnu away. Maybe he was struggling still, or maybe he had become a dead weight at which the men were spitting out filthy curses. Did I really hear them? Did I dream it or see it? I cannot have seen it all, someone must have told me of the men grey and white in the moonlight, rushing down the sand towards a stormy sea. The sea from which Jugnu had come and all the rest of us had come, hidden in boat-holds.

Nobody knew he had ever been here. Nobody would know he was gone again, forever.

On the seventh day of my confinement I was made to wash my hair with shampoo and bathe with a new bar of soap. The soap was pink and round. Padma Devi lined my eyes with kajal saying, "Can you see colours with black eyes? Or is everything black?" She gave me a set of new clothes. A long blue skirt with silver sequins and a blouse of darker blue printed with scarlet flowers.

I waited as I had been told, for Guruji to arrive and perform his rituals. The prayer bells rang at the puja hall. Midday. The conch shells. The end of prayers. The school bells. Lunchtime.

My hands were icy and my knees shook, I remember, counting the bells. I did not know why.

I remember how Guruji came in, locked the door, sat down and patted his thighs. How he stroked my legs as he spoke. How he told me I was a nun in the service of God. I was the chosen one. How he had always known there was something special about me and so, from the time I was seven, he had been training me for this day. He said again that he was God on earth and I would be purified by serving him. He held my face between his hands and stuck his greasy lips on my lips, pushed his tongue in. It felt like a wet snake. I remember the way he kept stroking my body at first over my clothes, then his hands went under them. I remember breaking away, trying to run, reaching the door, pulling a stool to it to unlatch it, and that when he stood up, he looked large enough to smash me against the wall.

196

My body felt as if it would tear into two when he forced my legs apart, then wider apart. He stuffed cloth into my mouth to stop me shouting for help. I remember my screams made no sound. There was blood. A burning between my legs. The sense that my body was being split open.

I remember how night after night I would run to a tap and sit under it, clothes and all, to wash it away: the smells, the touch, the bad taste in my mouth after Guruji summoned me to his room.

I remember how Piku was punished for not going to Guruji. They tied a big bag of dung to one of her ankles and she had to drag it with her wherever she went. She wasn't allowed into the school or the dining hall. She ate outside, tied to that smelly sack, flies buzzing around. I remember how I was punished for trying to untie her: three days in the kennel shed, no food. The kennels had six dogs and their smell was close and sharp. The dogs growled at first. They came to me to sniff me with flattened ears and snarling lips. Later I slept among them, ate scraps from their bowls and when they licked my face their tongues were rough and their breath was hot. One of the dogs was called Pinto. He was red like a fox, with a pointy nose. He slept against me in the afternoons, his rear wedged into my stomach.

Sometimes, journalists would come to interview Guruji. They printed articles about the ashram which were pinned up on the walls of our school. My picture was in the paper once. We were a line of girls standing in front of a tree in the square between the classrooms and our dormitories. I was third from the right. I had two pigtails tied with ribbons. My face was sulky, my eyes were screwed up, I was knock-kneed. Guruji stood behind me. He was smiling his fatherly smile. I remember I could feel his flabby belly and his stump pushing against me between my shoulder blades. But you couldn't tell that from looking at the picture.

THE FIFTH DAY

Suraj woke at dawn and decided to go for a swim. There were only two days left for the work in Jarmuli to be finished and he had not swum once. Swimming in every new sea he encountered was one of his life's unbreakable rituals, like making a boat every year or adding a dash of water to a malt whisky or taking the first drag from a cigarette only after a sip of coffee.

From his room he had to walk for ten minutes down brick-bound hotel paths to reach the sea. He swivelled his shoulders and stretched his arms, drinking in the early morning's grey-blue. After he had flung aside his slippers and torn off his T-shirt he realised his mobile was in a pocket of his swimming trunks. He couldn't go back to his room to put it there: the perfect air and light would last no more than another half hour. He scanned the beach for a safe spot to hide it. It was too expensive to risk leaving on the sand.

He saw Nomi's favourite tea stall being set up. The bent old baldhead was placing blue benches along its front and had busied himself with kettles, pans, jars. A boy was walking towards the tea stall bent sideways by a heavy looking iron pail and further down, a monk was meditating in the water. There was nobody else.

Making his way to the tea stall he asked the man if he would look after his things. He left his shirt and slippers in a heap on the bench, covering his mobile with them.

Suraj lay at first at the edge of the sand, fingers trailing in the white, lacy spume. Then he moved further in, lying on his stomach in the water, feeling the sand being sucked away from under him in the backwash, each time a little more, sending him further and further out. It had been four days of hard work — that girl was a workaholic, dogged beyond the call of duty. She had dragged him over every inch of Jarmuli. They had mapped out the whole town, walking every street to make notes about possible locations for shoots; they had visited shrines, big and small, and almhouses for indigent pilgrims; they had done bits of video recording in the kitchens of roadside shacks; they had gone out with fishermen in a boat, photographing as they cast their nets; they had taken night-time pictures in the red-light area and, dreaming of photography awards, Suraj had gone into a brothel to take more photographs on the sly. He was thrown out, and they were chased down the street by a pair of foul-mouthed pimps as they ran. He certainly needed a swim. Now there was only a sun temple left, and that would be their last assignment together this time.

Thoughts streamed in and out of him as he swam. He went back to the evening before, he and Nomi drinking again in their private garden at the hotel, she telling him about her visit to a village sculptor's and he telling her about his afternoon with government babus sorting out permissions to film. He had sat with her

202

sipping his whisky, smoking his cigarette, fiddling with his half-finished boat, thinking how pleasant it was to spend evenings this way, rather than alone as he was trying to get used to now. Nomi had turned out fun to be with after working hours. She changed. She cracked jokes, chattered about nothing in particular, and laughed at his stories until she had tears in her eyes. He liked that. It was sexy when she laughed that way, throwing her head back, helpless, showing a beautiful long neck. But now there were only a couple of days left. And after that? More internet searches?

By degrees, the swell of the waves was below him, and he was swimming with long strokes. There were no big waves, the water was gentle against his skin. A long distance from the shore he found the absolute solitude he had been hungering for at dawn. It was as if he had become a shark slicing through water unnoticed, no connection with human life. Across an infinite stretch of aquamarine was the arc of the horizon holding in the sea. Last night, after leaving Nomi in her garden, he had idled in bed, typing a text message to her which said, "The bottle's finished, but the night is not." He had neither sent it nor deleted it, and was now relieved he had not been drunk enough to send her such corny drivel. The future was obvious. She would go home to some Nordic hulk of a boyfriend and he would go back to divorce papers from Ayesha.

Floating on his back, he opened his eyes against the light. The sky was now a bright cobalt and an aeroplane crossed it miles above him, toy-sized. After the boat was done he would make a plane. He hadn't told Nomi how

203

in each of his boats he tucked in a letter to his father. Nobody knew about it. A handwritten note, barely legible, on a piece of paper that he then wrapped in clingfilm and twisted into a roll that fitted inside the boat's cabin. The letter would sink unseen, along with the boat, somewhere far away.

He felt weightless, his limbs loose and limp. Nomi's story of missing her train came back to him. How she had said, "Don't you feel like disappearing from your life sometimes?"

He stopped moving his legs, felt his feet fall away down, felt them pull him in after them. Something was sucking him downward and outward.

The dog he battered had lived. Lame, blinded in one eye, but alive. He had fed it scraps of meat and bowls of milk every day in atonement. The dog would drag itself away when he came with the food to its street corner. It would inch back to eat only when Suraj was out of sight.

He would not move his arms. He would not move at all. The sea could have him. Out there somewhere his wife was drinking beer, eating sandwiches, making love with his friend, and that dog was dying.

His legs followed his feet, his hips followed his legs. He sank further down. Nothing mattered any longer but this sense of letting go and never having to try again. Not his wife, not her lover, not the dog, not the first boat that he made at sixteen and sailed alone after his father died. When the water closed over him, all sound disappeared. Not another living thing in the world, nothing to go back to.

204

Just when his lungs felt as if they would blow up and he was about to open his mouth and let the water fill him and take him, he found he had instead erupted into the air gasping, coughing and flailing. He struggled to stay up, sank, let out a choking cry for help as he swallowed a bellyful of seawater. Thrashing around with all he had in him, he fought himself out of the water again. A boat had appeared from somewhere, it was bobbing next to him. It was painted green and yellow. Four fishermen were looking at him over its side, saying things he could not hear. One of the fishermen pushed an oar in his direction. He managed to get his hands on it.

He was dragged into the boat, fell against rusted tin and nets and ropes. The four men looked at him, pulled at their oars. He was very far from the shore, they said, these were dangerous waters with strong undertows and people were often sucked under. The fishermen were bare-bodied, their arms were sinews and muscles and veins held in by parchment-skin. Each man wore a head-cloth against the sun. It was more than half way up the sky now, fierce enough already to have burnt away the dawn.

Suraj sat gasping for breath, listening to the fishermen cackling about their lousy luck, tossing insults and jokes back and forth. After an entire night at sea all they had caught was a man! What's a man good for, eh? Can you eat a man? Can you fry it and feed it to your children? Now a fish: you can use all parts of a fish from its head to its fins to its tail. You can chew on its spine. You can fry its roe or eat your rice with its oil.

The tiny ones you can eat whole: heads, bones, eyes and all, fried to a salty crunch. Fish can swim and sing and fly, they can even kill men. If not fish, a woman was a better find. If you fish a woman out of the water you can lay her or sell her or set her to work. But what use is a man? If you had netted a man you might as well throw him back in.

One of the fishermen pointed at him and said, "You'll be back as a big fish in your next life. And we'll catch you."

The boat stank of fish and kerosene oil. Suraj could see damp boards, cans and rags, a tangle of dead squid in a net. The oars sliced the water with slow splashes. One of the fishermen bared a mouthful of yellow teeth and said, "Wanted to die? There are better ways." Suraj heard their words as if from far away. His head was brimming with water.

When they reached the shore the men forgot all about him, busying themselves hauling their boat in, unloading their nets. The beach was more crowded with early morning walkers and fisherwomen. Suraj needed to find that tea stall, but did not know which way to go. Sand in both directions, infinity curving inward and out. Where was his hotel? He had thought he had swum straight, but he must have gone far out in a diagonal. Nothing was familiar on this stretch. He sat on the ground, limp as a puppet without its strings. He could not move, not yet. He watched the fishermen. It was hard work, pulling in those heavy nets and ropes, tugging and rolling in unison. Their teeth jutted out in their thin faces as they grimaced with the effort. They were like their own boats, bony spines for keels, ribs for frames.

He watched them until the sun had dried the seawater on him into sparkling, itchy salt crystals. When they had finished their work and were about to leave he went up to one of them and said, "I've got no money on me now, but tell me the way to the hotels and if one of you comes with me, I want to, I mean . . ." He had nothing but the trunks he was wearing, he was crippled without his clothes and mobile. He wished he had his wallet and could give them all the money in it.

When one of the men had taken him back to the tea stall he found his clothes in a heap on the bench, where he had left them. The phone was gone. Johnny Toppo said, "Babu, what do I know? I didn't touch that bundle. You left it, I was serving customers. The bundle was there — nobody came near it." Then something seemed to occur to him and he yelled "Raghu!"

Far down in the other direction, Suraj could see that the boy who had been struggling with an iron bucket was now talking to a man — he could not be sure, but he thought it was the surly guide with the long red fingernail, the fellow who had taken him through the temple. They paid no attention to Johnny Toppo's shout. Suraj felt a deep fatigue overtake him and sat down on the sand to wait.

Johnny Toppo strode forward, cupped his mouth with his palms and yelled at the top of his voice. "Raghu! You little prick. Are you deaf? I swear today's your last day with me, I swear it. I've had enough."

This time the boy appeared to hear Johnny Toppo. He left the guide in mid-sentence and ran towards the tea stall, arrived panting. Johnny Toppo snarled, "Take your time, you'll have plenty now that you're sacked. This Babu left his telephone with his clothes here, have you seen it?"

Raghu shrugged and said, "I've got better things to do than look after someone's old clothes." Johnny Toppo flung his arm out and hit the boy's head. "Rude bastard," he said. "Better things to do, eh?"

He turned the boy around and patted his clothes. His hand stopped when he reached a pocket on the boy's shorts.

The boy shouted, "I haven't taken his phone! This is my phone! I just got it, this minute."

Johnny Toppo picked up his iron ladle from the pan steaming with tea. The stall was hot and smoky, he was sweating from being at the stove.

"Your phone, eh?" he said. "What d'you take me for? An old donkey? Your phone, you lazy scum? Where did you get the money for a phone?"

He slammed the ladle into the boy's back. "Did you steal the money from me, or the phone from him?" he shouted. "My shop's got no place for thieves."

The boy howled with pain. "I haven't taken it, I haven't taken it! This is my phone! That temple Babu gave it to me!" He pulled out the phone from his pocket. "See Babu," he begged, holding it towards Suraj, "is this your phone?"

Johnny Toppo had the boy by a tuft of his hair. He hit him again. The more Raghu howled, the harder

208

came the ladle until Suraj snapped out of his stupor and managed to stand up. He held Johnny Toppo's arms back and shouted, "Stop! Stop right now. That's not mine! Leave him alone! He's a kid!"

He turned away from the tea stall and started towards his hotel, but his knees buckled, his stomach cramped, and his feet kept sinking into the sand.

Vidya and Gouri were still troubled that they had forgotten to fast yesterday on Shivaratri. A day which their mothers, and their mothers' mothers before them, had spent without food or a drop of water till their prayers at sundown, fasting first for a good husband; then for the health of that husband; and after his death for their children's well-being. "Instead we were eating heaped plates of food! At a restaurant full of pilgrims," Vidya exclaimed. "Of all places."

How could they have forgotten the faith of a lifetime?

"Oh, the breeze from the sea blew away all of that. You're allowed to break rules on a holiday!" Latika sounded impatient when the discussion showed no signs of ending. They were being driven to the Sun Temple in a car from the hotel. The driver was a handsome man, who looked "not a bit like a driver" — Latika had whispered this almost as soon as she entered the car. The man was in his mid-forties, his clothes were not inexpensive, and he did not have the slightest hint of subservience. He was courteous but not ingratiating, obliging without appearing servile. A prince in disguise, not a driver on hire. When the thought crossed Latika's mind she hid her mouth behind her hand and smiled to herself. She had always been self-conscious about her prominent teeth.

They drove for two or three hours down tree-shaded roads, with the ocean sometimes on their right, sometimes obscured by trees, then filling the horizon with its miraculous blue. By mid-afternoon they were at the Sun Temple. They looked at each other for confirmation. Vidya, mustering the appropriate tone of voice — neither too eager nor too peremptory — said to the driver, "Would you like to see the Sun Temple too?" This temple was a ruin, a tourist sight and not a religious place, so it seemed correct to offer. The man agreed with a smile, and she felt she had got it right, her tone and how the words had come out. They bought him a ticket and a green coconut to drink before starting the walk to the ruins.

The sun was furiously close here, its white heat wanted to burn and destroy. Walking down the corridor formed by tourist stalls that bordered the road on each side, Vidya and Gouri bought themselves straw hats and looked questioningly at Latika, who shook her head. "You're bound to regret it," Vidya said. "The sun will give you a headache in two minutes." They put their hats on, settled the elastic bands into the folds of their chins. Some way down the road to the ruins, Latika turned back and started off at a brisk pace to the stalls they had just left behind. "Don't wait," she cried, "I'll catch up." She disappeared into the throng of tourists and shops.

Vidya gave an exasperated shrug. Given Gouri's stately pace, she thought, it would not be that hard for anyone to catch up. She and Gouri walked ahead. The driver followed at just the right distance, telling them he was there, but he was not going to intrude.

Past the shops came an open area fenced in by railings that held the cliff back from the sea that flung itself at rocks hundreds of feet below. Looking down over the edge, Gouri was visited for a moment by the sense she had had of flying into the sky on the wings of a kite — was that years ago or just days ago? Among eternity-old ruins, it was hard to tell.

The temple's central shrine rose straight from the cliff like a monumental rock. They had paused to look up at the tower when Latika came back to them holding a red parasol with a yellow frill. "Isn't it pretty? So Japanese!" she exclaimed, twirling it this way and that, holding it over her shoulder, making them feel foolish in their clumsy straw hats. "She's acting eighteen," Vidya said in an undertone to Gouri when Latika was out of earshot. "She always does when there's a good-looking man around. The way she repeats stories of her college conquests. And keeps mentioning how people say she looks half her age."

"At almost seventy!" Gouri said. "Really!"

Their misgivings were confirmed halfway through their tour of the ruins. At each shrine they had to climb rock-cut steps to look at the sculptures. And all the while, the blazing, blinding, ever fiercer sun radiating off the stones. Confronted by the tallest of the shrines with the steepest stairs, Gouri dropped onto a bench below a tree and said, "Oh no, that really is too high, the sun is too strong. My head feels as if it'll split open."

"No escape from the sun at the Sun Temple," their driver said, his first contribution to the afternoon's conversation.

"You go ahead and have a look," Vidya said to him, sitting down beside Gouri. "We'll rest here and wait for you."

"I don't want to rest," Latika said, spinning the handle of her parasol. "I'm not going to leave without exploring the whole place!"

Vidya heaved a tired sigh, and said, "Latika . . ." She started to get up from the bench, holding a knee with one hand. Was that twinge her back pain coming back?

"Why are you getting up?"

"Well, you can't go alone, can you? What if you fall?"

"Nonsense, I won't fall. If it makes you feel better, I'll go with . . . him." Latika darted a quick look at the driver. "You stay here with Gouri."

Before Vidya could say anything more, Latika had begun following the driver towards the tallest shrine. They watched her walking rapidly away. From the back she seemed no more than forty, slim and quick-footed, in a bright salwar kameez and sensible shoes. Her parasol bobbed near the driver's shoulder. She looked up at him and said something; he was much taller and he had to bend towards her to reply.

Vidya sighed. "Did you notice how many age-defying creams and serums she has on her bedside table? And foundation! All these years she claimed she used nothing on her face at all."

212

"I visited her once the day her daughter arrived from abroad," Gouri said. "You should have seen the mountain of moisturiser bottles she'd brought for her." She smiled. "Those of us who weren't pretty to begin with don't get into a tizzy about wrinkles and fat." She contemplated her words, then said, "I am happy to spend my last days with my grandchildren and prayers. But good tea is important. I have to have good tea, that's all."

"And a bit of cold cream," Vidya said, and they both laughed. Gouri's grandchildren loved pinching her cheeks and the loose skin of her upper arms. Soft as soufflé, her granddaughter called them.

Latika and the driver had begun climbing the steps to the main shrine, the one with the rearing horses and the chariots of the sun god. The day before the first ceremony at the temple centuries ago, a mason had toppled to his death from the tower; not long after, the king had been struck by leprosy. Because of the bad omens, the temple had never been used for worship and even now had a menacing, secretive look. The steps became forbiddingly vertical as they went higher. The people at the top looked ant-like in the distance, they appeared and disappeared behind pillars and corners. Vidya saw the driver offer Latika his hand at the steepest part and pointed this out to Gouri. They both saw her take his hand, then she and the driver vanished from view, into the shrine.

Vidya gave a sigh of resignation. "Now they'll be gone for God knows how long, and we'll have to wait here in this heat while he explains all those sculptures of a hundred different Kama Sutra positions to her." They giggled at the thought and it dissolved their irritation. Vidya told Gouri of the time she had come to the temple decades ago with her husband and various other relatives. Deadpan they had walked from edge to edge, exclaiming only at the artistic brilliance of the great carved wheels and the stone lions or the otherworldly expression on the Sun God's face. Uncles, nephews, aunts, and cousins, all had pretended not to notice that the stone couples on the temple walls had for thousands of years been entwined in complicated variations of coitus. One of her vulgar uncles had paused for long minutes before a particular panel. Vidya had a vivid memory of it: the sculpture of a man caressing the breasts of a woman who held his penis, which was as ponderous as a bottle-gourd, even as another woman sat playing at his feet with his over-sized testicles. The uncle had remarked in a loud voice on the yogic and gymnastic powers of Indians in earlier times, their free-spiritedness, but the rest of the group had walked ahead as if they had gone mysteriously deaf.

"Really," Gouri said, "Latika can still become such a giddy teenager . . . can you imagine how embarrassed we'd have been looking at these kinds of sculptures with a strange man? A *driver*!"

"Someone's walking on my grave," Vidya said with a shiver. "This place has so many mysteries. Do you know, I've heard there's an underground way to the sea from here? They used it to drown enemies?"

214

"Don't think about all that," Gouri said. "It'll make you feel unwell again." She placed a hand on Vidya's arm. "You look hot, are you feeling alright?"

Vidya pulled a newspaper from her handbag and fanned herself with it. She dabbed her forehead with her sari. There wasn't the faintest breath of a breeze under the implacable sky. The voices of other tourists came from far away, their words indistinguishable. In the tree above them a lone bulbul sat pecking at the figs, letting fall scorched leaves now and then. Vidya opened the newspaper. It was that morning's, a good thing she had had the foresight to stuff it into her bag — she always had some reading material with her for just such unexpected stretches of idle waiting.

Gouri examined her bottle of mineral water and informed Vidya that it was from a Himalayan spring, pure as water from the holy Ganges. Then she observed how the Ganga's purity had been destroyed by the very people who claimed to worship it. The paper rustled as Vidya turned its pages, the bulbul overhead sang a song. "Another bus accident," Vidya exclaimed. "Twenty-five people dead this time. Does it make a difference?" Gouri closed her eyes and tried to listen only to the bulbul. She wanted no news. She did not want to think about anything. Then something on an inside page of the newspaper caught Vidya's eye. She held it towards Gouri, showing her a photograph. "It's that evil godman. He's quite striking, isn't he? In a creepy sort of way. Look at those eyes — something hypnotic about them."

"I don't want to look at such men." Gouri turned away. "They finish off your peace. How sweetly that bird was singing. I wonder where it went."

"Oh, come on, Gouri," Vidya shook her head. But she said no more, returning to the paper.

"The papers are full of bad news," Gouri said. "That's why I seek out peaceful places like this, far away from newspapers."

"Well, it all happened very near here, you know," Vidya began again. "Just down the highway . . ."

"Look," Gouri said, "Pilgrims. Japanese, I think, Buddhists." She did not want anything to soil the purity from sea and sky, the blueness and serenity she had managed to collect and store within herself after more than an hour of prayer on her hotel verandah that dawn.

Vidya folded the paper and began to fan herself with it. "Disgusting," she said, "Unbelievable." Her lips were pressed one against the other as if she were stopping herself from saying more with great effort. Above them a raucous battle broke out between crows, causing them to look up at the tree. Sooty feathers were flying, leaves rained on them. They had to move to get out of the way.

The diversion gave Gouri a chance to change the subject. "Let's think of what we'll do this evening. Maybe I'll go to the temple again."

"This evening I want to go to that other beach where the open market is. I missed it the day you two went. I want to buy some things, have the tea you talked about."

216

Gouri recalled something and lit up. "Do you know who we saw on the beach when we were having that tea?"

"Who?"

"Suraj! We saw Suraj there!"

As soon as she had uttered the words, Gouri clamped her mouth with her palm. She was not meant to tell Vidya about her son. Of course she was not meant to tell her! Suraj was not supposed to be here at all. Latika would be livid.

"Suraj?" Vidya said. "How could that be? He's on an office trip to Hyderabad. Why would he try to meet me here?"

"Oh no," Gouri's smile was forced. She felt short of breath, managed to say, "How stupid I am, always muddling people up. I meant to tell you about my terracotta tea stall, but then . . ."

"What are you talking about? You said you saw Suraj!" Vidya stood up, agitated. "Did you see him or didn't you?"

"No, really, I meant that husband of Parul's: you know my niece Parul? Oh, I thought you'd met her. Well, her husband looks very like Suraj and I thought . . ."

Latika returned, full of news. "He isn't a driver at all. He's the hotel's manager. He's only brought us because, last minute, the driver didn't appear for duty. So knowledgeable about ancient sculpture! He knew each one of them, explained what they really mean. I'll tell you everything later."

Vidya had no ears for any of it. She confronted Latika, hands on her hips. "Suraj was on the beach yesterday, that's what Gouri says. Did you see him too? Why didn't you tell me?"

Even as she spoke, her son was closer than Vidya could have imagined: in a different part of the same ruins, climbing a flight of stone stairs bracketed by a pair of gryphons. Suraj selected a shadowed eave to sit in. He had a handful of tourist pamphlets with him and a notebook. He could see Nomi nearby, crouched, changing a lens on her camera. She straightened, then spotted something else and this time went on her knees, bent almost to the ground. She was wearing a dark blue kurta too large for her, one of the Indian clothes she had bought for herself in her bid to blend in. She had chopped the kurta's sleeves off because of the heat and wore it with shapeless white pyjamas to her ankles. Her feet were in red sneakers.

This was her notion of dressing demurely in Indian clothes. A lazy grin dislodged Suraj's cigarette and he held it between thumb and forefinger, sucking in the smoke as he observed her. The kurta hung on her as loose as a shift and kept slipping off her shoulders. It was an angular shoulder that led to slender but muscular arms. His own biceps had long since softened, but she was young, she worked on hers, he could see.

He looked at her focusing on a frieze of elephants in procession. She was at work. He was not. He needed to recover from the scare of his near-drowning that

218

morning. His chest still hurt, and his stomach had felt as taut as a drum ever since. He would not have come had it not been for Nomi's impersonal tone of command, as if the woman from the evening before, who was fascinated by everything he said, had never existed.

So he had come, but all he had done was to roll a joint and take a drag. He felt too old at this game to bother. Greying men shouldn't have to rush about over monuments making notes and taking photographs, there were things they should be forever exempted from. He leaned back and shut his eyes, savouring his smoke, listening to the penetrating voice of a guide doing his rounds with a group of Western tourists. After a while he heard one of the women in the group ask accusingly, "Is that a child? There in that . . ."

Nomi, straggling along behind the group, looked at the panel the woman was pointing to. It showed a buxom, narrow-waisted, naked woman in ecstatic embrace with a man, their lips pressed together, her legs curled around his hips. At their feet, caressing the man's leg, was a figure so small it might have been a toddler.

"Not a child, Madam, no child. No children in this kind of sculpture. Not in Indian culture," the guide said.

"Well, you've just about everything else, haven't you?" The woman turned to Nomi, her grey eyes twinkling. "There's some weird stuff out here — men with horses, women with camels, foursomes, eightsomes! Have you seen them?"

"No children, Madam," the agitated guide said. "Look."

He would not say the words, but what he was pointing to were the round breasts on the tiny figure. It was a woman and not a child, there was no doubt about that.

"A midget then." A straw-hatted man in the group said. "Not a child, just a midget who's seen a lot." The whole group tittered and the grey-eyed woman said, "They've all seen a lot more than you and me!"

"Some panel show children — but only playing." The guide was upset by their levity and pointed with a vehement, jabbing finger. "In ancient India no barrier between life and love. Erotic is creation itself, so it is celebrated in our temples. Nothing wrong. Please understand!" A voice from the group was heard muttering, "You don't say!"

The guide's voice grew fainter as he and his group went further away. Nomi kneeled to look at the tiny figure at the bottom of the panel. No, it wasn't a child, the guide was right. Were there any children at all in those scenes of abandon? She went from panel to panel, inspecting one spasm of ecstasy after another. She felt composed despite the fornication on the walls surrounding her. The certainty that she would be revolted must have steeled her. Not many children in this temple, the guide was right, and certainly no little girls being fondled by old men. If there was a child at all, it was in the arms of a maternal-looking woman.

She wondered what her foster mother would have made of this temple. Unbidden, a pang of remorse stabbed her. Two mothers. One she had lost and been tormented by a lifelong need to find; the other a woman she had found but never allowed close.

Just before the trip to India, she had gone from her own studio flat to her foster mother's house to pick up some things. She had found her sitting alone in the living room with the T.V. soundlessly on. Her foster mother did not move from her chair. She sat watching Nomi go up the stairs, listening to the sounds of cupboard doors opening and shutting, yet she asked no questions and Nomi knew that her foster mother could not speak for the dread that she was going to India because she had found some trail she would not reveal. To her biological family? The air between them was taut with unasked questions.

Nomi was overwhelmed then by an unexpected rush of compassion for the woman in the armchair, and with a terrible weariness at the burden of all that she could never speak of. She went to the drinks cabinet and poured shots of Aquavit and glasses of beer as her foster mother looked on in astonishment. They never had a drink together except dutifully, at Christmas. She kept topping up their glasses until the old woman started to smile, said they should eat something too, and warmed up meatballs that she heaped onto the white and blue plates from years ago. Afterwards Nomi made coffee and even washed up. When she left they didn't hug, but she had reached out and squeezed her foster mother's arm and said a gruff "see you soon" before hefting her backpack and walking out at the dark rain.

It was all so far away: that cold rain, the darkness at noon, her foster mother. Here the sun was burning her head up and there were many shrines to get through. She decided to find Suraj, time she turned professional again. There he was, still dozing. When she called, he struggled awake. There was a gap between his decision to open his eyes and the act of it.

"Hey, why are you sleeping? Get up! Make some notes. Come with me."

Understanding the meaning of her words, that too happened with a moment's lapse, like talking on a bad international line. He said, "Been here, seen this, binned it." An infinite slowness came over him. He watched a bird sail over them. A very white cloud inched sideways in the blue sky.

"Up." She held out a hand. He looked at it. "Come on." He put his hand into hers and she yanked him up, let his hand go, strolled ahead, then bent down to squint at a sculpture at knee-level. "Can you tell what this is?"

"Some kind of animal," Suraj yawned. "With a football for a belly and moustaches. No animal that I've ever seen."

"It's a lion, can't you tell? I saw one like this . . . not exactly, but very like it. At the sculptor's yesterday. He was telling the truth after all!"

He was surprised by her excitement. He heard her out when she explained how the lion on the wall was evidence of some unknown man's claim that he was descended from the same temple sculptors. She would go back to him, she declared, buy something to prove

222

she believed him. Suraj did not think it worth pointing out that local craftsmen everywhere made copies of temple art. Was she really so gullible, to believe everything she was told?

They climbed down the stairs and crossed the courtyard to go towards the tallest tower. The people already at its top looked to his smoke-filled eyes as if they were regiments of mice scurrying over a mountainous pile of stone. His head swam. He groaned, "Oh . . . forget it. I've seen it before. It's not such a big deal."

A guide with a few Japanese tourists glowered at him and raised his voice. "It is one of the great wonders of the world, this renowned temple to the sun." He went ahead with his group and Nomi said, "Come on, Suraj, it's a temple to you. Let's try and see it. You have the sun in your name."

"I've been here with my parents. I can truthfully say that I've already seen it."

Parts of the tower had high stone stairs etched into the sides of walls without railings or handholds in any form. Nomi stepped carefully, eyes on her feet. "That must have been years ago," she said. "You don't remember a thing. Not enough to write a report on it for a film company." Suraj lost sight of the words he was about to say in reply, feeling a perilous, airy sense of vertigo, a feeling he had to fight, of letting his body fall, as he had in the sea that morning — to let go, to float and fall from a great height. He stopped and shaded his eyes against the sun. If he looked at Nomi now, following him up the steps, he saw the earth far below, the sky immeasurably remote. The steps were steep, she was struggling up, her camera equipment was heavy. He should give her a hand. Then he saw that her kurta was sliding off a shoulder again. He noticed a black mole on the bare shoulder. Tiny. Perhaps raised — you couldn't be sure unless you touched it.

He leaned forward, a finger stretched out.

Even as he leaned forward, and Nomi put her hand out to him thinking he was trying to help her over the steep bit, he saw his mother's friend, Latika, climbing the stairs further away. When she faltered, a tall man, much younger than her, held her hand as if they had known each other for years. Suraj shut his eyes, opened them again. They were still there. He was truly stoned. High as a kite. Seeing things. Had he popped pills too that morning?

Then he remembered, as if from a great distance, that his mother had been going on for some time about a holiday with her friends. He never listened with much attention when she was on the phone, her patter registered dimly if at all. Mostly he browsed the web as her voice went on playing in the background, like music he wasn't really listening to. Once he had put the phone down in the middle of a call for a full minute to find his cigarettes and light one. He had been proven right: she had not noticed him being gone.

Hurriedly, he withdrew his hand and Nomi said, "What are you? Straight off the Sistine Chapel ceiling?" She took another step up.

Suraj was clambering down the stairs. He stumbled, almost fell, but then righted himself and ran down.

224

"Hey, you'll fall, careful!" She watched him bewildered. "Where are you going? What happened?"

"I've got to go. Right now. Something's come up," Suraj shouted to her over his shoulder. "I'll wait for you in the car, O.K.? Come to the car when you're done." No trace of his drowsiness remained, he moved down the stairs and across the courtyards so swiftly that he was gone before she could ask another question. She looked around, confused — what was he running from? There was nobody she could see following him.

Nomi stood watching him weave into the crowds far below. Two thin-waisted, broad-belted men in flashy sunglasses and tight trousers were looking at him as well. Once Suraj was out of sight, they trained their eyes on her. One of them breathed out a soft whistle and the other said, "Sexy, sexy." She moved away from them, up the stairs to the next level, and her eyes met those of another man staring at her. He arrived instantly at her elbow and in a whining voice began, "Madam, guide services! Authorised guide. Hundred Percent. Madam, this Sun Temple was built in . . ."

She ignored him and started on the next flight of stairs, but it felt pointless all at once and the carvings of men and women cavorting on the panels looked obscene. She could not bear to be among these stone people copulating, fondling, standing on their heads to have sex. It was so hot, her head was splitting open with the heat. Why was the sky that ghastly blue? Why was everyone wearing bilious orange saris? Were there no colours in this country that were muted? She felt her head swim, saw blue and purple and pink stars when she shut her eyes. She was on a sandy beach. A dog was inching closer. The shadow of the boat was receding and the sun was on fire. She was hungry and thirsty and alone and when she cried out, nobody came.

Late in the afternoon, Badal parked his scooter and walked to Johnny Toppo's stall, his hand in his pocket, caressing his mobile. The last two days had been hell, not knowing if Raghu was ever going to return. Badal had gone to the beach to find him two, even three times a day, to explain that he did not care who he drank beer with — and each time he had found Johnny Toppo cursing because Raghu had not turned up for work. But early that morning he had glimpsed the familiar red T-shirt and broken into a run. He had given Raghu the phone at last; he could call him any time. From now on, there would be no uncertainty.

A thrill of happiness shot through Badal. The next instant he remembered he had not taken down the new mobile's number. He felt unhappier still thinking back to the clumsiness with which he had pressed it into Raghu's sweaty palm, interrupting his push-ups. He had wanted that moment to convey everything he needed to tell Raghu and could never find the words for. Instead?

"What's that?" Raghu had said, sounding suspicious.

Badal struggled for coherence, but right then, before he could say anything that meant something, Johnny Toppo yelled for the boy and yelled for him again, more impatiently. Badal wanted to shove the man's tongue down his wrinkled old throat just so he would shut up for a few minutes.

226

He told himself it was an expensive gift that needed no words of explanation. Raghu knew what it meant and had accepted it because he knew.

But he would take anything he could get from anyone.

Badal sighted a bit of red and grey that seemed to be Raghu and again his steps turned into an involuntary run. The boy was crouched over the iron bucket filled with clay cups. The cups let out soft bubbles as they absorbed the water in the bucket. If you didn't soak earthen cups for hours before they were used, their porous bodies grew fatter on the tea poured into them, Johnny Toppo had once explained. Raghu was lifting them from the bucket and making a neat stack on a table next to him. When Badal put his mouth close to his ear and said, "You're back! Where were you?" Raghu fumbled in alarm and the four cups he was holding dropped to the ground and broke. He looked up to see if Johnny Toppo had noticed and growled, "What the hell are you hissing like that for?"

He got up, set the washed cups on the barrow, and began taking an order from a couple who wanted tea, one with sugar, one without and yes, maybe two of those biscuits . . . no, three. Johnny Toppo was at the other end, dealing with children whose parents were saying, "Horlicks, Horlicks, chocolate flavour. Don't you keep any?"

"There's something . . ." Badal whispered to Raghu. "Come away for just a minute, Johnny Toppo can manage."

"*Johnny Toppo can manage*," Raghu mimicked. But he moved away from the stall.

"I just wanted to ask you . . ." Badal began. But he had never been good at saying things and even now, when he had come especially to talk, he did not know how to say it. He was distracted by Raghu scratching something on his arm — another drying scab — where did he get all these wounds from? It was as if he cut himself on purpose just to be able to worry a scab. But he was so beautiful — impossibly beautiful in his ragged old red and grey clothes and those blue rubber slippers. He wanted to ask him, did you like the phone? Did you notice I fed my own number into it? Do you know what that means? Do you understand the full force of what that means?

Yet he found himself saying, "That afternoon . . . by the boat . . . you ran off . . . did you take my scooter away and then put it back near my house? Did you take the scooter keys from my pocket?"

Inevitably, it came out wrong. Still, he tried to look as if he was amused by the keys and missing scooter. He attempted a smile.

"You think I'm a thief as well? First they say I stole a phone, then . . . What's got into all these old buggers? What's there to grin about anyway with all your thirty-two teeth? You couldn't pay me to steal that pile of junk."

"Don't shout," Badal begged. "That's not what I meant, not what I meant. I thought you were playing a prank . . . just fooling around." He had not intended asking the question in that way. All he wanted was to remind Raghu of that afternoon, of what had happened before the scooter was lost. Maybe he had actually wanted to ask about the monk in sunglasses and the night when he had seen Raghu with those foreigners.

No, he had not wanted to ask about that, there was no need to.

Raghu went back to the stall and crouched over his pail again. Badal sat on his haunches next to him. Raghu turned his face away and started with single-minded zeal on the pile of clay cups in the water. He picked up another four and swilled them out. "Get lost," he said, "I've no time for this now." Hunched over the cups, his hair a dry, sun-bleached nest, he looked so childish and vulnerable that Badal wanted to put his arms around those thin shoulders and tell him, you never have to work again, I'll look after you.

"I thought you were just fooling around with the scooter," Badal said in an urgent whisper. "What else would I think? Why else would I buy you a gift? I got you that phone to . . ."

"That phone got me a beating, that's what it did."

"Can't you see . . . ?" Badal begged.

"What? What can't I see?" Raghu spoke slowly, biting off each syllable. His voice had a belligerent edge. It was raised — too much. Badal looked around hoping nobody was listening.

"Can't you see how things are between us?" he whispered. "You can see as well as I can what has happened between us. That's why I bought you that phone. So that, any time . . ."

Even as he spoke, he felt his voice drying up, his hands go clammy. A suffocating darkness rose from inside him, yet he could see everything now with agonising clarity.

The crowds shielded them. They were in the eye of their own private storm. Around them was the roar of other people. This was not how he had meant it to be, but this was how it was. This was always how it was with important things, the things that made or shattered your life.

Johnny Toppo shouted, "Arre Raghu, hurry up with the cups. I've got people here waiting."

Raghu gave Badal a twisted smile and said, "So *that's* how things are, is it? You don't say!"

Johnny Toppo hobbled towards them. "I've had enough of you, you punk. I told you I was sacking you," he said. "You begged to stay. Either you work or I get someone else. I haven't signed a bond to feed you for free."

Raghu stood up saying, "Take it easy, Uncle, I'm just entertaining one of your customers. That's work, or isn't that work?"

He threw another half smile towards Badal before going back to the stove. The scent of the tea came out from the pan in a cloud when he pushed aside the lid: thick, brown, boiling, sweet, gingery tea. He poured a cupful, imitating Johnny Toppo's technique of filling half the cup with froth, then held it out to Badal. There was something malicious in the way he held it just out of reach over the boiling pan for a second or two before handing it over. The cup felt too hot and Badal could not understand why he had been given it. He never drank this kind of tea and Raghu knew that. He had known it all these months when he had served Badal unsweetened lemon tea, unasked. He stared at the boy through the cloud of steam. He wanted no kind of tea. When Raghu did not look at him again, he walked away from the stall and tilted the cup over a grey crab that looked as prehistoric and lifeless as a stone, watching it skitter for cover under the sand which drank up the tea.

He crushed the cup underfoot. Sharp-edged waves puckered the surface of the granite sea as far as his eyes could reach. He thought he could walk into its measureless sweep until he became a barely visible speck going further and further away. Holiday-makers milled around him, everyone with friends or relatives, shopping, laughing, chatting, finding things, running into the water. Nearby were a young man and woman. Badal could see they were in a world that contained nothing but themselves — no work, no family, no yesterday or tomorrow. They did not look at each other or speak or hold hands, but they stood very close, their bodies touching at the hips and at the shoulders, as if a moment's break in contact might snap a fragile spell.

It took Badal no more than ten minutes to get home on his scooter. Nobody expected him at that hour. They knew him to stay out as long as he possibly could. He heard his uncle's hoarse shout from the balcony, "Who's that downstairs? Jadu? Jadua!" Badal didn't answer, nor did he go to the tap to wash his face. He went to his room and fell into his string cot. His bones ached with fatigue, a pain that filled the room and drained him with every breath.

He tried to sleep. After a while he realised he was staring at a nail in the wall above the door. It was an iron nail of the largest possible size. A deep, cold shudder shook him. His head hurt as if that nail were going through the centre of his forehead, the way it had hurt watching a relative hammer it into the wall after his father's cremation. He could not remember the relative's face, but he had a hazy memory of another man, shrunken and stooped, who had come for the funeral. "It's what people do," the man had explained, stroking Badal's nine-year-old head as the nail was being banged in. "To protect the room against evil spirits when someone dies in it." Badal did not know who that man was, but after he had held the ritual flaming torch to his father's head on the funeral pyre, he and the man had stood together, a child and a wizened ancient, watching the body burn. The man had held his shoulder and tried to console him saying the body that turns into a handful of ashes is nothing but meaningless flesh. The soul is eternal, he had said, you have not lost him, he will always be with you, only you can't see him.

A dry sob burst from Badal like a gasp. The solid, reassuring bulk of a body. The body that we embrace, hold, stroke — what is left when the body is gone? Nobody else would sleep in the room where his father had been found dead. Badal would sleep nowhere else.

He thought of his only friend at the time — a boy who lived down the alley. They walked together to school, studied and played together. Once, crawling through an unused sewer pipe by the road for fun, they had come face to face with the head of a just-slaughtered goat that someone was holding at the other end. Its teeth were big. Its eyes bulged. Its pelt was lathered to its neck with blood. The head shook because the person holding it was laughing so hard he couldn't keep it still. When the two boys had tried crawling away from it, backward through the pipe, fright had made them do all the wrong things and they had got stuck inside. He no longer remembered how they came unstuck, how they got out. But he remembered how gently his friend's mother had washed his face that afternoon, then sat him on her lap and fed him soft, warm parathas and sugar before sending him home.

He felt starved thinking of those parathas. He had not eaten since morning. He hauled himself out of his cot and went to the kitchen on the other side of the courtyard. He opened the latch on the kitchen door and saw a row of shining, upturned pots. In the basket where his aunt stored vegetables were three potatoes and an onion. The room smelled of overripe guava. He tracked down the smell to a single fruit, soft as a banana now, and blackened in patches. He swallowed it in two bites before its putrid smell could invade him. He looked around the kitchen. Through the mesh on the cupboard in a corner he could see three covered bowls of food. The cupboard was locked. He yanked the lock to check if it would give. That hammer began driving the burning nail through his forehead again.

233

The lock would not budge. He went to the line of tins on the kitchen shelf and opened them one by one — rice, flour, dal — weevils crawling among the grains of rice. A bottle of oil.

He saw his hand pour the oil onto the floor, then empty out the rice and flour and sweep through the line of washed pots. They fell with a deafening series of clangs. He turned on his heels as his uncle began screaming, "Jadua, the cat! It can't be the cat! Thief! Stop the thief!" Badal knew that if he had found a box of matches, he would have thrown the kerosene stove to the floor and put a flame to it.

He went to his room only to pick up his scooter keys and the tin box where he had, years ago, hidden away his father's spectacles and rosary, a Swiss army knife, and a pocket-sized glass model of the Taj Mahal. An afterthought propelled him to his cupboard and he collected a few clothes and the papers and chequebook for the bank account his uncle knew nothing about.

On his way out he uprooted what remained of the shiuli he had planted.

He burst out of the door, slammed it behind him, stuffed everything he had taken into the basket of the scooter and kicked it alive. The roar of its rackety old engine made his muscles jangle to his fingertips.

He had gone only a few hundred yards when he had second thoughts and skidded to a halt.

The scooter's wheels scooped up some more dust as he turned and made his way back down the road, retracing his journey, slower this time. He came to a halt near the old woman's shrine. A wisp of smoke

234

trailed from the incense the woman had lit. Badal touched his head to the floor before the tiny idols inside the shrine and saw that the images were decorated with red roses today.

The woman who tended the shrine was balled up in her usual place on the pavement, in the shadow of the neem tree. Her spectacles were askew, she had fallen asleep without taking them off. A thread of drool shone in the trench that went from her lips to her chin and it had collected in a damp patch on the bundle she had placed under her head as a pillow. Three thick white hairs sprouted from a spot on her chin like the roots on an onion. Her steel plate lay beside her, in its usual place on the pavement. It held five rose petals and a rupee coin.

Badal took his wallet from its usual place in the left pocket of his kurta. It had a hundred and fifty rupees. Keeping no more than a few tens and twenties for himself, he emptied the rest of his money onto her plate. Then the thought struck him that the money might be stolen while she slept. He had a sudden irrational urge to wake her, bundle her onto his scooter, take her with him. Instead, he picked up the plate and edged it into the shrine for her to find when she woke.

The Sun Temple's parking lot was a square of baking grey cement patrolled by a sun-shrivelled attendant who stopped giving Suraj meaningful looks after his first few glances at the packet of cigarettes went unacknowledged. The excitable clamour of tourists and guides was no more than a distant murmur here. Suraj perched on a low wall shaded by the bulk of a four-wheel drive. He counted the dents on the car, speculating about their causes. The owners must be slobs: the car was dirty both inside and out, muddy and scratched. His own car, when he could buy something that wasn't a dinky Korean toy, would gleam, it would smell of leather. He would never smoke inside it. He had always wanted a four-wheel drive — a real, heavy, roaring Jeep whose top could be rolled away so you could drive with the wind in your face. He would drive to Ladakh in that Jeep, right from Bangalore, taking a month, maybe more, wandering coasts and forests along the way, foraging for food in wayside dhabas, picking up hitchhikers, letting them go, stopping when tired, then carrying on, filming the journey.

If he had told her about it, Ayesha would have called it another of his schemes to run away from life — as if life were something that you had to grit your teeth against and endure. She said he was an escape artist — when all he wanted was the freedom to just be, to come and go without a hundred accusatory questions from strident wives and anxious mothers. He lied to them both for no reason at all sometimes, merely to feel himself free. Why *shouldn't* he tell his mother he was in Hyderabad when in fact he was in Jarmuli?

It struck him that he should call Nomi. He had left her so suddenly up there on the way to the tallest tower, shooting off like a bullet the minute he sighted Latika Aunty holding hands with a stranger. Maybe Nomi hadn't heard him when he told her he would wait for her in the car. What if she thought he was going to come back to the ruins for her? He slid his hand into his pocket for his phone.

It wasn't there. Of course. It had been stolen on the beach that morning.

He got up from his wall and found his driver chatting nearby in a knot of other waiting drivers. He borrowed the man's phone — then was stumped trying to recall Nomi's number. He had never needed to memorise it.

He retreated to the warm shade of their hired car and sat inside it, sweating, wondering if he should go back and find her — but if he went back he would very likely bump into his mother and her friends. He decided to wait. He fidgeted, drank some water, smoked a cigarette. He thought he would stretch out on the car seat and take a nap, but it was full of things. He stowed away a tube of Nomi's sunscreen and bottles of water. One of the many elastic bands she used for her hair lay on the seat too. It had a plastic daisy on it. He slipped it round his wrist like a bangle to give her later.

Then his hands fell on her computer. She had left her laptop in the car. He sat tapping the lid, listening to his nail on its surface, a metallic sound. It had a sleek body, slim and light. He had never seen one of these machines, they had just come out. He opened the lid. He shut it again. Should he go on?

What if she happened to arrive just then and saw him? She would be furious he was snooping. But he wanted to snoop. He had to know: where had she disappeared to that morning when she abandoned him at the Vishnu temple? And then yesterday, when he thought they would go together to clear a few permissions to shoot, she had made an excuse and not come back till the evening, when she came up with that cock and bull story of going to see a sculptor.

He opened the laptop's lid again. There was the lit screen — she hadn't even shut the machine down and he had to tap no password to access the files. Really, people as careless as her deserved what was coming to them. His fingers revelled in the familiar pleasure of trackpad and keys. He navigated her machine swiftly and surely. He was good with computers, it took him seconds to find his way around new ones. He opened her photo application and found it empty. That was odd. He had never come across people who didn't store pictures on their machines. He started up her e-mail programme — it wasn't configured. That meant she used e-mail off the internet, but since there was no connection here, he wouldn't be able to see what she did on the net.

He began searching her folders. Quite a lot of notes and writing — he couldn't linger too much on those — she might come back. There was a folder named after him. He paused over that, but it contained only copies of his own e-mails to her.

The door of the car clicked open and Suraj slammed the laptop shut, his mind racing to find explanations to give. "I was hunting for your phone number," he would say. That was the most plausible.

But it wasn't Nomi. It was the driver. "We should go," the driver said. "It's getting late, we have a long way to go and it'll get dark. We can't wait any more.

There are buses from here also — she must have gone back to Jarmuli on one of those."

Suraj agreed with the driver — she must have misunderstood and taken a bus. Why else was she taking so long? The car slid out from its slot in the parking lot, the air conditioner came back on, and its first cool currents made Suraj sigh with relief. He opened the laptop, this time with no sense of urgency or stealth. He tapped the trackpad.

Latika seemed to be in the grip of a curious exhilaration for hours after her visit to the ruins at the Sun Temple. She swatted away Vidya's questions about Suraj. "You know how confused Gouri is about faces! She thought she saw him, but it was someone else entirely. Who was it, Gouri?" She insisted she would sit in the front seat on the way back because she had felt squashed between Vidya and Gouri during the drive from the hotel. She ignored Vidya's troubled glances and chattered on, even with the driver who was really the hotel's manager. He was no longer the taciturn man who had driven them out, and Vidya caught snatches of their conversation from the back, the two of them sounding as comfortable as old friends. At times they heard Latika humming "Are you lonesome tonight" in her husky voice which an admirer had once described as sand and smoke. When they stopped midway to look at a confluence of river and sea, Latika walked into the mirror-still water, unconcerned about wetting clothes and sandals. She would not come out of there until

Vidya said, "Really, Latika, be reasonable, it's getting dark."

The rest of the drive down the highway was suffused with a sense of things ending. Vidya was already tense about her electricity bill. She was sure it had come by now and if the bill wasn't paid on time she might lose her connection. And then? In a few minutes her mind felt as if it were an undone skein of wool: impossible to find the beginning or end of the problem of the unpaid bill. The car speeded down the last of the twilit roads and secretive trees. "At day's end, like the hush of dew comes evening," Gouri murmured to herself. "The kite wipes the scent of sunlight from its wings." She could not remember the next few lines or where she had read the poem. Perhaps at college. After a moment some snatches came back to her and she whispered, "All birds come home, all rivers, all of life's tasks finished, only darkness remains." Looking out of the window she said sadly, "It's over so soon." They were approaching street lights, cars, buildings, Jarmuli's market.

"It's not! Let's get off at the bazaar! I don't feel like the hotel yet." Latika twisted herself back to look at them. "Come on now, you two, let's have some fun."

"Aren't you tired?" Vidya said. "We can go tomorrow. We were there just yesterday." The sense of misgiving which had taken root in her after hearing that Gouri had caught sight of her son weighed her down, and tired her out. First her ill health, then that molten sun pouring down on her head all afternoon, then Suraj. She tried reminding herself of the many times Gouri had confused one person with another. But the

240

same thought went around her brain in concentric circles that tightened into an aching noose. Why had her son followed her to Jarmuli? Did he need to speak to her about something? But then they had spoken the morning she left, when she had phoned him. Had she imagined his unease, his attempt to hang up minutes after she called? He had been sounding evasive and abrupt for many months — one had to be grateful he answered his phone at all, which was more than she could say of her daughter-in-law, Ayesha.

Latika was still urging them to stop the car and get off at the bazaar. "Let's, please!" she begged them like a child. "We can take rickshaws back to the hotel, it's only ten minutes away. It's such a lovely evening." Vidya drew breath to snap at her, then counted, as she had taught herself, a slow fifteen. "Fine," she said after her pause. "Fine, we'll do as you want."

They were in a dilemma about the driver's tip and held urgent whispered consultations. How did one deal with a tip when he was not really a driver but the manager of the hotel? It was difficult conferring when he was inches away, listening. Ultimately, Latika whispered, "Gift, gift," and they got off. Now that there was a purpose to the market trip, Vidya did not feel as irascible, and after a long cold gulp of a fizzy drink her anxieties over Suraj and the electricity bill receded.

After leaving his uncle's house for the last time, Badal drove out of town towards the Sun Temple, down Marine Road, shaded by the casuarina trees that flanked it. It was a lonely stretch, close neither to

Jarmuli nor to the huddles of earth and straw that made up the dismal villages which lived off the temple. At one point, where he sighted an opening in the foliage and a pale stretch of sand, he abandoned his scooter and walked down to the shore. White-topped rollers came crashing in, a wind had risen in the orange sky.

Why had Raghu shown not a sign — not the tiniest flicker — that their afternoon by the boat had meant something to him as well? The cruelty of his indifference opened an abyss inside him. It wasn't indifference alone, there was ridicule as well. He could not stop himself thinking about it. He reworked every second of their togetherness into separate images, as in a slide show, as though this would keep him from losing them. He wanted to throw himself into a thorn bush, cut himself with a razor, smash his toes with a stone — anything to fight pain with pain. He stood by the sea and the song Johnny Toppo had been droning that morning played in his head:

> Where is my mud-brown hut?
> My young guava tree?
> Where's the black cow that came
> When I called her to me?
> Where is that pretty stream
> As blue as the pure blue skies?
> The only streams I know now
> Flow from my two sad eyes.

He sat on the sand, head in his hands, clutching his hair, trying to drive the song and his headache away.

242

Once he had asked Johnny Toppo, "Can't you sing a happy song? Why are all your songs so gloomy?" And Johnny Toppo had said, "They aren't sad for me. They're all I have left of my world. I've no cameras like these tourists — clicking all the time. Smile, smile! Click!" He had tapped his forehead. "I keep it all here. It makes me happy to remember."

"So what was your world?" Badal had asked him. "Tell me, why don't you?" Johnny Toppo had turned away. After a while he had said, "I sell tea, I was born ten years after the great earthquake in Bihar, I live in a tarpaulin shack, I have nobody, nothing to worry about, nothing to lose. I'm happy I'm above the water and below the sky and I've got beeris to smoke and a half-bottle to drink. I know from the songs in my head that I used to have another life long ago. That's all there is to say about me, Babu."

In the far distance, across the water, a line of lights glimmered. Fishing trawlers, living their secret lives. The lights dipped, disappeared, came back. Their nets went deep down to the floor of the sea. They would be at work all night, trapping and killing thousands of gasping creatures.

Badal had had a trick since childhood, of sitting by the sea with his back to it. He would position himself close enough for the waves to wet him with spray, knowing that if a big breaker came it might sweep him out to sea. He knew all about waves and currents, about riptides formed by winds hundreds of miles away that sucked swimmers under or sluiced away people standing on the shore. If you fought the current and tried swimming back against it, you would drown. The thing to do was not to oppose it but to fool it and swim away from it, in a diagonal. Badal had seen the washed up corpses of those who had battled the currents and lost. But he still sat with his back to the water, as if at the edge of a cliff, playing with death.

A wave crashed onto the beach and he moved away from long instinct. The nearby waves told him which ones would come further inland than the rest. Still, this one had managed to wet the bottom half of his clothes. Two more waves followed, lapping at him. At times he wanted to stop their rush and roar, freeze them mid-charge for a moment's stillness. To know how absolute silence sounded.

He grew tired of his game and turned to sit facing the sea. He had grown up beside it, yet its endlessness was a thing his mind could not come to grips with. This coast he was sitting on — going towards the Dolphin Hotel, the Swirling Sea Hotel, past Vishnupada Road and the Vishnu temple and beyond it to Grand Road and the market and Matri Mandir and the Kanakot highway — went onward, curving voluptuously past the tigers and honeycombs of the Sundarbans towards Burma, and downward towards Pondicherry, where the same water flowed, and the same winds that blew here blew there too, pushing that water into waves that travelled towards the southernmost tip of this tongue-shaped country before they curved upward again on their journey past Bombay and Goa to Karachi and Iran, Arabia and Egypt — names from dreams and textbooks.

Jarmuli radiated outward to Asia, the world, the solar system, the universe — it was every child's incantation in school, and even now, when he wanted to be out of the reach of his aunt and uncle, he dreamed of living on Jupiter and sleeping under its many moons. When his teacher had told their class it had sixteen moons he had wanted to ask her if this meant that there was a full moon on Jupiter every night. Or were there crescent moons and half moons and round moons all at once in that other sky?

If he put his feet into the water here at the beach in Jarmuli, he was dipping them in the universe. If he could only step into the sea, swim and swim, and land in Zanzibar. He knew nothing about it, had never wanted to know anything about it beyond its place in the school atlas, merely loved the sound of its name: Zanzibar.

Badal rose, not knowing where to go. He trudged to his scooter. Where did Johnny Toppo live, he wondered. In all these years of drinking his tea he had never found that out — where was that tarpaulin shack?

Where would he go now? What was he to do?

He was fiddling with the key to his scooter when he heard a woman's voice.

"Whose is that camel?" the woman was saying. "I'm going to untie it."

Badal saw the tasselled leather bands on the woman's ankle, the coloured braids in her hair. That girl in the wrong clothes at the temple. She was still in strange clothes, he saw, an overlarge kurta whose sleeves appeared to have been hacked off. It was being whipped around her by the breeze. Billowing pyjamas. Red sneakers. But she had made an effort: he had to admit these were Indian clothes, after a fashion.

The girl was pointing to a forlorn, barrel-chested camel tied to a post by a shuttered souvenir stall. Its hump had collapsed, its eyes were rheumy. Its coat was moth-eaten and its ribs showed through. The girl stroked the camel's side. She looked at Badal as if she had had a brilliant idea and said, "Shall we untie it? Let's!"

"Where will it go?" he said. "It has nowhere to go. And what will it eat?"

"It can be free for some time. Here it'll live without ever knowing anything else. No?"

Was she merely whimsical, like many of the foreigners he encountered? Or was she addled enough to think the camel had emotions and spent all its life yearning for freedom? He had always seen camels in Jarmuli, brought there from thousands of miles away for tourists to ride on the beach. They were replaced by others when they dropped dead. They were so timeless in their solitude it had never crossed his mind before how far away from their natural homes these animals were.

And he? Could he live if someone cut the invisible threads that bound him to the great temple? The temple that had been his life and his heart and his soul from when his memory began.

The girl said, "I'm going to untie him."

Jarmuli was quite far, it struck him, and the sun had almost set. "What are you doing here?" he asked her.

"It is not safe. A woman was . . ." He stopped himself from telling her a woman had been attacked nearby the month before, left for dead.

"Let's find something to cut the rope with," she said. "Unless we can untie it." She began to prise open the knots.

Badal pulled out his tin box from the scooter's basket and extracted his father's Swiss knife. It had never been used and the gadget had rusted. The springs were stiff. After a struggle he managed to open the blade, and held it towards her. How odd he had the knife with him, he thought, as if he had known all along they would meet again, she would need a knife.

She said, "Will you hold him or will you cut the rope?" She had a small, pointed face, now split open by a comic-book grin that showed all her teeth and a bit of her gums.

He held the rope. The camel smelled of hide and dung and mould, a strong animal stench that made him gag. It had tearful eyes and drooping eyelids fringed with long lashes. Its nostrils quivered as the girl sawed at the rope — on and on until first it frayed, then frayed some more, and then fell apart.

She patted the camel's side and said, "Go! Run! Far! You're free now!"

The camel did not move. It hung its head, looking too weary to take another step.

The girl pushed the camel and said, "Shoo, go . . . before they come back!"

The camel stood its ground. It had never heard these words before, nor the tone of voice. The girl pushed with all her strength as if the camel were a stalled car. "Move!" Then half giggling, half annoyed, she sighed. "O.K. I give up. It's your life."

This time the camel took one tentative step to the left, then another.

"Good!" Nomi said. She walked away from the camel and stood gazing at their surroundings, hands on her hips. "Bleak, no? This place? Not on the tourist trail, right?" She fidgeted with a lighter and from her bag pulled out a bottle of water. She was talking in English now, assuming he understood. He did, after a fashion, but his answers were halting and slow.

The girl lowered her face to shield her cigarette from the wind. She was exactly the kind of person he usually found repellent. Those rings in her ears. That crazy hair. And a woman smoking? He should walk away and leave her to her fate — such people invited trouble. He looked towards his scooter and fingered the keys in his pocket. The girl circled the cigarette to light it. She kept the lighter flame on, waving it at his face and saying, "Want one?"

Badal said, "I don't smoke, I work at the temple," and simultaneously put his hand out for one. When she leaned over with a smile to light it for him, he saw that, like Raghu, she had a dimple. Hers was in the right cheek while Raghu's was in the left, as if the two of them had two halves of the same face. A black smog of grief rose to his throat, choking him.

She shrugged and said, "I don't really smoke either. But I stole these from a friend of mine when he wasn't

248

looking. He dumped me at the Sun Temple and left. No explanation, nothing."

"That is not good," Badal mumbled. He knew the man she meant, someone drunk, rude, disrespectful, the kind of man he did not want in his head. He had spotted him early that morning on the beach with Johnny Toppo. That man was the reason Raghu had to rush away when he was being given the phone.

"I had to hitch a ride on a bus. It turned off at some village and they told me, Get off. Just like that. Serve that driver right if they found my chopped up body in the bushes. What a relief to find you. I recognised you in a second. You don't recognise me."

They sat on the sand. She looked over her shoulder to see where the camel was going. It had hardly moved. "Have you ever seen a donkey's eyes?" she said. "They're so beautiful. This camel has eyes like a donkey's. I'd have loved having those eyes, you know?"

"No," he said. "I have not looked carefully at a donkey's eyes."

He was puzzled by her question. Her eyes — he hadn't considered them before. Now he saw they were long-lashed and very dark and large, like Raghu's.

She said, "When you see a donkey, it looks so alone. Like it has no mother or father or friends. Cows never look so isolated." She flicked her lighter on, then off, then on again. She held up a finger and passed it through the flame, then said, "Don't you love that it doesn't get burned when you do that?"

He could make no sense of her talk. And her English, when she spoke so fast, was hard for him to follow even though she broke into sentences in Hindi. Still he followed her logic without missing a step, as if he were a blind man who had counted the number of paces between rooms so that he didn't need sight any longer.

Having grasped that he couldn't understand much of her English, Nomi fell silent. The sea rushed towards the beach, then retreated with a roar, as if coming in had been a mistake. There was moisture in the air, Badal could feel it. It smelled of fish and salt-water. Something made an odd grunting sound nearby — the camel, Badal thought. Then he wondered, what sounds did camels make? Did they moo like cows?

Nomi gazed out at the sea and thought she had had its sound in her ears forever. Her first memory of the sea was of being alone by the sea, her mother walking away. A dog came and sniffed at her. How alone she had felt, and how hungry. Her mother — she had spent the last ten years of her life looking for the sea where she had lost her mother. She had been in the sea in Greece — the water was purple and green and blue there. She had seen — she counted — the Sargasso Sea, the Chilean Sea, the North Sea, the Bass Strait, the South China Sea. She'd even dipped a toe in the Baltic Sea — that was icy — and grey like slate. Whole shiploads of children drowned in the Baltic Sea during the Second World War. Think how they died. Frozen. And then there was the Dead Sea — she had not seen it, but she knew that people floated in it, not needing to swim. At every sea, she would sit down like this and wait for it to tell her something, she didn't know what, but she'd know it when it came. She would be sitting by the sea where she had been left, the one she could sense from her cement cage in the ashram.

Badal felt the wind rise. He could see no clouds, but the sky was lumpy and old, too heavy to stay up. He sensed an approaching storm. High tide too would come in a while and the next morning the beaches would be littered with sodden rubbish. Once he had found a rusted harmonica and had coaxed a few tunes out of it.

Nomi rested her chin on her arms. Those trawler lights on the water, she had thought there were buildings — a whole city across the sea. When she chanced upon a spellbinding place she kept it a secret, as if it existed only for her. Now look: this beach, the trawler, the storm coming — wasn't it actually a magic show or a stage set? Afterwards they'd dry the wind, clean up the sand, wipe up the sea, fold away the sky, stow the camel and unstring those lights and nobody else would find this place again.

Badal drew lines in the sand with a twig. When Raghu had given him the thick milky tea he had known it was all over — worse, he had known nothing had ever been. The afternoon by the boat, his mouth on Raghu's, that was a spell he alone had been under and understanding this made him feel as if someone had pushed a hand down his gullet, grabbed his blood-slimed heart and intestines and pulled them out through his mouth the way fisher-women cleaned fish. His throat came up with an involuntary choking sound. The girl did not seem to hear it. She pulled out two more cigarettes and lit them, putting both in her mouth together like one who chainsmoked every day. She passed him one and he took it from her as if from long habit.

She was fiddling with the jewellery in her ears. Several silver rings. Two tiny ruby studs at the top of the left ear. One gold ring at each lobe.

He had not realised he was staring until she said, "Weird, no? So many? I didn't plan it that way. I just collected them over the years."

Badal swallowed this information with a smile and a nod. She did not seem to expect more.

For a long time after their cigarettes finished they sat looking out to the horizon. She was humming a song — one of Johnny Toppo's songs. Badal could not remember which. How did she know the song? Johnny Toppo's songs had no melodies stolen from any movies he had seen, neither were the words those of a poet. It came to him that Raghu never hummed Johnny Toppo's songs even though he listened to them all the time; he didn't hum any songs at all. But he would not think of Raghu. He would not think.

Then, as the wind dropped, something in the air changed, as if the storm were drawing breath before it broke loose. The trawler's lights had faded.

The girl fished around in her bag and brought out a box of mints. She held it out to him. "You'd better have one of these," she said. "Then nobody will know you smoked."

She looked hesitant; she was going to ask a favour. He knew what it would be.

252

"Give me a ride?" she said. "Till somewhere?"

"I will drop you near the market in Jarmuli. You can take a rickshaw from there to your hotel," he said to her. "And then I leave. I won't go back there ever again."

He put the mint into his mouth, felt its icy charge wipe every other taste away.

It was when they were looking for a gift for their driver who was not a driver that Latika had her brainwave. They were in a badly-lit alleyway lined by a series of shops that looked like rusted cupboards on stilts. Crowds of evening shoppers were jammed against each other looking at displays of cheap clothing, bags, shells, and statues. Here, set somewhat behind the other shops, as if it needed to be hidden, was a grilled window in a wall flaky with torn posters from the recent elections. A few men who had been glued to the window slunk away from it, tucking half bottles of liquor into their waistbands, then pulling their shirts over the bottles as camouflage.

"Let's get a bottle of vodka." Latika's eyes were shining.

"Have you lost your mind?" Vidya had not paused to count to fifteen this time and her question came out as a furious bark.

"She has. What is wrong with you, Latika? Let's go back and have some hot cups of tea. From that man on the beach." Why she needed that tea so badly Gouri could not explain. But she did.

"Tea, tea, tea! I'm sick of tea. Haven't had one cup of real coffee for five days. I'm going to buy some vodka. Wait here, Vidya."

"Wait here? What will those . . . those *loafers* at the shop think? Respectable old women queuing up with that riff-raff to buy . . . liquor!"

"I've never drunk alcohol in my life," Gouri said, pursing her lips and looking away.

"Neither have I." Vidya's words came rapidly, as if the very thought rattled her. "What an absurd idea. Look how those men are staring. What if they follow us? Let's just go from here." She pulled at Latika's thin arm.

"They'll never see us again. Come on! We'll never be out together after this, away from children, away from family."

"What's happening to you in your old age, Latika? Since when have you been drinking?" Gouri wanted to sound sarcastic, but she never managed irony and this time too it came out sounding like a real question. It infuriated Latika. "Oh, old age! Old age! I'm tired of this." She stalked off towards the grilled window.

"What's got into her, really . . . Latika? Oh, this is all so exhausting, and after such a long drive and the hot sun all day . . ." Vidya followed her, calling, "Latika! Slow down."

Gouri stood where they had left her, in the middle of the market, with its piles of garlands, fruits, rotted vegetables underfoot, the chaos of vendors shouting under gas lamps that seemed to create more shadows than light. She wondered if she too should try and stop

Latika. She stole a look at the dingy shop as if a glance, however quick, might be enough to contaminate her. "INDIAN MADE FOREIGN LIQUOR" a sign said in blotchy red paint on the walls around the window. That decided her. She stayed where she was.

Out of the mess of rickshaws and people with shopping bags and laden carts that were being pushed through the crowd, Gouri saw a young woman approach her. The face looked familiar, but she could not place it. The woman — a girl, really — was looking at her. Gouri turned away. She wanted to avoid their eyes meeting.

The girl came towards her, as if she knew Gouri. "Do you remember me? This really is a small place, no? I'm so glad you're here! My friend abandoned me at the Sun Temple, then I took a bus and then I got a lift on a scooter, but now someone is following me. A monk . . . see? Behind that shop with the saris? That one, with the long hair. Haven't you seen him standing in the sea with his beads? He's been after me from the first day I came here."

"Child, a monk will never do you any harm. He is a man of god. Why should he follow you?" The girl looked deranged, what with her matted hair and and her strange clothes.

"Please." The girl looked at a group of people some distance away, then turned to Gouri again. "I mustn't look that way, he'll see me. Just . . . if we could leave together from here? Then I'll be fine. Please?" She put a hand out and Gouri shrank back. "If you're going in a rickshaw, I'll share it? Where are you going?"

Her voice was shaking. Gouri could see she was terrified — but for what reason? A monk? Monks were good. They would never touch a hair on a girl's head. There were any number of monks at the temple: pious, holy, revered.

"I am waiting," Gouri explained. "I can't leave."

"For what? For how long?"

Gouri had to think — for what? For some moments she could not recall what exactly she was waiting for. Then — of course, she remembered — she was waiting for the guide to the Vishnu temple. Vidya and Latika had gone on ahead in a rickshaw. The guide had told her he would take her on his scooter. He had asked her to wait till he brought his scooter from the parking lot, but then he had not come back. She had been waiting quite a while, her tired legs told her that. They felt as if they had been walking all day when all she had done was to rest in the hotel, praying and preparing for this evening's trip to the temple.

She might as well take a rickshaw with this child, do her a good turn while she was at it. Perhaps the guide couldn't find her in the crowds. What was the point of worrying about it? Whatever would be would be. They only needed to reach the temple, and then she knew her way about. They would get there right in time for the evening's prayers and change of flags. That was such a spectacle. Young people loved that kind of thing. She would tell the girl what it all meant.

She waved towards the line of waiting rickshaws with a magisterial finger. A rickshaw broke away from its rank by the road and creaked to a halt next to them.

256

Holding the seat for support, she heaved herself in and beckoned to the girl, who clambered in as well. "To the temple," Gouri said.

At the Indian Made Foreign Liquor shop, the men by the window made way for Latika without being asked, too astonished to catcall or whistle. Latika leaned in at the window, unzipped her handbag, fished out some money and said in an authoritative tone, as if this were an everyday thing and she was buying onions or potatoes: "One small bottle vodka."

She was stumped when she was asked, "Which brand, Madam? What's your usual?" The pig-eyed man behind the grill was smirking, he underlined the word Madam when he spoke. He had a hairline moustache over a puffy upper lip and was picking at his teeth with a pin. The other men were sniggering too.

All of a sudden it came to Latika that she would stop colouring her hair. No more chestnut or black, no more visits to Wendy at Sunflower every month. She ran her fingers through her wind-tousled crop. She wanted it to turn grey and white that minute. She looked straight into the man's piggy eyes, pushed up her glasses, said, "Smirnoff, of course, if you have it." Her handbag was big enough for the bottle he handed over through the window-grill. He watched her put it away and took her money without another word.

When she and Vidya got back to the place where they had left Gouri, she was nowhere to be seen. She must have wandered off, attracted by some bauble in a shop. Exactly like that morning when she disappeared from the hotel and they found her after an hour of pointless panic, sitting on an upturned boat.

More exasperated than worried, they divided up and went in opposite directions to look for her. Whoever found her would phone the other and then they would take rickshaws back to the hotel. And not let Gouri out of their sight for the rest of the trip.

Neither of them had found her after a quarter of an hour. The street was full of people, and not one of them was Gouri.

When Nomi knocked on his glass door and pushed into the room the moment Suraj had opened it a crack, he realised it was quite late. He must have dropped off. She was shouting, "Why did you rush off like that from the Sun Temple? How did you think I'd come back?"

He had gone from horizontal to vertical so abruptly his head spun and he had to hold on to the door. Her voice seemed far too loud. If he tried not to think about it, he felt less dizzy, but he wanted her to stop shrieking. He put his hands to his ears. The sea was rising inside him, a tide of sour, stale liquid.

"Can't you hear me?"

He could muster up no more than a mumble. "Why didn't you come to the car? I waited. Then I left — why didn't — I feel really sick."

"I couldn't find the car! I looked everywhere. It wasn't where we parked it."

"Had to move — too much sun. Just for shade — only a short distance." He needed to sit. He sat heavily on the bed. His head hurt. His eyes couldn't bear the

258

light. He had come back to the hotel a while ago — when? He could no longer remember. Then he had raided the minibar, finished the last of his dope, and fallen asleep. Had he eaten? Maybe a few peanuts.

She stood over him beside the bed, remorseless. "Why weren't you picking up your fucking phone? How could you *do* this?"

"My phone was stolen. I left it on the beach when I went for a swim and it was stolen." He spoke as if each word was a sentence with a full stop after it.

For a while neither of them said anything. She couldn't very well blame him for a stolen phone, did not know what to blame him for next, he guessed. She threw herself into a chair, said, "At least give me a drink."

"We ran out last night. Remember?" He pointed to the empty whisky bottle on a table by the bed.

Again, the shrill whining. "So why didn't you buy some more? You had the car all bloody afternoon!" He felt her petulance stirring that old rage inside him. A voice demanding, "Why do I even have to repair the plugs? Can't you do one thing around this house?" Shouting, "What do you mean you didn't get the eggs on the way back? Didn't I ask you to?" And, "Why the *fuck* didn't you pick up the phone?"

"So sorry," Suraj said, taking care to stay calm. "My service standards appear to have slipped. There is always the minibar . . . don't think I've emptied it."

"Don't bother." She ran her fingers through her hair, tangling it even more than it usually was, as if at a loss over what to do next. She spotted his packet of cigarettes in the circle of light from the table lamp. "O.K., if I can't have a drink I'm going to have a smoke instead."

She pulled a cigarette out after some moments of struggle with the packet. She reached for his lighter. Her lips circled the cigarette in a pout. She had tucked her feet under herself as always, and turned the chair into a shell in which she fitted securely.

He lay with his arms cradling his head. "I'm going to enjoy this," he said. She looked so unlike herself with that cigarette, he could not take his eyes off her. He relaxed into his pillows, as if lying back to watch a movie. So what if he normally didn't like people in his room. This was worth the price.

She exhaled through her nostrils. "I'm fagged out. So hot. And it took forever coming back. Do you know whom I met? The fat old lady from my train. I dropped her off at the big temple. She was hell-bent on dragging me in too, but I managed to give her the slip."

His throat felt very dry. His skin had a crawling itchy feeling. He recited, "When Nomi has a smoke, It is a fucking joke," as if to himself. "A pome." It wasn't such a bad rhyme, he thought, it did actually rhyme. He opened his mouth to repeat it, but his poem had set something off in her again. "Do you know how dangerous it was to leave me out there? Even that temple guide said so. An albino monk with long hair was following me half the time. I thought he was going to attack me."

"An albino monk. An albino . . ." He began laughing, first a giggle, then another, then a helpless guffaw. "You're wild, you know that? I bet you're writing a novel. 'The Gooroo and his Slave Girls'. Who's Piku, tell me that? Raunchy stuff on your laptop, man!" There was something unbelievably erotic about her indignation, that cigarette in her mouth, kurta slipping off her shoulder again.

She got up, looking for a place to stub her cigarette. He pointed through his laughter. "The ashtray's right there, in front of you. See? On the table?"

"You've been snooping around my computer," she said, crushing the cigarette. She was stammering, her voice had a tremor. "You abandon me in the middle of nowhere, you don't give a shit how I'll get back, you don't answer your phone, and now you're being a smart ass."

Her words turned his blood to acid. He sprang up off the bed. "I'm not your fucking bodyguard. I've had enough too." A vein in his forehead throbbed. His face was hot. His ears rang. He lunged for her before she could move and grabbed one of her arms. It was thin and bony. He could break it in two as if it were one of his cigarettes, a limp tube of paper filled with shreds of leaves. He gripped her arm harder, pulling her towards the door. He'd fling her out of his room and never see her again.

"Hey, let go! That hurts!"

Her voice was far too loud. He needed to stop that voice.

She shook her arm, trying to free herself and her kurta started slipping further off her shoulders. Something caught his eye. He loosened his grip, his voice dropped abruptly to a whisper. "There is one thing I need to check — about that spot on your right shoulder — that mole — is it —"

"Get some sleep, Suraj." Her fingers were at work, prising off his. "I'll see you in the morning. We're here to work, you're supposed to do what I need done. I'm out of here. Breakfast at eight tomorrow. Where's my laptop?" Her voice wasn't trembling any longer, it was a curt, superior voice. And her unidentifiable accent was starting to get on his nerves. He wanted to chuck her out of his room, not hear that voice any more, but that shoulder — that hacked-off sleeve, he could focus on little else — that sleeve had come off entirely — and now, somehow, his hands had torn most of the other one away too. He did not know how or why her kurta ripped. He hadn't pulled on it, she had moved away too quickly. And then — how did they end up in the shower? They were both in the cubicle, he had turned the water on full — jets of water. He held her under it, the water made her braids stick to her skull. He was rubbing shower gel all over her, but she was wriggling free, slippery with soap, just would not hold still even when he shook her and slapped her. And then she slipped from his hands — she slipped out of them, fell against the cubicle door, which swung open and she was flung out with it. She slammed down full length on the hard, shining floor. He giggled. "Hey, that is bad, shit, man!" Her legs were splayed, and she was looking upwards at the sink.

A slow red trickle appeared from somewhere behind her ears. It edged across the beige stone of the

262

bathroom floor towards the drain below the sink. There was a creamy bathtub with a fresh white towel draped over it. He wanted to put the towel on the blood stain to stub the red out. He would have to step over her to reach the towel.

He was soaked. Cold, canned air streamed through the bathroom. He shivered.

She was not shivering. She wasn't moving.

Now that she was flat on the floor, much of her kurta gone, he saw her breasts were no more than flattened pancakes topped by chocolate buttons. They were small. Not big enough to fill half his palm.

He found himself looking at his hands. His hands were shaking. He was shaking all over.

Not a sound but for the air conditioner shuddering.

He had to do something. What? He staggered into his bedroom towards the phone — he should call reception for a doctor. But then they would ask what had happened. He had no idea what had happened.

He heard a knock on a door down the corridor followed by a voice saying, "Turn down your bed, Sir?" They arrived every evening, drew the curtains, lit scented candles in the rooms, patted the pillows as if they were babies. In a few minutes the housekeeping service footsteps would close in. He needed time to think. He locked the door. Turned the lever twice to double-lock it.

A sound told him someone else was in the bedroom. He swivelled around. Nomi, in the shreds of her kurta, bleeding from her head, dripping water onto the floor.

He wanted to shout with relief. She wasn't dead. He hadn't killed her.

She held her wet clothes closer. Her teeth were chattering in the cold. He could hear them, like soft castanets.

"I'm going to tell them everything," she said. She was looking straight at him. No, not exactly at him, past him, at the door. She was holding something in one hand, he couldn't quite see what.

He would sort it out with her if only he didn't alarm her. It was all a stupid misunderstanding, couldn't she see that? They were fooling around and it got out of hand. He needed to make her see that. He inched towards her. "Listen, it was an accident, I was drunk, it was bloody awful, but . . ."

The housekeeper's footsteps were coming closer. He could hear them on the flagstones. If there was no privacy sign on the door they usually knocked twice, then let themselves in after a pause. Could they do that even when rooms were double locked?

"Listen . . ." he began again.

"You don't scare me," she said. She was still looking past him as if her eyes were seeing something else. That look made him feel more afraid than he had ever been. He was trapped with a psycho.

"I don't believe your bullshit," she said. "I'm through." She lifted her hands as if holding a gun. She pressed. His hands flew to his eyes, but it was too late. He felt something in one of his eyes, was blinded by a fiery pain. He covered it with his palm. The pain shot through the eye into the back of his head. He could

264

smell his anti-mosquito spray. The can in the bathroom. The bitch. His eye streamed tears, he could barely see anything. It felt as if it had burnt away.

"You don't scare me. I don't believe your bullshit." The words came from Nomi in a low monotone that was not her voice.

Suraj felt a sharp, stabbing pain in his forearm. One eye open, he could see the white sheet had splashes of red on it. He looked down at himself — his arm had a gash. The blood was spreading warm and scarlet, all over his arm, his hand, the bed. And she was coming at him again with a knife. His own carving knife from the toolkit on the bedside table.

She lunged for his eyes, he ducked, and this time the knife ripped open the skin on his cheek. He could taste the salt of his own blood as it streamed down his face. His shirt was soaking red. He tried to move away and she threw the whetstone from the tool kit at him, splitting the skin on his forehead. He fell to his knees, but she would not stop, she flung all his gouges and chisels at him, one by one, as if he were a dartboard. He cowered, trying to shield himself with his arms and she aimed a vicious kick at his side. He doubled up with a howl as her foot slammed into his crotch.

Suraj managed to get to his feet despite the agonising pain. He struggled with the glass doors to the private garden at the back, stumbled out of them into the lawn. Hauled himself up over the wall that separated the lawn from the waste lot at the back, where the eternal buffalo was lowing. He was wheezing for breath, he was staggering away as fast as he could. His arm bled, his face bled, his stomach hurt, he could barely see. He had no sense of where he was going, except forward. He pushed through the undergrowth, between trees, bushes, bulrushes, tearing his clothes, feeling his skin rip.

The grassy ground turned to sand, the darkness lightened. He was on the beach. It was the grubby part of the seafront, smelling of sewage, strewn with the detritus of many meals: discarded water bottles, plastic spoons, foil plates, plastic bags. He slipped on something, trod glass shards and puddles. Then the sea was before him. He ran to its edge. His slippers floated away in the water — or had he run out barefoot? Dogs barked somewhere nearby, a stray pack. The waves crashed towards him. The barking came closer. "What did I do!" His brain sobbed, "What did I do?" The beach was lit sickly green by a strip of fluorescent lighting. He ran without looking, collided into a man watering a twig pushed into the sand. The man shoved him out of his way, went on watering the twig.

Suraj wanted to tear his eye out, he needed to stop it burning. He ran, fell, picked himself up, cursed, ran again. He came to a stop where the waves tugged at his feet. He held his head in his hands and collapsed on his knees in the water, choking on brine, throwing up.

Something emerged from the churning green water. A pillar was moving towards him. In the eerie glow of the green light it was an apparition from a nightmare. When it came closer it became a man. Yellow robes slid off the man's powerful shoulders as he moved. White hair fell to his shoulders. In spite of the darkness, he wore sunglasses. Suraj kneeled in the surf, transfixed, as the man came closer.

Piku, I promised I would come back for you.

I tried to explain then, I couldn't. I'll try again.

They had locked me up with the dogs for trying to untie you. Every feature of the days that followed has been playing in a loop in my head these past thirteen years. When I came out I walked into a thick silence. It was as if fear had become a real living monster panting one step behind. I had eaten very little for those three days. My eyes were crusted with dirt, my clothes were sticky with sweat and grime. I did not see you anywhere. Instead, there was Champa. She was waiting for me when I came out of the bathroom. She looked around us to see if anyone was listening, then she asked me if I knew what Guruji had done when I was locked up.

She spat on the floor and I wondered what made her brave enough to do that. Some months ago she had disappeared for a fortnight and come back thinner, her eyes dark and sunken. The girls had whispered she had been sent away because she was pregnant and her baby had to be killed and removed from inside her. Some said she had gone with the driver of the school van. Others that it was with one of the guards. Nobody had done anything to help her. Champa had a recklessness about her ever since.

"He came into the dining room and went straight to Minoti," she said. "He smashed her head against the wall. She bled and he laughed."

"I don't want to hear any more. Leave me alone."

"That's not all," she went on in a breathless whisper. "He threw her down to the dining room floor, in front of all of us. He pulled her skirt up and pulled her knickers down — why are you blocking your ears? You're only hearing this, you didn't go through it. And you didn't see it. Think of Minoti. She was screaming her lungs out and he was still cracking up. Then he pushed a big spoon into her. All of us saw it. The girls were crying. She was bleeding. There was food everywhere because the plates fell and the serving dishes fell."

Do you know what I thought then, Piku? I would spend my whole life in this hell, that there was no beginning and no end. I had known nothing else since I was seven years old. I would never know any world other than this. Neither would you.

"We're going to run away. There's nothing to lose," Champa whispered. This is what she said to me, Piku.

I said, "You ran away twice. The police brought you right back."

"This time I won't go to the police. I know better than that."

"There's no place for us outside. We have to stay hidden or they'll put us in jail."

"Forget it, they told us lies all these years. If we had run away long ago, nothing would have happened. And jail's better than this, I can tell you. Anyway, look . . ."

Joba came in. Champa and I tried to look as if we had not been speaking. We didn't know how long she had been out in the corridor or how much she had heard. Joba wrinkled her nose at me and said, "You're stinking."

She smiled at the mirror, re-clipped her hair and said, "You smell just like a dog."

We wouldn't allow Joba to run away with us. No. Who else would run away with us?

"Don't be a fool," Champa said two days later when we got a chance to whisper again to each other. "Nobody else."

"Piku. I'm not leaving Piku behind."

"She'll give everything away. She doesn't have a brain. She can't speak properly. All she can do is bang things and yowl."

That's what they thought of you, Piku. But I knew better. We had a secret language, you and I, and we had spoken it for five years.

"Piku's not like that," I whispered back as vehemently as I could. "She's just slow and she doesn't speak, but she understands everything I say. I know how to calm her down."

"Ssssh! Don't raise your voice!"

"I'm not going without her. She'll be finished without me. I'm the only one who knows what she's saying!" I had tears in my eyes. I didn't let Champa see them.

270

"You can come back for her. There'll be no space in that manure truck. It's too small. What if she has one of her screechy fits? What if Bhola hears? What then?" She did not need an answer to that question, Piku.

Champa said, "Look, the only reason I've even told you about the plan is because I like you. And I need you to get me into that manure truck. But if you try anything funny, I'll figure out another way of leaving. Remember I've run away twice before? Without your help. You can stay with your Piku."

I went quiet. I could not get out without Champa, I knew nobody in the world outside. Champa was older. Because she had escaped before and been caught she knew what not to do. She said that during her time in the hospital she had found out about a home for girls like us, abandoned or orphaned. They would tell nobody about us, they would look after us.

Now that freedom seemed within reach, Piku, I could not let it go. I began to think our only chance was if I managed to get out. Then I would come back for you.

"I've heard they find parents for children at these girls' homes, rich parents. Parents abroad. It'll be a different life," Champa said when we were sitting side by side one evening making garlands from a pile of jasmine. It was almost time for the puja and we had to have all the garlands done and ready in another half hour. My red thread flew in and out of the white jasmine at the ends of fat needles while Champa whispered the details of our escape to me.

I said, "Those adoption things must be for babies. I'm twelve. You're fifteen. Who's going to adopt us? We'll just get caught and have to come back."

"If you don't want to come, don't come. I'll find another way of leaving."

The manure van used to come from far away a few times a year. I can't recall how often. I felt as if scarcely a month passed between each delivery of cowdung and sodden leaves. Since Jugnu went, it had been my job to unload the van. I shovelled the manure with a spade into a smaller basin that I carried on my head just as he used to, and tipped it out into a heap by the shed. It took me two days. At about six in the evening on the second day, the driver came to where I was working and stood watching me. "How much longer? She looks like a stick and tries to do the work of a man," he said. "That bastard Bhola has no brains. I should've been out of here hours ago." He spat a red stream towards the basin I was filling.

He went off to the hut where Bhola and the others were smoking and drinking. "Call someone to help," he shouted, "I need to get going in an hour."

This was as Champa had planned. I waited for Bhola to say I could get someone else to help.

In a minute, Bhola's voice: "Go get someone. Move that skinny ass."

I shouted, "Is anyone there? Is that you, Champa? Can you come here? I need help." She had been waiting nearby.

272

She ran towards the van saying, "What do you want? Don't expect me to do all the heavy work!"

The two of us scurried about emptying the van. There were still five sacks left to unload. My legs trembled and my arms shook as I struggled back and forth with the basin. Our heads and bodies stank of manure. My hair was crawling with dung beetles.

Before the driver came back, Champa and I hid ourselves under the heap of empty sacks in the back of the van, among the rest of his junk. There was a spare tyre, empty liquor bottles, flower pots meant for delivery to some other place. I was suffocating under the scratchy sacks. They smelled of rotted dung. Bugs and ants crawled over me. I was itching all over, but we had to keep still. It felt days, those minutes of waiting. I thought people would start looking for us at the ashram. There was a desperate moment during the wait when I thought I could run back, fetch you, Piku, and smuggle you into the van as well. There was enough space, and you would have taken up so little. But it was too late: we could hear the driver coming. He came towards the back. Then we heard him lurch off towards the front and get into the seat. The door banged shut. The van jolted forward. Long minutes later it came to a halt. We heard the scraping of metal, the clank of latches and chains. A voice said, "Still here? Want to spend the night or what?"

The driver said, "Nope, I can find better chicks out in the city. More flesh on them." They tittered and someone thumped the side of the van. It sounded like a bomb blast inside, where we were. You would have started screaming for sure, Piku. You were always scared of loud sounds. The van began to rumble along again. There were jolts and bumps that threw us against each other.

I cried all the way in that van, thinking of the smile on your face the evening before when I stroked your knobbly legs and arms in the way that always soothed you. I kept telling you I would come back for you. Did you understand that? I was the only person who knew what you were trying to say with your whimpers and squeals. That evening you made no sounds at all.

The van stopped after quite a while. I did not know why or for how long it would stop, but Champa poked her face out of the sacks, then stabbed me in the ribs with her fingers and said, "Out. Get out." The two of us had barely scrambled out from the back when the van started again. It trundled ahead and then it was gone. It took only a few seconds.

My knees felt weak. My eyes were blinded by the beep-beep-beep of horns. A woman's high-pitched voice was singing on a loudspeaker. Bright, white headlights from cars. And people — I had never seen so many people. I didn't know the world had so many people in it. They didn't pause for two scrawny children fighting their way down a street.

Champa held my hand and dragged me towards a line of auto-rickshaws. She pushed me in and she told the driver where to go. The auto-rickshaw began to move. Then moved faster. We were breathing open, fresh air. Gas lamps peppered with insects hung over hand-carts selling everything from boiled eggs to hot parathas. And in the distance, all along the road, was a frill of white foam on black cloth — the sea that Jugnu had told us was very close.

The sea he had been thrown into.

Champa had told me what to say when we reached the girls' home. We were cousins. We had no parents. Our uncle used to beat us and so we had run away. We had enough scars and bruises and cigarette burns for this to be convincing. "Not a word about the ashram," Champa said. "Everyone rich and famous is his disciple, they all think he's a god. They'll never believe anything bad about him. They'll take us straight back there and then we'll be dead, like Jugnu."

"What about Piku? What about the other girls? We can't just leave them there. We should tell the truth."

"Just stop being such a saint," Champa snarled. "I'll throw you out of this auto right now."

I spoke to you in my head then. I speak to you in my head all the time. Do you know the taste of betrayal? How would you know it? It's as if your clothes are full of sand, so full of sand that the grains bite you and pierce you and scratch you. You shake out your clothes, you wash them, you wash yourself, but even then, days later, years later, in the crevices of your toes, in the lining of the pockets, the grains pierce you. They're unbearable, those grains that don't go away whatever you do. You no longer know the real from the nightmare. Your heart, mind, mouth, everything is filled with sand.

For a month, maybe three or six months, I stayed at the girls' home. They put Champa somewhere else soon after we got there. I don't know where she went — to another home or to a family. The home never told anyone where its children were being sent. I did not see her again. They had told me that they would soon send me off as well. They were hoping to find foster parents for me. Nobody would know about me either. Not even you, Piku.

I did not talk about the ashram to them, but I wrote. All day I wrote. Half the evening I wrote. I used an exercise book with many pages. I wore out pencils. I started with the day my father was killed and wrote everything I could remember. I wrote especially about you. I wrote about how you would die if you were left in the ashram because of the way you were.

When I had finished writing, I kept the book safe until it was time. I was to be sent off to my new home: first to Delhi, then to some other country. A happy future, they told me, with a woman who had waited a long time to adopt a child.

I stole out of the home the day before I was to be sent to Delhi. I had taken down a newspaper's address from the copy of it that came to the home every day. It was the same newspaper that had written about us once — the article which had a picture of me and some of the other girls with Guruji. I had pasted together sheets from the exercise book to make an envelope and written the newspaper's name on it, then put in my exercise book and stuck my envelope fast with glue. I walked more than an hour, asking every second person on the road for directions, and found my way to the newspaper office. After a moment's panic that I would lose the book if I let go, I dropped it into the big letter box at the gates of the office. It fell in with a hard thump.

I wrote that for you, Piku, so they would read it and get you out of there, and get the others out of there. They would come to know what went on in the ashram, then they would go and see for themselves.

Out there, far away, years later, I found a picture of Guruji on the internet and glued it to a wall. I looked him in the eye every day, I stuck pins into his face. He will not scare me again, not from a distance, nor when I stand face to face in the same room with him and say I was there: I was there from the start, I know everything. In my dreams I tell everyone the truth, I leave nothing out, even if it makes me sick to the stomach.

You are standing beside me. You haven't changed at all. You cannot speak, but you still smile the same way.

It was when Latika had worked through half the vodka that a radio somewhere began to play an old Geeta Dutt song. "*Piya aiso jiya mein samae gayo re, ki main tun-mun ke sudh-budh gawa baithee,*" the voice from years ago sang. "My lover has so dissolved into my being/That I have lost all control over my mind and body."

She was sitting alone in the hotel verandah. Below the verandah were the tops of young palm trees and beyond, the sea, which heaved and sighed. The fronds of the coconut palms were tossed in the rising wind.

After the heat of the day, the mild night air spread a gentle languor through her limbs. Her head felt as if someone was slowly, very slowly, stuffing it with clouds. The whoosh of the sea became a roar in her ears.

They had come back from the market without Gouri. The day had ended in calamity. Latika tried to digest what had happened, but her thoughts kept wandering and Vidya's voice, when it came, came from far away. What was she saying? Something about getting things under control, organising a search party. The hotel manager had gone with a few other men, driving around to look for Gouri. Jarmuli was a small town, they were sure they would find her, after all she had only gone missing in the market and it had been just a few hours. Of course the darkness made it difficult, but they would not give up. If they did not find her by midnight they would go to the police. Vidya approved of this plan. She had found her runaway secretary long years ago, and that was in a big city. This was almost a one-street town. They would cover every possible angle.

"I'm so desperate I even looked in her room, Latika. On the off chance . . . she wasn't there of course. I told the manager to search the Vishnu temple. Remember how she kept saying she wanted to go back there? If there's anywhere she'd be . . . but it's such a maze . . . how will they ever find her even if she is in there? I phoned that guide for help — Badal — he knows the place inside out. But he was so rude. Just said he was too far away and could not come! Latika? Latika! Are you listening?"

Vidya sat down beside Latika and looked at the third chair in the row. Empty. How perfect and peaceful it had been until yesterday: the evenings in that verandah, the three of them chatting late into night, the sea, this trip, the hotel, life itself. Everything had been in place. It was as if, overnight, a tornado had ripped things apart. Suraj was probably in Jarmuli, maybe in trouble, and they had lost Gouri. She would have to phone that pompous son of Gouri's to tell him if they did not find her. Because Latika was too tipsy — could that be possible? — certainly too tipsy to make a difficult phone call. Really, she was no help at all. Latika *drunk*. What could be more unreal?

"Oh Latika, what are we to tell her son!" It was a despairing cry.

Latika opened her eyes with an effort. "The manager will find her. He'll do it. He is a . . . most capable man."

"But he isn't God. Latika, how can you be this way when there is such a crisis?"

Latika had another sip of the vodka. She took off her glasses, closed her eyes, and rested her head against the wall. When she spoke her voice was so soft that Vidya had to lean forward to catch her words before the wind threw them away.

"I was in college when I fell in love with a man who lived at the other end of my street. He was from a religious, traditional Konkani family. Handsome, green-eyed, tall, Greek-looking, as Konkanis can be. His family had a beautiful house with ancient tamarind trees, sculptures in the garden, tame doves. They were very rich. We met because he would come every day in a grey car to pick up his daughter from the junior school next to my college. One day he gave me a ride home along with the girl. Over some weeks it became a habit and nobody thought anything of it because he was married and a neighbour and of course his daughter was in the car with us. Then we started meeting each other in secret — I would skip a class and he would come earlier to the college so that we had an hour in the car without the child. I knew it was mad, but there was nothing I could do to fight it. We loved each other. It didn't feel wrong or bad. But of course nothing was possible and then bits of gossip began floating around . . . someone saw me getting into the car alone, someone else saw me with him far away from home. My brother was ragged about it in his school . . . so that was it. I was packed off to Bhopal to live with an aunt. It was an overnight train I had to take and my brother was sent with me to guard my chastity. Those old second-class coaches. The bunks on top were divided with such a low partition you could touch someone on the other side through it if you tried. My Konkani had somehow managed to get the next bunk. All night, we held hands through that jolting partition. I could hear him crying. Not sobs, but ragged breaths, sniffing sounds, as if he had a cold. My wrist ached, it got a bruise from being twisted through the partition. I felt as if I could hear my heart break. I was very young, you see. My brother was sleeping just a few feet below me in the lower bunk, and he had no idea."

"And then?"

"Then . . . nothing. The Konkani got off the train before daybreak. His family moved to some other town altogether, so we couldn't meet even when I came home for holidays. I never saw him again."

The hotel was in darkness, and now that the radio had stopped they could hear the frenzied barking of dogs in the distance.

"I haven't thought about all this for years," Latika said. "Why am I babbling this way?"

Vidya opened her mouth to reply, but Latika went on, "It's the sea. The sound of it. It brought back so many old things I thought I had forgotten. I should have been thinking of Gouri, not myself."

"Do you think we will find her?" Vidya sounded too tired now for despair.

"We will," Latika said. "Tomorrow the sun will be up again and everything will change."

There was nothing in their ears but the deep roar of the ocean.

Latika looked beyond the verandah's banister, at the sky. It had a pale red glow, a storm was imminent. The moon and stars, so clear the evening before, were hidden behind low clouds.

"Shall we go for a stroll?" she said.

"Might as well. We have to stay up till the manager comes back with his search party."

The hotel staff had furled and tied away the big striped umbrellas that dotted the lawn. In the yellow glow of its submerged lights, patterns of blue and green rippled across the surface of the swimming pool. Latika thought she saw a frog swimming in it. The grass of the lawn felt dew-wet already, and they could taste salt on their lips. They walked down the path to the gate at the back of the hotel's garden and unlatched it.

A guard came running out of the darkness and shouted, "Aunty! Madam! Where are you going?"

"We want to walk to the sea."

"It's not safe this late. A storm is coming, can't you see? I cannot let you go. I'll lose my job if you are swept off the beach. It's too dangerous."

Latika walked ahead and opened the gate. The sea brimmed at the horizon. The charging waves ate up most of the sky before flinging themselves onto the sand, battering the upturned boats. Not another soul there, nothing apart from the shadows of two men further down the beach, one apparently kneeling in the sea, another emerging from it. The man coming out of the water was very tall. The man kneeling was trying to get up.

"Look! On the other side of the creek. How strange, in the water . . ." Vidya pointed at them.

"Is that man trying to kill him or save him?"

"I think the tall one is pushing the shorter one into the water."

"No," said Latika, "I think the tall one is saving the other one from drowning. I can't see that well in the dark. But look, out there. The lights."

Vidya turned her eyes to the lights on a ship far out in the sea. Then she turned back to the two men, except that now there was nobody. Nothing but the dissolving darkness, and the sea swallowing up the sand.

The wind gusted at them, tugging them ahead. They walked to the very edge of the beach. They lost the ship's lights, then glimpsed them again where the sky met the sea, bobbing in and out of the water, and then gone.

They stood with their ankles in the water, feeling the earth disappear from beneath their bare feet with the tug of each receding wave. Latika took Vidya's hand. Each time they were buffeted by waves they felt their ankles sink and they held each other firm.

"Do you really think we'll find her?"

"Yes, we will. Just hold on. Everything will be sorted out tomorrow. Wait and see."

THE EIGHTEENTH DAY

It is long past midnight when she cycles up the road and reaches the pathway through the woods. She gets off, wheels the bike some distance in, thrusts it into the bushes. The trees have dimmed in midsummer's brief twilight. She must note the spot where she left the bike if she is to find it again. She digs into one of the many pockets of her jeans. Pieces of chalk emerge. She chooses a couple of tree trunks, marks them.

She walks down the pathway, dusk soaks her, she becomes a black shadow flitting between trees. Overhead, leaves slice the pale sky into slivers. She can hear herself breathe, hear her shoes crunching earth. She steps through brambles that claw at her jeans. She smells marsh rosemary and woodsmoke. It is more light than dark, more dark than light, as is usual on midsummer nights this close to the Arctic. As she is thinking this, all at once before her is the sheet of silver that she has dreamed of before sleeping every night these many years. When she reaches the clearing she slips her jacket's hood off and arches her back. The beads and the braids are gone. Her hair is cut so short that her head is a fuzzy bud on a thin stem. The rings in her ears catch the light.

She shrugs her backpack off her shoulders and for a long time sits by the water, chin resting on her knees. When it is almost light she slips out of her clothes. She slides into the lake, gasps at the first chill of it, starts swimming towards the centre. When she can no longer make out the shore, she comes to a stop and floats on her back in the shining water. She is a leaf, the water can take her where it will. The air is warm against her skin. She is barely moving, eyes on the stars until they start to fade. Your mother and your father and your brother have become stars, a woman had said once. Whenever you want to be with them, look up at the sky and there they are.

As daylight stains the grey trees green, she flips over. She swims back to the lakeside, climbs out of the water, dries herself and gets into her clothes. She bends to her backpack, takes from it a small stone statue. She traces its lines with a forefinger, holds it close for a moment, then drops it into the lake's water. Its ripples widen in the light.

She digs into her backpack again and takes out a rusted metal object that is no more than two narrow bands on a rudimentary spindle. She tests several spots with her feet, plants it into the sodden mulch on the bank. She looks up to orient herself: one side of the opal sky is turning pink. She swivels the spindle until its arrow points north.

Acknowledgements

My mother Sheela Roy and her sister Sunila Rudra were my companions on a research trip for this book. They were game for everything, opened doors to worlds I wouldn't have known existed, and even thanked me for taking them along.

For their clear-eyed comments and sympathetic reading of drafts, I am indebted to Arundhati Gupta, James Scott Linville, Manishita Dass, and Myriam Bellehigue.

I am grateful to Gina Winje and Karin Marie for help on Norwegian foliage and birdlife. Abhishek Roy for untangling the intricacies of relationships in the *Mahabharata* and *Ramayana*. Prateek Jalan for years of keeping me out of trouble, Rajesh Sharma for his unwavering support and interest, and Koukla MacLehose for a peaceful desk by the sea.

For getting the book ready to step out into the world: Katharina Bielenberg, Monica Reyes, Poulomi Chatterji, Thomas Abraham, and Victoria Millar.

Constantly beside me through the writing of this book were John D. Smith's translation of the *Mahabharata* and A. K. Ramanujan's translations of bhakti poetry; the lines in the epigraph are based on a translation by Ramanujan, published in his collection, *Speaking of Siva*. The snatches of poetry that come back to Gouri are from the Bengali poet Jibanananda Das' poem "Banalata Sen", written in 1942.

There are countless horrific cases of child abuse and sexual violence in India. I have drawn on the legal and investigative history of many such incidents; this book is not based on any particular instance.

It is a great sadness that Per Bangsund isn't around to see where his walks with me in the Norwegian woods led.

Other titles published by Ulverscroft:

NOT FORGETTING THE WHALE

John Ironmonger

When a young man washes up on the sands of St Piran in Cornwall, he is quickly rescued by the villagers. From the retired village doctor and the beachcomber, to the priest's flirtatious wife and the romantic novelist, they take this lost soul into their midst. What the villagers don't know, though, is that Joe Haak is a city analyst who has fled London, fearing he may — inadvertently — have caused a global financial collapse. But is the end of the world really nigh? And what of the whale that lurks in the bay?

THE SUMMER OF BROKEN STORIES

James Wilson

England, 1950s: While out playing in the woods, ten-year-old Mark meets a man living in an old railway carriage. Despite his wild appearance, the stranger, who introduces himself as Aubrey Hillyard, is captivating — an irreverent outsider who is shunned by Mark's fellow villagers, and a writer to boot. Aubrey encourages Mark to tell stories about a novel he is writing — a work of ominous science fiction. As the meddling villagers plot to drive Aubrey out, Mark finds himself caught between two worlds — yet convinced that he must help Aubrey prevail at any cost . . .